Madame ZeeZee's Nightmare

By

Pat Bertram

Deep Indigo Books
Published by Indigo Sea Press
Winston-Salem

Deep Indigo Books
Indigo Sea Press
302 Ricks Drive
Winston-Salem, NC 27103

First Deep Indigo Books edition published July, 2017
Deep Indigo Books, Moon Sailor and all production design are trademarks of Indigo Sea Press, used under license.

For information regarding bulk purchases of this book, digital purchase and special discounts, please contact the publisher at indigoseapress.com

Cover design by Pat Bertram

Manufactured in the United States of America

ISBN 978-1-63066-470-1

For Jeff
Forever

Chapter 1

I didn't want to kill Grace—it was her idea. I've literarily massacred hundreds of thousands of people, so it shouldn't have been difficult to do away with one petite older woman, but the truth is I couldn't think of a single reason why I—or anyone—would want Grace Worthington dead. Though most of us humans frown on murder, we do grudgingly admit some folks are so villainous they need to be eliminated, but no one would consider Grace a villain. She is charming, kind, with a smile for everyone, and the ghost of her youthful beauty is still apparent on her lovely face.

Besides, killing a friend is a good way to lose that friend, and dance class would not be the same without Grace.

I was still trying to make up my mind about killing Grace when several of us dancing classmates met for lunch. After nibbling on salads and sandwiches, we rose and gathered our belongings. I'd hung my dance bag on the back of my chair, and I yanked the bag with more force than I intended. The bag swung out and narrowly missed hitting Buffy Cooper, a tanned, elegant blonde a couple of years older and a couple of inches shorter than me.

Buffy deadpanned, "I'm not the one who volunteered to be the murder victim."

That cracked me up, and right then I decided I had to follow through with the project. I mean, really—how could I not use such a perfect line?

I turned to Grace. "How do you want me to do the deed?" Since she'd initiated this lethal game, I thought it only right that she got to choose the means of her demise. So much fairer than the way life works, wouldn't you say? I mean, few among us get to choose our own end. Life, the greatest murderer of all time, chooses how we expire, whether we will it or not.

Grace laughed at my question and said she didn't care how she died.

But I cared.

Death is often messy—and smelly—with blood and body wastes polluting the scene, and I did not feel like dealing with such realities, especially not at Madame ZeeZee's Dance Academy.

I'd never taken dance classes when I was young, never had any interest in dancing. After my husband died, however, I had to do something to reconnect to the world, so I ventured into the dance studio, hesitantly enrolled in a jazz class, and fell in love with dancing. By the third month of my initial enrollment, I'd signed up for as many classes as I could, sampling not only jazz but also tap, Hawaiian, ballet, Arabic, Tahitian, Italian. Now, almost two years later, dancing has become a pilgrimage—a soul quest—and I didn't want this sacred place to be haunted forever after by the scent of a gruesome end for Grace. It would put a damper on the pure joy of dancing, and I couldn't allow that to happen.

"No blood, body wastes, smells, or any other unpleasantness," I said. "This needs to be a nice gentle murder befitting our nice, gentle victim."

"What about poison?" Buffy asked.

"Blunt force trauma." Sixty-eight-year-old Lena Thomas danced around like a prizefighter, giving a one-two blow to an imaginary opponent. Lena sometimes sported black spiky hair, sometimes blond Shirley Temple curls. Her personalities changed with hair color, raucous when black, babyish when blonde. Her changes seemed less of an affectation and more of an illness since each of her personas didn't always remember what the other had done. Today, her hair looked unfathomably black.

"Insulin overdose!" Buffy gave a nervous laugh as if embarrassed by the way the words had burst out of her mouth.

Lena shook her head in time to her continued punches. "Grace isn't diabetic."

"Doesn't matter." Buffy's quiet words seemed even quieter coming after Lena's strident tone. "She can still die if she gets more insulin than her body can handle, and almost all of us have access to insulin. Most of us are either diabetic or are married to a diabetic."

I nodded slowly. Poison, a blow to the head, or insulin would all work for my scenario. None of those means of murder would be particularly gentle on Grace, of course, but then, it's not her sensibilities I'm worried about. She'd be dead and beyond such matters.

"How would I give her the insulin?" I asked Buffy. "It would have to be an injection because the pills aren't strong enough. But she'd know if someone in class injected her."

"What about putting the insulin in an EpiPen?" Buffy said. "The next time she had to use the pen, she'd give herself the insulin. But that would only work if you didn't care when or if she died."

"I'm not allergic to anything." Grace shivered as if suddenly spooked by our talk.

"It doesn't matter," I assured her. "My pen is mightier than the EpiPen. It only takes a couple of words to give you allergies."

Lena punched the air one last time, then let her arms drop to her side. "I'm allergic. I almost died of anaphylactic shock once."

"Me, too," sixty-nine-year-old Deb Gillespie said. "Several times. The last time I died the doctors didn't think I'd make it back. Now I carry an EpiPen. I have to use it a couple of times a year or that's the end of me. Maybe I should be the victim." She laughed, but I didn't see the joke.

The truth is, I would love to kill Deb off not just because she annoyed the hell out of me, but because I could think of a dozen reasons to kill her. No matter what successes anyone celebrated, no matter what traumas anyone suffered, Deb had been there, at least in her own mind. She'd survived thyroid cancer. She'd died of a heart attack and come back from the dead. She suffered from neuralgia, arthritis, and extremely low blood sugar. She'd been a professional dancer, an award-winning swimmer, a photographer, a makeup artist.

I'd never been able to sort out the truth from her exaggerations, so I didn't bother to try anymore. I found it easier simply to assume everything out of her mouth a lie.

Should I forget Grace and kill off Deb instead? But Grace might feel slighted since the project had been her idea. Besides, Grace as a victim would be a much more challenging than Deb. It's hard to kill someone you like and keep their friendship at the same time. Maybe if I went easy on Grace, it would be okay. And anyway, we really weren't that close.

***

On Tuesdays, ballet comes first, then Arabic. We'd just finished practicing our final combination of ballet steps—*glissade, arabesque, pas de bourrrée, assemblé*—when Grace arrived, already dressed in her green and beige silk belly dance skirt.

I waved at the older woman. "I brought my camera. I need a photo of your corpse. Will you play dead for me?"

Grace laughed. "Sure. Where do you want me? Over there by the barre?"

I glanced at the corner of the studio she indicated, and shrugged. "Sure. Anywhere is fine."

I'd expected to have to take several shots to get the pose I wanted, but Grace sank to the wooden floor as gracefully as she did everything else, and lay in the ideal pose.

Right then I knew I could kill Grace. She was just too damn perfect.

Kim Saunderling, a lithe woman of unknown years (unknown to me, that is) with wonderfully flawless dark skin, entered the dance studio. She was the type of woman who could randomly pull two or three unmatched items out of her closet and look as if she'd spent hours dressing herself for a Vogue photo shoot. This seemed especially remarkable to me because she was legally blind. That day she wore her purple practice skirt, which wrapped twice around her hips (mine barely wrapped once, if you must know), a maroon scarf tied into a turban-like affair, and a bluish-purple long-sleeved shirt with the tails tied at her waist. It wasn't only her age Kim was reticent about, but her earlier years, too. Perhaps she had been a model at one time. Or maybe she had reason to be secretive—a woman with a sordid past.

Kim stood by while I took another photo of Grace in her death pose below the barre. "How are you going to get Grace into that exact position when she's killed?"

"I hadn't thought of that," I admitted.

"Maybe she was trying to reach the barre so she could die dancing," Buffy said.

Grace gave a little laugh. "That's too true to be funny." Then, more seriously, she added, "Dying while dancing is how I'd like to go out. I just wouldn't want to die on stage with all those people watching like a friend of mine did."

"*Dying to Dance* would be a good name for the book," I said.

"Or maybe *Sashaying with Death*. Or *Death en Croix*."

"Why does it have to be *death*." Madame ZeeZee said with a moue of distaste. Though Madame ZeeZee is seventy-nine years old, she has the body of a woman half her age and the legs of a teenager. When she dances, you can almost see the years melt away, and she is young again.

"We could call it Madame ZeeZee's something," I said.

"*Madame ZeeZee's Nightmare*." Madame ZeeZee giggled, sounding about seventeen. "Maybe you don't really kill Grace. Maybe I wake up and find that I dreamt the whole thing."

"Great name," I said, hoping the teacher wouldn't notice I didn't comment on her idea about Grace's death being a dream. It's a time honored ending, of course, but I thought if I were going to go through the trouble of killing Grace, it should be for real. I did like the title, though—we were a dance teacher's nightmare. Many of us were out of shape and overweight, some of us had no sense of rhythm, and all of us were many decades past any hope of a dancing career.

Glee lit Madame ZeeZee's beautiful dark eyes. "I could be the murderess. I have experience."

I felt my jaw drop. Madame ZeeZee had experience with murder? It seemed impossible that anyone who danced with such expressive moves—moves that spoke of life—could have a history of violence.

"It was a murder weekend," Madame ZeeZee said. "I was the murderess, a princess from a foreign country. I even wore a tiara."

I blew out a breath of relief, glad I didn't have to alter my impression of the dance teacher, at least not yet. "But why would you want to murder Grace?"

Madame ZeeZee exchanged glances with Grace, who had risen fluidly and was smoothing her skirt. "Maybe she stole my choreography."

I understood the need to protect one's artistic work any way one could, yet in truth, Madame ZeeZee routinely gave us her choreography. Every step she taught gifted us with her work.

Still, such an irrational theft, as minor as it might seem to the danceless, could be a killing offense, especially if Grace were to give Madame ZeeZee's work to a rival instructor. (I've lost track of how many dance classes Grace took. Three or four from Madame ZeeZee, and at least a couple more from other teachers. Now that I think about it, in the dance world, such promiscuity could be motive enough for wanting someone dead.)

"Do you know how long it will be before the cops get here?" I asked Grace, thinking how disappointed I would feel if class had to be cancelled.

"A long time. Maybe a couple of hours."

That seemed excessive to me, but I figured Grace should know since her husband is a retired criminalist.

I looked around the dance studio. The place wasn't large, perhaps fifteen feet wide by sixty feet long. Mirrors lined one long wall and a barre stretched across the opposite wall. A nook at the back of the studio next to the small restroom had been furnished as a miniscule waiting room, and a corner had been cordoned off with a counter and cabinet for an office. Pictures from Madame ZeeZee's past and inspirational posters hung on the walls, but other than that, the studio was empty.

"If we have to stay here for a couple of hours waiting for the cops, we might as well have a class," I said. "The floor will be mostly bare since Grace's body won't take up much room, we'd be dressed for the occasion, and our minds would not yet have processed the truth. I like the idea of a group of aging women dancing in the face of death."

By this time, the rest of the class had arrived. Everyone stared at me with various shades of disbelief, but I shrugged off their attitude. This was my story, my murder, and I could choreograph it any way I wished.

Grace shook her head with mock sadness. "I am truly hurt that no one will mourn me."

"Of course, we'll mourn you," I told her. "But it will have to wait until after class."

Grace smiled, but I don't think she found my comment amusing.

I stowed my camera in my dance bag, unwrapped my ballet skirt from around my waist, and donned my orange and turquoise Arabic practice skirt. I moved to the barre and waited for class to begin. Kim found a place at the barre next to me.

"When did all this happen?" she asked.

I turned to face her. "When did what happen?"

"I don't know how it all started with Grace. Was it your idea?"

Buffy had been silent during the picture taking and the between-class bustle, but now she spoke, sounding surprised at Kim's question. "It started a couple of weeks ago when we all went to see the Trocks." By "Trocks" she meant *Les Ballets Trockadero de Monte Carlo*, a glorious and gloriously funny all male ballet troupe. "At lunch before the show, someone mentioned that Pat was a writer. Grace suggested Pat write a book about us and even volunteered to be the victim."

"Oh." Kim slid one slender leg behind her in a deep lunge and stretched her body forward. "I sat at the other end of the table that day, so I didn't know."

"I'm a writer," Deb announced.

My fingers curled into fists, and I could feel my jaw tightening. Cripes, the woman really did annoy me. Just once, it would be nice if she didn't butt in.

I loosened my jaw enough to put a pleasant expression on my face, reminding myself that anyone with such an overpowering desire to trump everyone else had plenty of problems already and didn't need attitude from me.

"You wrote a book," I said as noncommittally as I could.

Deb gave a single emphatic nod of her head. "Yes. A bestselling novel about a woman figure skater who teams up with a hockey player and wins the Olympics."

I had no idea what to say. Part of me felt envious she'd achieved such a status while I still struggled in the ranks of the unknown, but mostly I had a hard time envisioning her actually accomplishing such a monumental task. She seemed too full of herself and her own importance to surrender to the power of words.

Buffy frowned. "Wait a minute. That sounds like an old movie I saw recently."

"I read a lot of bestsellers," Nancy said. "But I don't remember your name, Deb. Do you write under a pseudonym?" Nancy Pahrump was in her seventies, and although she looked a lot younger, she had problems indicative of her age, such as extra weight and a bum knee that sometimes kept her out of class.

"I'm not strictly published yet." Deb tapped the side of her head. "It's all in here. I just have to get it down on paper."

My fists unclenched and my jaw relaxed into a smile. I might have to dance with Deb, but at least I didn't have to share my meager literary fame with her.

"Pat's a real writer," Nancy said. Her greenish eyes twinkled with pixyish delight. "Maybe we should all tell Pat a secret that will come out during the story."

Kim continued to stretch, and Lena drew *tendus* on the floor with a pointed toe. Their so obvious lack of response to Nancy's suggestion made me wonder what secrets they were hiding. Was it my obligation as a writer to pry out those secrets, or did my obligation as a friend demand that I leave them alone?

"I don't have any secrets," Buffy said. "I'm the most boring person in the world. No crimes. No affairs. No problems with my parents growing up. No calling in sick at work when I wasn't. The worst thing I ever did in my whole life was copy a quilt I saw once."

"I don't have any secrets, either," Rhett said. Rhett Norris is our lady in red. It's not that she always wears the color—in fact, Deb wears red and other bright colors more often than Rhett—but Rhett is as zestful and vibrant as the color itself. But now, beneath her relentless optimism, I sensed a strain, as if she did indeed have a secret she was keeping even from herself. Or perhaps the strain came from continued dealings with an ex-husband who had divorced her after forty-two years of connubial unbliss. He'd hidden their assets and moved to the Philippines. She ended up with only her social security and small pension, and he'd tried to take those from her, too. Rhett seems radiantly happy now that she's remarried, and yet there is that telltale strain.

The exotic notes and strong percussion of Arabic music sounded in the studio. Madame ZeeZee stretched with us at the barre, moved to the center of the floor and led us in a series of steps—figure eights with our hips, common motion, hip lifts, *ronde de jambs*. After we warmed up, she watched us practice the dances we'd already learned.

As we danced, I thought how much I would miss Grace when she was gone, then I paused midstep. What the hell was wrong with me? I wasn't going to kill Grace for real. It was a story, a game.

Madame ZeeZee stopped the music. "You're not together. When you dance in a group, Pat, the group has to act like one person. Let's start again."

Chapter 2

Madame ZeeZee's Dance Studio is located in the Mojave Desert community of Peach Valley, (nope, no peaches, and not much of a valley, either) in an old L-shaped strip shopping center filled with a dozen independent businesses,. The shop spaces were so small they could all be piled into a single big box store with space left over. What the shopping plaza lacked in charm and style it made up for in safety because it was hidden behind the brand name gas station and a Mexican restaurant positioned on the street side of the parking lot.

We were standing outside the studio, waiting for Madame ZeeZee to open the door for our Thursday morning ballet class. *"I'm a dancer, not a clock watcher,"* our teacher often told us. I wondered if her lateness could be a reason for someone to want to kill her, but lateness didn't seem a dying offense especially since the class ran for the allotted time no matter when it began.

And anyway, Grace was to be our victim.

"Who is going to be the murderer?" Nancy asked.

"I don't know who's going to be the murderer," I admitted. "I'm having a hard time wrapping my mind around this whole death scenario."

"Eddie said he'd do it." Eddie was Nancy's new roommate. Saying his name put a smile on her crinkly-eyed face, and it did me good to see that she'd found life after the death of her husband.

"But why would he want to kill Grace?" Deb asked. "Does he know her?"

"Maybe it wasn't Grace he wants to kill," Rhett said. "Maybe it's Madame ZeeZee he wants dead."

I nodded slowly. Grace being killed accidentally in place of Madame ZeeZee did seem a logical conclusion. Not that Madame ZeeZee acted less kind and generous than Grace, but she had an enviable talent, a business, and a reason for being at the studio during off hours. And a door key. After all, if Grace were to be killed in the studio in Madame ZeeZee's absence, Grace—and her murderer— would have to find a way into the locked studio.

So maybe Madame ZeeZee needed to be the murderer to make

the story work. But no—even as a game, I could not countenance such an eventuality. Without Madame ZeeZee, there would be no dance classes.

"Okay," I said. "I'll consider Eddie for the role of murderer. But why would he want to kill Madame ZeeZee?"

Nancy chuckled. "Maybe he thinks I'm spending too much time at dance class."

Inspiration hit me. "And maybe he wants your DeLorean. That could be why he's wooing you, and he sees dance class as a rival for your attention. If he can't have you, he can't have the DeLorean."

A wistful expression settled on Nancy's face. "I would like to get the DeLorean working again, and Eddie said he'd help me."

I held out my arms as if in offering. "See? It all fits."

The door of the nail salon next door opened, and the owner, a darkly bespectacled Korean, walked out, cigarette in his mouth, lighter clamped in his hand.

Rhett glowered at him. He wheeled and went back inside.

"I hate that guy," Rhett said. "He's always smoking in front of the studio and stinking up the room."

I pivoted toward the door of the salon, thinking of the man inside. The smoker would be a good suspect. Or maybe the murderer. The man seemed to have little fondness for Madame ZeeZee and her eclectic mix of students.

"We could kill him." Rhett adopted a fighting stance and kicked up her leg in what would have been a vicious blow if it had landed on someone's head. Although she'd recently turned seventy-one, her years in no way impaired her martial arts skills. "And then we could kill my ex-husband."

Lena threw a couple of punches. "While we're at it, there's some people I wouldn't mind killing."

I closed my eyes. *Madame ZeeZee's nightmare, indeed.*

"We can kill whoever we want to." I spoke mildly in an effort to defuse the combatants' wrath. "It's our story. Maybe when you see how easy death is, Rhett, you take off and go kill your ex-husband."

"No." Rhett kicked again, narrowly missing my face. "I mean kill that bastard for real."

I backed away, wanting to distance myself both physically and emotionally from her violence.

She laughed at my retreat. "Joking." But the glint in her eye told me she'd been more than halfway serious.

"If I'm lucky," she added, "That bitch he's living with will kill him for me. She doesn't take his crap the way I always did, and sooner or later he'll find another woman. I doubt the bitch will back away. She's too used to living off his money. *My* money."

"Divorce is worse than death," Deb said in her usual pedantic tone. Like Rhett, she had gone through a painful divorce, but was now remarried to the greatest guy on the face of the earth, or so she claimed.

"When they die, you don't have to deal with the rejection," Rhett added. "And they don't keep coming back."

The two women continued to extol the virtues of death over divorce. I turned away, shutting my ears to their blather, but I couldn't stop the sudden spurt of tears. The divorced didn't know about the pain of continual rejection you had to deal with when your beloved husband slowly embraced a new mistress—death—while you struggled to live. They didn't know about the feeling of amputation when your soul mate left, taking half of your soul and most of your shattered heart with him. They didn't know about the agonizing bewilderment of standing on the edge of eternity, unable to go where your mate had gone., or about the great yearning to see the beloved one more time.

They didn't know I would give anything to have him lost to divorce, to another woman, another family. At least he would be alive.

Nancy put her arm around me and whispered, "They don't know."

I smiled through my tears, grateful for the kind words, grateful someone understood.

"What's with her?" I heard Deb ask.

"Frankly, my dear . . ." Rhett answered.

I stiffened at her oft quoted words, then took a deep breath and willed myself to relax. There was no reason for her to give a damn about my grief. My grief wasn't her problem. It belonged to me alone. Maybe making a game of death would help me put the grim reaper in his—or her—place, would make death seems less deadly and heartbreaking.

The sound of a car drawing near caught my attention. If I had any doubt the cream-colored Kia belonged to Madame ZeeZee, I had only to glance at the license plate—MMZZ.

"Sorry I'm late." Madame ZeeZee stuck her key in the door lock. "You'll never believe what happened." She turned the key, grasped the handle, and pulled the door. It didn't open. "What's wrong?" She yanked on the door again. It remained locked.

"My door always sticks," Deb said. "Let me try." She rattled the door, almost pulling it off the hinges.

"It's probably still locked," I said, trying to keep the disdain for Deb's interference from my voice.

"I unlocked it. You saw me." Madame ZeeZee turned the key again and pulled on the handle. The door opened easily. She wrinkled her brow at me. "I know I locked the studio when I left yesterday. I even shook the door to make sure it wouldn't open."

"It's happened before," I reminded her. The door was more than forty years old, installed when the building was new. Something always seemed wrong with the door—it blew open in the middle of class, didn't always lock properly, and sometimes got stuck on a screw sticking out from the frame.

Madame ZeeZee stood aside to let us troop into the studio. "I'll have to call someone and get it fixed."

"Hey, there's Grace." Nancy pointed to the floor where Grace had lain when I took her photo. We all turned to look at the corner of the room. No one lay on the wooden floor, though I fancied I could see an outline of Grace's body. Nancy laughed, apparently pleased she'd made us look. "I guess Eddie hasn't killed her yet."

"The cops are here." Rhett gave a throaty chuckle. "Maybe they know something's going on."

We watched a uniformed police officer climb out of her squad car and swagger past the studio, probably on her way to the Italian restaurant three doors down. Feeling tension seep from my body, I thought it a good thing I weren't murdering Grace for real. I couldn't handle the pressure. I'd read enough mysteries to know there was no such thing as a perfect crime. Uncanny circumstances and strange coincidences tended to wreck the best plots—squalls that clouded a clear-sky day, witnesses who appeared out of nowhere, and cops who showed up unannounced.

Even writers have a hard time creating perfect plots, but the benefit of writing is that you can rewrite a scene as many times as necessary to get things right. In life—and death—there is no rewrite. What's done is done.

Class had started during my musings, and I'd automatically followed along with what my classmates were doing until I heard Madame ZeeZees's sharp, "Point your toes!"

I knew she meant me, and I sighed. I don't know what I'd hoped for by taking ballet—maybe grace or strength. Even if I were young and slim, I could never become a ballerina. I don't have a ballet body, or even ballet feet. I have a hard time pointing my toes, and when I stand on the balls of my feet, my heels barely lift off the ground. Luckily, dancing was like writing. I could practice over and over, trying to get it right.

We did *chaine* turns across the floor, and most of us stumbled as we tried to keep our balance, but Jackie spun like a top, doing a dizzying number of turns. Jackie McDerr looked like a Buster Brown doll with strong cheekbones, bright eyes, and salt and pepper hair cut straight just beneath her ears. She'd taken ballet classes for decades, and I comforted myself with the thought that maybe ten or twenty years hence, I too, could spin across the floor instead of making the few wobbly turns I now managed.

At lunch after class, most of us drooped wearily onto our chairs, but Jackie sat straight and cheery as always. "So, Pat. Have you started to write the book?"

I thought of lying, meeting her perky question with a perky response of my own, but all I managed was the feeble truth. "Nope. Not a word. There's still so much I haven't figured out. Everyone needs to have a secret that's unveiled in the book, but I don't want to reveal anyone's real secrets, so I'd have to make something up. And I'm afraid of hurting people with my fictions."

I imagined a conversation that might result from an untruth:
Husband: Character B is you, right?
Character B: Yes. Isn't this great?
Husband: And it's based on your life.
Character B: Yes, but it's fictionalized.
Husband: So who is this guy you're having an affair with?
Character B: I am not having an affair.

13

Husband: You said Character B is you.
Character B: It is. A fictionalized me.
Husband: And Character B is having an affair.
Character B: Yes, in the book I am having an affair.
Husband: So who is he? Do you want a divorce? Is that what you're saying?
Character B: No. I'm saying I'm character B.
Husband: Do you want to leave or do you want me to leave?

"It's a big enough responsibility shaping one's character's life," I said, "and to have the real person influence the character. Having the character influence the real person's life is more responsibility and guilt than I can handle."

"Maybe it doesn't have to be a secret, even a made-up secret." Jackie took a bite of her vegetarian burrito and chewed it slowly. "Maybe you in the book can find out things about us that you in the real world don't know."

I took a second to unravel that convoluted sentence. "But how could my character find out things that I don't know in real life? And what sort of things? They'd have to be relevant to the story."

"Well," Jackie said. "Something you don't know is that I'm a pilot. Maybe that would have some relevancy."

"Cool!" Rhett shot a fist in the air. "You can fly me to the Philippines to kill my husband, and no one will know I went there."

Jackie looked from me to Rhett and back to me as if she couldn't decide if Rhett were being facetious. I shrugged, unable to guess how far Rhett would go to get her way. Nor did I know how far her frankly-my-dear attitude carried her. Did she really not give a damn, or was the attitude merely a conceit she'd adopted because of her name? Maybe it worked the other way—the attitude came first, and then the name.

The whole murder project suddenly seemed impossible. I thought I knew these women I danced with, but I didn't know them at all. I didn't even know if the names I knew them by were their real names or nicknames. Or aliases.

What secrets were they hiding behind their innocuous names?

Madame ZeeZee claimed to be Russian, but nothing in her looks, attitude, or unaccented English revealed her to be anything but a California Girl.

14

Grace seemed graceful and gracious, but could those characteristics be illusions created by her name? If her name had been something else—Jan, perhaps—would she be any different?

Buffy looked like a preppie grown up to be a golf matron, exactly as her name implied. (The nineteen forties version of the name, that is, not the nineteen nineties vampire slayer version.) But Buffy had once laughingly called herself a cracker and hinted at poor-southern roots that belied her upper crust appearance.

I heard my name and jerked myself to attention.

"Pat, what do you think?" Madame ZeeZee asked.

I held out my hands, palms upward, hoping our teacher would take the gesture to mean I didn't know how to respond rather than I hadn't been listening.

"Me, too," Madame ZeeZee said.

The women dumped their trash, scooped up their belongings, and left the fast food restaurant in a swirl of chatter.

I sat by myself at the table, thinking that twice in a few short hours I'd missed out on a bit of information, once when Madame ZeeZee had tried to explain why she'd been late, and now at lunch.

A horrible thought struck me. I hadn't missed something important, had I? I hoped this story didn't turn out to be one of those wretched mysteries I so hated where the truth had been told at the beginning, but the inept detective hadn't been paying attention.

But I was no detective, and this was no mystery.

A patrol car pulled up to the taco bar, and my stomach tightened. I grabbed my dance bag off the end of the chair and escaped out the opposite door.

Chapter 3

When I plan a new book, I spend too much time obsessing over insignificant details, and Grace's murder was no different. Instead of figuring out the plot—the many conflicts that would arise during the investigation, the secrets that would be revealed, the final unmasking of the killer whoever it might be—I lay awake most of Thursday night worrying about the ages of my characters. Should I give everyone pseudonymous ages to protect the innocent and age conscious? Would anyone but the families of the women involved be willing to read a story about not-young women? Would people understand the truth behind the number of their years? While the women might not be able to do everything they could when young, they weren't decrepit by any means. In fact, though so many were in their seventies, such as our forever young teacher, our lovely victim, the perennially gung-ho lady in red, they were in better shape, more energetic and more active than many people half their age.

I also worried about a lack of character arcs. At our ages, we are what we are. Our idiosyncrasies have been polished through the years and have become indistinguishable from our personalities, like knotholes on a sanded plank. We might have a change of heart, but a change in character would be highly unlikely.

And I worried about how the book would affect my friendship with these women. Writing, like dancing, has a way of reaching inside a person, dredging up emotions and feelings you might not consciously be aware of. Would I unwittingly show truths about the women—and me—that none of us wanted to accept?

I decided to tiptoe warily into the story, ready to draw back if the words played rough.

***

The hardest thing for me as an author, even harder than figuring out the plot or dredging up the necessary words, is having to deal with questions about my progress, so before class the following day, when Rose jokingly asked if I'd finished writing the book yet, I pretended I didn't hear, though I felt bad about ignoring her. Seventy-year-old Rose Rowland had indeterminate health problems that made the weight melt off her body. She'd once been very heavy, but her tee shirt with "Madame ZeeZee's Dance Academy" emblazoned on the back, now billowed with every step. Her gray hair, fluffed out around her head like a helmet, never moved at all.

"Pat can't have finished writing the book." Rhett grinned at Grace. "Grace isn't dead yet."

"But the cops are still hanging around," Buffy added.

I glanced out the door. Two patrol cars had pulled into adjacent parking spots, one facing in and one facing out so they could talk to each other through their left front windows.

I put a clamp on my uneasiness and wondered if I should go out to talk to them. Tell them I was writing a book about a murder, ask what the local procedure would be when we found our dead victim.

But no . . . I'd rather not bring myself to their attention. Besides, I'd see firsthand what their procedures were after Grace was killed.

I banged my head with a fist. *What the hell was wrong with me?* I never considered myself suggestible, but this whole murder scenario spooked the hell out of me, maybe because I'd never killed anyone I knew. All my previous murders had been strangers— faceless mannequins conjured out of words for the sole purpose of slaughter.

"Are you okay, Pat?" Rose leaned forward and peered at me, acting as if she'd welcome a fellow sufferer.

I nodded, unwilling to admit that the lines between fact and fiction were starting to blur.

"Who is going to be your sidekick?" Deb asked. "You need a sidekick."

No I don't. I forced a smile onto my face to hide my rebellious thought. "Are you volunteering?"

"No." Deb's eyes widened and her brows rose in a parody of shock. "I can't be. I'm not black."

I gaped at her, my mind blank.

"All women detectives now have a black girlfriend. Or a gay guy friend. April's black friend is a lesbian. That way I get two for the price of one."

"April?" I asked.

17

"My heroine." Deb sounded surprised I didn't know. Apparently, I wasn't the only one mistaking fiction for fact—in her mind, her unwritten book had truly become widely known.

Maybe all authors were nuts. Maybe I should rethink my place in the writing business.

"Unless you want to make someone up, Kim will have to be your sidekick," Deb added.

"Kim is no one's sidekick," Buffy said. "She'd never allow Pat to turn her into a cliché."

Lena giggled. "Allie should be your sidekick. Allie. Ally. Get it?"

Allie Shaffer, a gorgeous woman in her fifties with toffee-colored hair matching her tanned unlined skin, had been leaning against the barre, arms folded, but she jerked upright at the sound of her name, an avid look in her eyes. Her greed for notice seemed to war with her self-effacement, though I could be wrong. I didn't know her all that well. She'd joined the class recently, and seldom spoke.

Rhett ogled herself in the mirror and tugged her red shirt down over slim hips encased in black leggings. "Will you cut twenty-five pounds off my weight when you describe me? I don't want to be fat."

I blew out an exasperated breath. I weighed a heck of a lot more than Rhett, and I didn't have a fraction of the body image problem she did. "You're not fat," I said for perhaps the hundredth time.

But the truth was, she did seem a bit pudgy to me right then. She'd told me often enough and emphatically enough about her excess poundage that I was beginning to believe her despite the evidence of my own eyes. This didn't bode well for my powers of detection. If someone insisted important information wasn't germane or that trivial details were vital, I'd probably believe them, leading me onto false trails.

I reminded myself this was my book. I'd create the evidence, the red herrings, the clues. To a certain extent, I'd even create the characters with my ability to put whatever words I wanted into their mouths, so there'd be no influence or persuasion but my own.

Since I found the concept of the book so confusing, I could only wonder how poor Grace was faring.

Grace had been talking to Madame ZeeZee and some of the other students, but she glanced at me over her shoulder and caught me staring at her.

"Are you okay with all this?" I asked. "Doesn't the talk of your murder bother you?"

She laughed. "No. But my family thinks it's funny. I don't know what that says about me."

"Family members are always the first suspects," Deb said with her usual know-it-all tone, but her words had an unusual ring of truth. Had she once been a suspect? Or a murderer? But if she had killed someone, she would have jumped at the chance to one up Madame ZeeZee when our teacher had announced her experience with murder. But what if there were a reason Deb had held her tongue? What if she'd never been caught?

No one else seemed to follow my train of thought. They were happily discussing Grace's demise and who would be the one to do her in.

I turned my back on the lot of them and took a place by the barre at the front of the studio. I fought the urge to walk out. The cops were gone; the coast looked clear. Then the sound of music filled the studio, and I found myself swaying to the jazzy beat.

After class, while we were changing from our jazz shoes into our tap shoes for the next session, talk turned once again to Grace's murder. I hadn't written a single word of the story, and the idea already sickened me. Everyone seemed excited by our game, but they wouldn't have to write the gruesome details. They wouldn't have to live through the reality of death. Even though I'd have Grace's presence during our shared classes to prove I hadn't really killed her, at night, in my writer's eye, she'd be dead.

Maybe I should use Madame ZeeZee's scenario where the whole thing turned out to be dream. Or maybe the murder could be a prank where everyone just wanted to trick me into thinking Grace had been killed. Or even better, what if I turned the tables on everyone and instead of writing a simple murder mystery, I penned a science fiction fantasy with Grace both dead and alive—or neither—like Schrödinger's cat.

Tap is a difficult class for me because, like writing, there are many elements that have to come together in a seamless whole. The music, the beat, hand movements, body movements, and always those dang taps clicking out their own rhythm. But that day, winged by my new outlook on Grace's murder, everything came together and I danced as if I'd found heaven on earth.

Still, I felt glad when the class ended and I could take a break from the stress of Grace's impending death. It seemed strange, this eagerness for a respite from class. For the past two years, ever since I started taking dance, the weekends had been hard to get through with nothing but sorrow to fill my mind. After the death of my husband Jay, I'd come to the high desert to take care of my father. My mother had died a year before Jay, and it made sense the two of us left behind would look out for each other. My father gave me a safe place to work through my grief, and I took care of him, making sure he'd be able to be independent until the end.

The end had come three months previously, leaving me adrift. I could never afford the mortgage on that immense house—what had my folks been thinking when they'd bought such a monstrosity in their old age?—so it had to go. Besides, the house belonged to my father's "estate" though the estate consisted of little besides the equity in the house.

Permission from the probate court to sell the house had been swift, and despite the sluggish housing market, the pristine place had sold immediately. Luckily, the buyers had requested a long escrow so I plenty of time to clear out the house and prepare for a move.

I spent the weekend sorting through my parents' possessions, boxing donations and setting aside things that had been earmarked for my brother and sister and their various offspring. I kept my mind focused on the task and refused to think of death or dance.

But Monday came, as it always did.

We were dressed in our pau skirts, ready to begin warm-ups for Hawaiian class when Madame Zee took note of all who were present. And absent.

"Where's Grace?" she asked.

We responded with a murmur of "I don't know"s and "She said she'd be here"s.

Madame ZeeZee checked her cell phone. "She didn't call."

"Maybe Pat killed her this weekend," Rhett said.

My stomach clenched in fear, but the others laughed along with Rhett.

Deb pointed to the parking lot beyond the studio window. "She's here."

We watched Grace hurry to the door and drag it open.

She looked from one of us to the other. "What?"

"We thought Pat killed you," Rose said.

Grace laughed. "Not yet." She took off her street shoes, pattered across the dance floor in her bare feet, and pulled on her pau skirt. "I'm sorry I'm late. Car problems. Charlie had to drive me." Charlie. The criminalist.

Hawaiian, for me, is a meditative dance, especially the Hula Kahikos, the ancient chants. The slow, precise movements, all of us flowing in sync as if we were one being, fed my spirit in a way other types of dances couldn't. Even the inconsistencies—Rhett a half step ahead of us, blonde Lena a half-step behind, Deb singing under her breath, Rose with her head turned toward Grace to follow the more accomplished woman's moves—didn't diminish our oneness.

The connection felt so strong and so electric, that when the music ended and Madame ZeeZee turned to go change the music, we turned with her and took a step in the direction she went.

We all must have realized our mistake at the same time because in unison, we stopped. And laughed at ourselves

Life—and dance—didn't get much better than this.

Chapter 4

I dawdled at my father's house on Tuesday morning. I wanted to get to the studio when everyone already stood in place at the barre ready for ballet class to begin, but when I turned into the parking lot, a cluster of women were standing outside the door of the studio. Jackie, Nancy, Rhett, Deb, and Buffy faced a tall, long-haired blonde, whose head was tilted at a listening angle.

Margot! She'd been absent the past couple of weeks. A vacation at the beach. I was glad to see she'd returned. I always enjoyed dancing with fifty-six-year old Margot Strand. She had a ballerina's body and a ballerina's lithesomeness she'd earned from a lifetime of ballet classes, but instead of intimidating me, she made me feel as if I, too, were light and airy.

Margot grinned at me. "I hear you're killing Grace."

My pleasure at seeing the blonde drained away, though I kept a smile on my face. "That's the plan."

"I had an idea for the murderer," Buffy said. "But it's nothing."

"Hey!" Jackie feinted a gentle punch toward Buffy's arm. "You can't lead us along like that and then not tell us your idea."

Margot and Rhett nodded their agreement.

"I'd appreciate any suggestions." I smiled apologetically at Nancy. "I can't figure out why Eddie—or anyone—would want Grace dead. Death comes soon enough for all of us, so it doesn't make sense to hurry it along."

After a brief pause, Buffy laughed, probably to dissipate the aura of doom I'd managed to draw around us. "What if we all did it? All worked together to kill Grace? Or maybe each of us independently had tried to kill her? But then, you'd still have the problem of why."

"I'm not sure it matters who the killer is." I spoke slowly, trying to grasp the elusive thought. "Maybe it's our relationship that matters. Our relationship to Grace and to each other, and how that relationship created the need for her death, and how it both sustained us and destroyed us afterward."

"Of course the killer counts." Deb scowled at me as if daring me to disagree. "The killer is the story. If there was no killer, there could be no hero. A hero is only as strong as the villain."

"True. A hero who vanquishes teddy bears isn't as strong as one who vanquishes dragons." The sentence seemed to echo, and I realized I'd quoted myself, though I couldn't remember where I'd used that analogy. *A Spark of Heavenly Fire,* perhaps. "But not all stories depend on heroes and villains, good and evil. Stories that do seem too much like comic books. I prefer more subtle story lines, where the hero is not heroic and the villain not villainish."

"So, who's the hero?" Jackie asked, dark eyes bright. "You?"

"Me?" I laughed humorlessly. "I'm no hero. I'm the narrator, and an unreliable one at that. I can write fiction because I can make up the necessary details, but I am not at all observant."

Jackie held her dance bag in front of her chest. "What color is my top?"

"Black," I said. It was a good guess—Jackie always wore black.

Jackie laughed and lowered her bag to show a new purple crop top. "You really are bad."

"So who *is* the hero?" Nancy asked.

"Maybe we all are," Buffy said. "If we can't all work together to murder Grace, maybe we can all work together to get the killer."

"Like at dance class." Nancy hooked a thumb toward the studio. "Madame ZeeZee always says we need to dance as one. Maybe we dance circles around the killer."

Rhett stepped back and savagely kicked an imaginary opponent. "And then I kill him."

Madame ZeeZee drove into the parking lot and pulled up in front of the studio.

"Sorry I'm late." She stabbed the key into the lock, fiddled with it, tried to open the door, turned the key again, and glanced back at us. Her usually youthful face had deep lines of exhaustion. "My mother is getting really bad. I've been on the phone with her caregivers the last hour."

She yanked on the door. It flew open, wresting itself from her grasp, and slammed against its hinges. "I have to get this door fixed." She reached inside the studio, flipped the light switch, then stood back so we could enter.

I stumbled into Jackie, who had stopped abruptly in my path. I peered around her to see what had made her pause, but all I could see were the backs of the other women. For a second, no one moved.

One by one, the women turned to look at me, then parted to make way for me. I gave them questioning glances as I picked my way past them. When I had a clear view of the room, I stopped and stared, my heart beating wildly.

Grace lay on the studio floor, dressed in her green belly dance skirt, in the very position she'd assumed the day I took her photo.

I put on my best trying-to-be-a-good-sport-but-not-succeeding smile. "Very funny. Ha. Ha."

Madame ZeeZee pushed through the knot of women. "What's Grace doing here? I didn't say *she* could spend the night in my studio."

Our heads snapped in her direction, then we all ran to where Grace lay still.

Margot held out her arms to keep us from crowding her. She crouched by Grace, put her fingers under the fallen woman's jaw, then rolled Grace on her back and put an ear to her chest. After a moment, she craned her neck to look up at us.

"She's dead."

I felt like crying as I so often had when as a child kids had played practical jokes on me. "This is not funny."

Tears glistened in Margot's eyes. "It's not a joke. I used to be an emergency medical technician. She's dead."

"I killed her," I whispered.

Everyone turned to stare at me.

I backed away from their accusing looks. "Wait a minute. You don't think I really . . . I didn't . . ."

Their unfriendly scrutiny stabbed deep. I tried to catch Buffy's eye—I thought we were finding our way to friendship—but she let her glance slide away from me.

"I didn't even want to play this stupid game." I wished I could weep to soothe my hot eyes and relieve the agonizing tension, but no tears came. "It was Grace's idea!"

Out of the mind-numbing silence that greeted my cry came Madame ZeeZee's voice. "I called nine-one-one."

I heard the sound of the door opening and wondered how the ambulance could have arrived so quickly. But it was only Rhett and Deb sneaking out of the studio.

Come back, you cowards! I held the words inside. I didn't blame them for leaving. I'd leave too if I could, but I felt tied to the horror of my story-come-true. No. Not my story. Grace's story.

Grace had initiated the deadly game. Grace had chosen her death pose, the very position and place she'd assumed when we found her. The tendrils of a monstrous thought poked through the confusion fogging my mind. Could Grace have committed suicide? Could the murder scenario she'd proposed have been . . . what? A way of making her death newsworthy? A way of getting even with me for some unknown slight? But suicide seemed even more improbable than murder.

Buffy leaned toward me. "You're not dancing."

I jerked away and stared at her. Buffy stretched her lips into what might have passed as a smile in other circumstances, but now seemed a rictus.

"What?" I asked, not certain I'd heard her correctly.

"Dancing in the presence of death," Buffy murmured.

And then I remembered my blithely naïve comment the day I took Grace's photo. *"I like the idea of a group of aging women dancing in the face of death."* What had prompted such a foolish remark? I knew how death affected me, how it numbed like the gathering waves of a tsunami, sucking up all emotion that would later crush me with its unbearable force.

The dance floor, empty of everything but Grace's body, beckoned me. I wished I were the sort of person who could dance in the face of death. I lifted one leaden foot, set it down and lifted the other, but the effort sapped all my strength. I stumbled to a chair, sank onto the seat, put my elbows on my knees, hid my face in my hands, and waited.

***

If I were a real writer—a writer whose passion for storytelling takes precedence over all else—I would have paid attention to the various folk who tramped into and out of the studio for the next couple of hours. Since I didn't pay attention, the only thing I can do is lump them all under that vague term often found in mystery stories but never heard in real life: "the authorities."

It must have been a slow day for emergencies because all types of emergency vehicles screamed to a halt in front of the studio—ambulance, fire engine, cop cars. Lots of cop cars.

Each of us—Madame ZeeZee, Margot, Jackie, Buffy, Nancy and me—were herded into a separate police car. I doubt the studio had been declared a crime scene so early in the investigation since there was no obvious indication of how Grace had died so I told myself being locked in a police car was standard procedure.

But I didn't believe it. I felt like a criminal.

An hour and a half after we discovered Grace's body, a bus for the handicapped pulled into the parking lot, circled around, and left. Kim's bus. I don't know why she hadn't stayed to find out what was going on—perhaps the confusion of people and vehicles were too much for her to handle. Rose came late for Arabic class, got caught in the swirl of official activity, and was released.

I peered over the front seat of the police car. The digital timepiece on the dashboard showed twenty-seven o'clock. I'd heard that sometimes cops played dirty tricks with those under their care, and I wondered if the erroneous time fell into such a category. I suppose I could have read the clock wrong, but I'd scrunched up on the back seat and didn't have the energy to unscrunch and look again. I'd used up all my reserves trying not to think about Grace, ignoring the odor of vomit and unwashed feet permeating the police car, and fighting to remain calm.

My cop, a sandy-haired fellow who didn't look old enough to be out of school, entered the vehicle, introduced himself as Officer Ephraim Ungar, and proceeded to ask me a few basic questions. Name. Date of Birth. Social Security Number. Occupation. Address. I gave him the information he requested, and recited the events of the morning—by then I'd turned the words around in my mind so many times they spilled out by rote. I didn't mention what I'd said about killing Grace, but otherwise I told everything I knew.

The officer had me sign my statement, said a detective would be in touch, and helped me out of his squad car.

I stood blinking in the harsh desert sunlight. I'd walked to the studio that morning and felt too drained after my ordeal to walk the mile back to my father's house. I'd hoped to hitch a ride with someone from my class, but I didn't recognize any of the cars in the parking lot. Most of the emergency vehicles had left, and only a couple of police cars remained. I suppose I could have asked Officer Ungar for a ride, but I couldn't bear the thought of climbing back into his odiferous vehicle.

As I dragged myself home, one dreary step after the other, I tried to make sense of Grace's end. By the time I got to the house—putty-colored stucco with a brown tiled roof and pinkish gravel instead of grass—I'd come to a single conclusion: In the game of life there is only one winner, and death had won again.

Chapter 5

No matter how often I replayed the past few weeks in my mind, hoping each time for a different story to materialize, it always came down to the same two sentences.

"You should write a book about us," Grace had said. *"I'll volunteer to be the murder victim."*

What if Grace had instead volunteered to be the queen bee in a women's lit novel, with all the rest of us swarming around her, trying to find our place in the world. Would she be alive today?

Or what if she'd volunteered to be the matriarch in a southern gothic novel, a medieval warrior in a fantasy, or the love interest in a cougar romance? Would her story have had a happy ending?

Now that Grace had died under suspicious circumstances, what role did she expect me to play? I had no experience as a private eye—I didn't even have experience *writing* a private detective. I couldn't be the nosy neighbor digging up everyone's secrets—I didn't know where most of my classmates lived. I couldn't be the village confessor, the woman everyone entrusted with their confidences—I doubted anyone would speak to me. And I certainly couldn't be a know-it-all mystery woman who was smarter than the bungling cops and who had an even more mysterious cohort who truly did know it all.

Me? I knew nothing, though I felt strongly that I'd been complicitous in Grace's death.

I haunted the local Facebook groups for a couple of days, hoping to learn more. I found many expressions of horror at Grace's murder, though her death hadn't yet been classified as a crime, at least not from what I understood. But no one posted any real news. I finally turned off my computer. Even if I learned something to put Grace's death into perspective, what could I do?

By now, most fictional detectives would be well on their way to solving the crime, but I spent my lonely days thinking of the metaphysical ramifications of those two powerful sentences: *"You should write a book about us. I'll volunteer to be the murder victim."*

On Friday, when the silence of my father's house and the

cacophony of my own overactive mind got too much to bear, I walked to the dance studio to see if classes had resumed, but yellow plastic cautionary tape sealed the door. I thought for sure the cops would have released the studio within a couple of days, but perhaps Grace's retired criminalist husband had insisted on keeping the scene sacrosanct until means of death could be established.

I called Madame ZeeZee to ask when classes would resume but got her voice mail. I left a message and trudged back to my father's house.

Sun glinted off the police car parked out in front. My footsteps slowed and my heart rate speeded up, but my mind stilled as I accepted the inevitable.

Officer Ephraim Ungar got out of his vehicle and waited for me. He had no partner with him, and he had a smile on his face, so perhaps he hadn't come to arrest me as I had feared.

"I've been wanting to talk to you," he said, eyes intense. "I'm a writer, too."

He continued talking, but I zoned out. I know I should be more sympathetic toward other authors, but most writer chitchat bores me. Besides, too many writers treat their craft with a messianic fervor that borders on arrogance, and from the tone of Officer Ungar's voice and the gleam in his eyes, I deduced he fit into this category.

I drew myself to attention. "Is there anything else I can help you with, Officer?"

He frowned at me like a petulant child being denied a treat. "I'm supposed to take you downtown."

I took a step backward. I sincerely doubted the other local cops called their single police station "downtown." Officer Ungar's use of the hackneyed term seemed to indicate he was playing a role, but I couldn't tell whether he envisioned himself as good cop or bad cop.

"Why do you have to take me to the police station?"

"I'm not at liberty to say, Ma'am." He opened the rear door, put a hand on the top of my head and eased me into the back seat as if I were a handcuffed prisoner in a dreary television show. Someone must have spritzed the vehicle with a deodorizer because now the scent of pine mingled with the odors of vomit and unwashed feet.

The officer scrambled around to the driver's side, started the car, and rolled down the street in silence. I felt a momentary pang for squelching his enthusiastic soliloquy about his writing, but when I fumbled for the door handle and couldn't find it, panic pushed all thoughts from my head. I put my hands on my knees in a vain effort to still my trembling legs.

For a second, a more dispassionate me peeped beyond the curtain of fear, and I wondered if in some recounting of this adventure, I'd laughingly proclaim—and believe—I'd turned the tables and interviewed the officer for a future character.

The truth—that I'd huddled in quavering speechlessness—would be too intolerable to remember.

At the police station, Officer Ungar shepherded me down a short hall into a small chamber furnished only with a table and two chairs. If not for the large mirror set into one of the cream-colored walls and the tiny camera in a corner of the ceiling, the room could have been any interview room anywhere.

But I wasn't waiting to be interviewed for a job. I was waiting for . . . what? I still didn't know.

After about ten minutes, a beautiful woman with masses of dark hair and sympathetic brown eyes strode into the room on low-heeled pumps. Though not tall, she exuded authority that seemed to fill the room, squeezing me into a too-small bubble of personal space.

She introduced herself as Detective Arsalee Morales, set a clipboard and a recorder on the table, smoothed the skirt of her navy business suit beneath her when she sat, and proceeded to ask me questions for which she already had the answer. Name. Date of birth. Social Security Number. Occupation. Address. The only thing new she asked me was why I'd come to that dusty desert town. She nodded encouragingly when I told her about relocating to look after my father. When I mentioned his death, she offered me the standard, "I'm sorry for your loss," and I almost thought her sincere.

She led me through the whole story—how Grace had proposed my writing a book about our dance class, how I had dithered, and how even after I'd decided to follow through with the project, I could not find the heart of the story.

"So that's why you killed her?"

I gaped at the detective. All softness had disappeared. Her eyes looked as stony as obsidian, her lips a blood-red slash in that implacable face.

I clenched my hands. I welcomed the pain of my fingernails digging into my palms because at least the unpleasant feeling made sense, a direct consequence of my action.

I took a deep breath and tried to sound strong and sure. "I did not kill Grace." Despite my best effort, the words came out wobbly, as if on a sob, and even I didn't believe them.

"So you're recanting your confession?

I have never liked being unjustly blamed for even small infractions and had gotten into the habit of explaining and re-explaining myself, which sometimes resulted in my saying too much or my being accused of contrariness. But now, when I needed to explain to save my life, no words came.

Finally I managed to squeak out a single sentence. "I never confessed."

"Three witnesses claim to have heard you say you killed Grace."

Three witnesses. Three women I'd considered my friends had thrown me to the wolves. I couldn't figure out why, and then I remembered my whispered, *"I killed her."*

Suddenly, the tears I had not been able to shed poured down my cheeks. *Cripes. What a cliché. A woman crying in a police station. How pathetic is that?*

I groped in my pocket for a tissue, then dabbed at my face, but the feeble attempt to wipe away the tears didn't stem the flow.

"Do you want a glass of water?" the detective asked.

I shook my head no. During the long days when my husband lay dying in a hospice care center, the tears never stopped falling, but I'd managed to get him the help he needed for his pain, nausea, and disorientation.

I now told Detective Morales what I'd often told the well-meaning nurses and caregivers. "Ignore my tears. They don't mean anything. Just a release of stress."

Detective Morales jerked her already erect body a bit straighter as if what I'd said surprised her. As if *I'd* surprised her. But perhaps I misread the situation. It could be she'd merely wondered what I had to be stressed about.

"I did not kill Grace," I said through my snuffles. "Words have power, and I was afraid that by writing about murdering Grace, I might actually have set her death in motion."

The detective tapped a sharp red fingernail on her clipboard. "But you claim you hadn't yet written the book."

The tears still flowed, but I found my spirits brightening. "That's true. I didn't write her death. We'd just talked about it. It was supposed to be fun. A game."

"And yet a woman is dead. Do you have any idea who might have killed Grace?"

"Did someone kill her?" I responded.

Again that slight upward jerk. Did she think I was playing with her, answering a question with a question?

She gazed at me, her dark eyes unreadable.

I broke the silence. "How did Grace die?" It must have seemed ridiculous, those words spoken so intensely by a woman with tears streaking her face, but the detective appeared oblivious of my distress, and didn't respond.

"Don't you see," I said as patiently as I could. "If she died of natural causes, then I couldn't have killed her." Even as I spoke the words, I knew I'd said the wrong thing.

Detective Morales pointed a finger at me. "So you did kill Grace."

"No," I yelled. "No. No. No."

The detective patted the air with a hand, as if telling me to calm down, but I'd already drooped in the chair, all energy spent.

The detective repeated her question. "Do you have any idea who might have killed Grace?"

I couldn't even find the strength to raise my head. "No," I mumbled into my chest.

"Come now. Surely you have some ideas."

An insane giggle arose in me, and I wanted to sass her with a "Don't call me Shirley," but I merely shook my head no.

"In your story, in your game, who had you picked for the perp?"

"That was the problem." I finally looked up, bleary-eyed, and met her interested gaze. "I couldn't think of a single reason for anyone to kill Grace. She really is—was—a lovely woman. I thought perhaps she'd be killed by accident or maybe someone would mistake her for Madame ZeeZee."

A tiny wrinkle marred the smooth expanse of the detective's brow. "The two women don't look at all alike."

"But what if the murderer didn't know Madame ZeeZee?"

Detective Morales put an elbow on the table and rested her chin in her upraised hand. "Why would someone want to kill Madame ZeeZee?"

I thought the detective was humoring me, but I'd shifted into writer's mode, and didn't care. "Nobody would want to kill Madame ZeeZee, of course, but I considered using someone from her past. Do you know who Ruth St. Denis is?"

Chin still propped in her hand, the detective managed a small shake of her head.

"Ruth St. Denis is the mother of modern dance. She was the first to incorporate eastern dance into her routines and was especially interested in Egyptian influences. In her later years, she had a studio near the Hollywood Bowl and taught many influential people. She died in 1968 at the age of eighty-nine, but her work still lives on. Madame ZeeZee was the protégé of a protégé of Ruth St. Denis, and some of the routines she's teaching us were created by Ruth St. Denis herself. It astonishes me to think I'm a direct descendant, artistically speaking, of the mother of modern dance, and I wondered if I could use that as a reason for murder, but I never developed the idea as a possible plotline."

The detective made a notation on a form attached to her clipboard, but I couldn't tell what in my recitation had caught her interest. For all I knew, she could have been reminding herself to pick up Chinese food for dinner.

"Who else did you consider for the doer?"

I hesitated. Deciding I owed no loyalty to anyone who smoked in my vicinity, I said, "They guy who owns the nail salon would have been a good villain, though a bit clichéd. Dark, foreign, enigmatic. A spy maybe."

"Anyone else?"

"Someone suggested that we should all do it, but that seemed too awkward to me. Ludicrous even. Since I couldn't think of a single reason someone would kill Grace, it would have been almost impossible to come up with a reason for each of us wanting her dead."

"So you did want her dead."

I didn't bother to answer.

"Who suggested all of you do it?"

"Does it matter?" I said wearily.

"Could it have been Buffy?"

"If you knew, why did you ask me?"

Without even a blink to acknowledge my response, she went right to her next question. "Are you going to finish writing the book?"

"I told you, I never even started. But if I do write the story, I'll like to get the details right. Will you keep me informed about your investigation?"

I didn't expect an answer to my brazen query, but she readily responded. With a smile, even.

"I'll tell you anything you need to know. In turn, I want you to keep me informed about your writing."

She rose and gathered up her accouterments. "Please wait here until I get your statement typed up." She exited and click-clacked down the hallway in her low-heeled pumps.

I watched her go, feeling as if I'd been played, though I had no clear concept of what her game had been.

I did know she had no intention of telling me anything about her investigation—saying she would served some function in her game plan.

And, after I'd waited an hour until a young cop came with the papers for me to sign, I knew she had no intention of getting me a ride back to my father's house.

Chapter 6

On Sunday, five days after Grace's death, I received an email from Madame ZeeZee saying classes were to resume on Monday. She included a new schedule. Monday afternoon—advanced jazz and tap. Tuesday morning—intermediate ballet and Arabic. Wednesday afternoon—beginning and advanced Hawaiian and Tahitian. Thursday morning—beginning ballet and beginning tap. Children's classes were Monday and Wednesday after the adult classes.

I'm not an advanced dancer, though Madame ZeeZee allowed me to follow along with the advanced classes as best as I could. In private moments of hubris, I thought I danced better than some of the advanced students. Deb was too full of herself to notice how badly she danced, so she never strived for improvement. Rose seldom made more than a minimal effort, and when she did take broader steps, her movements looked painful. She'd lost weight so fast, her tendons hadn't yet tightened, and she seemed all jutting bones and loose joints, like a marionette pulling her own strings. Lena, of course, was always off beat, either too fast or too slow.

But I was nowhere near as good as the best dancers in the class. Although Allie was too new to know all the routines and she made her steps too tiny, she learned fast as if she'd spent a lifetime studying dance. Buffy looked elegant in all her movements, making even the most complicated step seem effortless. Grace, of course, was graceful in all she did.

Monday morning, I dithered about going to class. I'd always thought Madame ZeeZee allowed me to take the advanced class out of friendship for me, but remembering the pained look she'd given me when the cops escorted her to a squad car, I couldn't be sure our friendship still held. Thinking of Deb, Rose, and Lena, I told myself that of course, I belonged and should go. Then, thinking of Buffy and Grace, I knew I had no business taking that class.

In the end, I couldn't not go. I missed dancing, missed the feeling of participating in something bigger than myself. And though I expected to be shunned by my classmates, I needed to see Grace, to make sure she was okay. I'd been present at both my dad's and my husband's death, so I'd known they were gone. I had seen Grace lying on the floor of the studio, but she'd looked peaceful, as if she were sleeping, and somehow, despite the involvement of the police and their interrogation, I could not believe the truth of her death.

Buffy, Rhett, Lena, Allie, and Deb huddled by the studio door. They seemed oblivious of my approach, but one by one they looked at me and gave me smiles of varying warmth, from Deb's glacial lip movement to Rhett's wide I-don't-give-a-damn grin.

I nodded my hello. Unable to bear their collective flinch if I stepped too close, I stopped a couple of yards from the group.

They shifted their weight from foot to foot and averted their gazes. Rhett cleared her throat as if she were about to say something, but remained as mute as the others. Buffy took a step forward, hand outstretched, then, as if pulled by the will of the group, she let her arm drop. I took it as a good sign that she didn't shrink back to her previous spot.

I knew it was up to me to break the anxious silence, but my stubborn streak took that moment to make itself felt. I had not done anything wrong, and I'd be damned if I'd I would try to make them feel comfortable.

Buffy's lips quirked, making me think she knew the powers at play and found us amusing. I responded with my own wry quirk, but our subtle reaching out got lost in Madame ZeeZee's arrival.

"Sorry I'm late." She unlocked the door, and only then did I realize the yellow crime scene tape had been removed. She reached inside the studio to turn on the light and stepped aside to let us enter.

As I passed her, our eyes happened to meet. I detected no censure. Still, I didn't let myself relax but held myself stiffly. I glanced at the floor by the barre in the far corner and did not see Grace lying there. I let my breath out in an audible rush that had heads turning in my direction.

I'd changed from my street shoes into my jazz shoes and was bending over to tie them when I heard the door open. I jerked myself upright and fought my disappointment. Rose shambled in, shedding purse, dance bag, shoes. Her soft-spoken hello sounded like a gunshot in the silence and shattered the constraints binding us. Lena and Deb talked over each other, and Rhett mumbled something about forgetting her water bottle.

Madame ZeeZee turned on a jazz tune, and we plodded to the dance floor to begin our warm-ups. I kept looking at the door, and finally burst out with the sole thought on my mind.

"Grace isn't here?"

Everyone stared at me in the mirror, eyes wide with shock. I stared back. I felt sickened by the cruel charade of Grace's death, and I wanted the grisly joke brought to an end.

Buffy turned to me, a sad smile on her face, and said, as if I were one of the children she had taught not long ago, "Grace passed away."

Tears stung my eyes. "No. Words don't kill. She can't be gone."

I looked longingly at the door, wishing Grace would arrive, wishing I could leave. But I didn't have the strength to break away from the group. And Grace didn't enter.

"How did she die?" Rhett asked. Usually Rhett, with her energy and the sensibility of a teenager, amused me, but I could not forget that she had sneaked out of the studio before the cops had arrived.

"Does it matter?" I tried to sound callous and must have succeeded because Rhett took a step back and flashed her don't-give-a-damn smile.

"I talked to Charlie," Madame ZeeZee said.

"Who's Charlie," Allie whispered to Deb.

"Grace's husband," Deb whispered back.

"They won't know for sure until the full autopsy is finished," Madame ZeeZee continued as if the two women hadn't spoken, "but the preliminary finding is that Grace died right before we found her. They don't know if it's what killed her, but her skull was cracked with something like a baseball bat."

I drew in a sharp breath. *Or like the ballet barre.* Could Grace have slipped and hit her head? But what had she been doing in the dark studio by herself? And why would she have slipped? Grace had a dancer's balance and sure-footedness. Could someone have pushed her?

"Being hit with a baseball bat wouldn't kill someone." Deb patted her head above her right eye. "I got hit with a baseball bat and—"

Usually nothing got through to Deb, but this time, the baleful look Madame ZeeZee fixed on the woman shut her up.

"When is the funeral?" Allie asked.

"Not until after the autopsy. Maybe another week." Madame ZeeZee moved to the front of the class. Although grief showed the age on her face, her step remained light and youthful.

We started with jazz plies and knee pops at the barre, then faced the mirror for stretching and easy aerobic moves. The room seemed crowded for so few of us. It took me a minute to realize the truth—we all stood far from where Grace had fallen.

I pushed the conflicting thoughts of Grace out of my head—Grace dead, Grace not dead, Grace still dancing in some alternative universe, Grace completely gone—and tried to give myself over to the magic release of dance. I blundered through the learned sequence of steps, aware of Grace's absence from her customary place in front of us.

Suddenly the music stopped, and I felt myself jerking back to reality.

"You're not together." Madame ZeeZee spoke harshly. "When you dance in a group, the group has to act as one person. Every one of you was doing something different."

"But Grace . . ." Rose's voice faltered under Madame ZeeZee's stern regard.

I felt a pang of sadness for Rose. If I were fumbling with the steps, how much harder it must be for Rose, who'd never taken her eyes off Grace when we danced.

Madame ZeeZee looked from Rose to me to Rhett. "I've told you for years that you need to know the steps. You can't rely on me or Grace always being here for you to follow. Try again."

She turned on the music, and we step-touched, step-touched our way across the floor, kicked and swung our hats while Madame ZeeZee watched us with a pained look on her face.

"Let's try again."

We did the dance over and over—"Chorus Line," a dance we all knew—but we couldn't get through the routine even once without a mistake. Finally, Madame ZeeZee turned off the music.

"Put on your tap shoes."

We practiced windshield wipers, shuffles and flaps, Maxie Ford's, on Broadway, Buffalo, and time steps. We worked on our new dance for a few minutes, "Anything Goes," a dance we'd been learning for months, but from the way everyone acted—pausing when there weren't pauses, running into each other, forgetting even the most basic steps like flap-ball-change—you'd have thought we'd never practiced the dance at all.

With a half an hour of class time remaining, Madame ZeeZee turned off the music and dismissed us.

No one spoke to me as we changed into our street shoes, but I caught sidelong glances from Rhett and Deb that seemed accusatory. I felt like twice a murderer. Not only had I killed Grace, I'd also killed Dance.

Tuesday seemed more normal, perhaps because we started out with ballet, a class Grace hadn't taken. And Kim showed up for Arabic, laden with her dance bag, white cane, and a whole lot of questions to fill the silence.

"When I called Madame ZeeZee last Tuesday to find out what happened, she told me Grace had passed."

We murmured our agreement.

"Someone hit her on the head," Deb declared, "but that couldn't have killed her. I was hit on the head with a baseball bat and—"

I clenched my hands into fists and raised my voice over Deb's. "It hasn't been established that someone hit her on the head with a baseball bat. It hasn't been established that someone killed her. She might have fallen and hit her head on the barre."

"That's where you found her?" A frown marred Kim's perfect brow. "Under the barre?"

Rhett pointed to the space on the floor we all still avoided. "Right there."

Kim turned her frown on me. "Where you took the photo. Was she in the same position?"

"Exactly the same." Rhett gave a broad smile as if she relished the game. And maybe it still felt like a game to her. After all, she hadn't remained in the studio with Grace's body.

But I had stayed until the cops came, and Grace's death didn't feel real to me, either.

Kim turned her head away from the spot. She still had some peripheral vision, and maybe she hoped to see Grace lying there. "How did she get in that exact position?"

"Maybe she was trying to reach the barre so she could die dancing," Buffy said.

I had the world-shifting sense of déjà vu, and I could almost hear Grace's laughing response, *"That's too true to be funny."* At least she hadn't died on stage with an audience watching, but if she'd been murdered and not simply fallen and hit her head, someone had watched her die. The thought made me shiver.

"Maybe she was trying to tell us something," Margot said.

"Like a clue." Jackie sounded excited to be able to make some sense of the senseless, then her excitement dimmed. "But what could she have been saying?"

Deb sneered at me. "Maybe she wanted us to know Pat killed her."

I reared back as if slapped. I knew Deb had as little affection for me as I held for her, but I hadn't realized the depth of her dislike.

Buffy sent me a sympathetic smile that helped ward off Deb's chill. "Pat couldn't have done it. Everyone knows the murderer in a classic mystery is the one least likely to have done it."

"Like who?" black-haired Lena demanded, her voice strident.

"Any of us but Pat." Buffy looked at each of the women in turn. "Jackie, perhaps, because she always takes everything in stride. Rose and Allie because they're both so quiet. And Margot, of course."

Margot's smile wobbled, as if she didn't know whether to take Buffy's words as an insult or a compliment. "Why 'of course'?"

Buffy held up one finger. "For one, you didn't have classes with Grace. If you didn't know her, you wouldn't have reason to kill her."

"And that makes me a suspect?"

"In a classic mystery, unraveling the motive is half the story, so the least likely murderer makes the most appealing villain. If a character has a motive, and we know the motive, and we find out that character did the deed, we feel cheated."

"But this isn't a story," Rose said quietly.

Jackie laughed. "Sure it is. It started out as a story, so why shouldn't it continue being a story? For all we know, Grace could still be alive."

I studied Jackie. Buffy had it right, Jackie did take everything in stride. She didn't affect a don't-give-a-damn attitude like Rhett, but appeared to accept life's vicissitudes with ready humor. Could that acceptance and humor come from the ability to mow down anyone or anything that got in her way? I had to admit life would be easy if you could simply make your problems vanish. But why would Jackie have wanted Grace out of her life? She wasn't even in it. Like Margot, Jackie only took ballet.

"Could Grace be alive?" Lena asked. "I never saw the body."

"You didn't?" Margot gave her a puzzled look. "I thought you were here that day."

Buffy held up two fingers. "That's the second reason you'd be the logical murderer, Margot. You're the one who said Grace was dead. And you also moved the body, so we don't know for sure how exactly the positioning matched Pat's photo. And if you'd overlooked any evidence, you could have removed it."

"Stop it!" Madame ZeeZee's shout more than her words halted our chatter. No matter how amateurish our dancing or how lacking in discipline she considered us, our teacher had never raised her voice.

"I know what you're doing," Madame ZeeZee continued in a more modulated tone. "You're trying to make yourselves feel better about Grace by distancing yourself from her passing, but you just have to face it and move on. Let's practice 'Ya Habibi.' Buffy, you come up front with me."

Buffy hunched her shoulders and took two tiny steps forward. My heart went out to her. I knew how much she hated being in the front where everyone could see her, and it would be even worse for her to be dancing in a dead woman's place. I felt grateful for the extra weight and ungainliness that kept me in the second row where I could dance in obscurity.

"I'll do it." Allie said, a glint of greed—or was it need?—in her eyes.

Buffy took a big step back into line with the rest of us.

Allie glided to the front of the class. Deb brushed past her and planted her feet.

The light in Allie's eyes faded, and she slowly slipped back to her usual place, but she shot Deb a look that made me shiver.

I glanced over at Madame ZeeZee, wondering if she'd seen the byplay, but she had turned away and was sorting her CDs. When she raised her head and saw Deb in Grace's place instead of Buffy, she said, "I don't care who dances in the front row. But you have to know the dances."

Deb lifted her chin. "I know the dances."

Madame ZeeZee stared at her a moment but didn't say anything further. Maybe she had seen the look of triumph on Deb's face and didn't feel up to tangling with her.

"Whew," Buffy whispered. I don't know why she was so self-conscious about dancing where we could see her—she was a wonderful dancer, tempering precision with style and a perfect sense of rhythm.

Jackie and Margot left, and the rest of us stumbled through our learned dances without a word of censure from Madame ZeeZee. Apparently she realized that we were doing the best we could, even though our best must have seemed nightmarish to her.

After class, as we were changing into street shoes, Madame ZeeZee asked, "Is anyone going to lunch?"

Those of us without other plans often went out to eat after class on Tuesdays and Thursdays. I'd wondered if Grace's death would make such a gathering feel frivolous, but Madame ZeeZee's question seemed natural.

Everyone else begged off, so only Madame ZeeZee and I walked to the Mexican restaurant across the parking lot. She acted glad to have my company. Despite her words—and belief—that you have to forget the dead and move on, I suspected she felt as confused as the rest of us.

We took our taquitos and drinks to a small table.

Madame ZeeZee poked a straw into her diet drink. "I shouldn't have yelled at you girls."

"It's okay." I took the cover off my cola and squeezed fresh lime into the cup. "We're all on edge."

"How are you going to find out who killed Grace?"

I jerked, rocking my cup, but caught it before the liquid could spill. "Me? I'm not a detective."

"But you're a writer."

"Just because I can write characters who go in search of the truth, it doesn't mean I can search out the truth myself. I wouldn't know where to begin. What if Charlie killed her? How would I find that out? It's not like I can go breaking into their house to find clues. I don't even know where Grace lives. Lived."

Madame ZeeZee picked up a taquito, then set it down untasted.

I peered at her. "Are you okay? You look—"

"I'm fine."

Her sharp tone bit deep. I held up my palms. "Whatever."

She narrowed her eyes at me. "Don't be so sensitive. Dancers have to learn to deal with criticism. Sometimes my teachers made me cry, but I still kept dancing."

I refrained from pointing out that I would never be a dancer and that she hadn't criticized me but nodded my head in agreement. My feelings did get hurt easily, as if I were a child and not a grown woman rapidly sliding down the banister of late middle age.

We crunched our taquitos, and when she finally spoke, I couldn't make out the words over the sound of my chewing.

I swallowed the masticated food. "I'm sorry. I didn't hear what you said."

"I'm worried. What if people think I killed Grace? What if they think . . ."

I waited for her to find the right words.

She took a deep breath and continued in a rush. "What if they think I'm a bad teacher? What if her dying gives the studio a bad name? What if Grace was killed instead of me?" She stopped and stared at me in surprise, as if she hadn't expected that final "what if."

I wrapped my arms around my middle to hold in a sudden spasm of grief. The fear in my seemingly fearless teacher made me realize, as nothing else had, that Grace's death was not a dream from which we would awaken. I remembered my dispassionate discussion with Detective Morales about possible motives for murdering Madame ZeeZee, and I felt ashamed of that glibness.

"I'm sorry."

Madame ZeeZee offered a small smile. "For what? You're not planning on killing me next, are you?"

"Of course not. If I did, I wouldn't have anyone to teach me to dance."

She chuckled as I hoped she would, but it sounded more like a sob than a laugh and vanished in an instant. "If Grace died instead of me, then . . ."

I remained silent. I couldn't think of anything reassuring to say, and I doubted she'd have wanted me to voice her unspoken words,

"Then someone could still be after me."

"Why would anyone want to harm you?"

She sipped her soda, her guileless gaze meeting mine. "When I was young, maybe another dancer if I got a part she wanted. Now? No one."

"What about your choreography? When you said you could be the murderess, you suggested that Grace could have stolen your choreography."

"That was for a story. There's no camaraderie among teachers here. No one would know about my choreography, and if they did, they wouldn't care. My dances are classical. Most studios in the area teach modern things like line dancing and hip-hop."

"Can you think of any reason why Grace would have been in your studio that morning? She didn't take ballet."

"Maybe she forgot her tap shoes and stopped by to pick them up on her way to her other tap class. Or maybe someone called, pretending to be me, and asked her to come to the studio." Her dark eyes lit up. "Then it wouldn't be me they were after!"

I played with the guacamole that covered my taquitos and kept my thoughts to myself. With the prevalence of cell phones, an unheard of technology in early detective literature, Grace would have known immediately the call hadn't been placed by Madame ZeeZee. Unless someone had stolen Madame ZeeZee's phone? But no—I remembered Madame ZeeZee that morning saying she'd spent the previous hour on the phone with her mother's caregivers, and I remembered her using the phone to call 911. And I remembered something else, something that had seemed strange to me at the time, but had been pushed out of my mind by the calamitous events of that day.

"When we saw Grace lying on the studio floor, you said, '*What's Grace doing here? I didn't say she could spend the night.*' What did you mean by that?"

"I don't know what you're talking about." Madame ZeeZee glanced at her watch. "It's late. I have to go." She gathered her purse and fled out the door, leaving me with two plates of mostly uneaten taquitos.

I shrugged, dumped her taquitos onto my plate, and munched to the tune of my roiling thoughts.

Chapter 7

In every mystery story, it seems, there comes a time when the author wants a way to present insights, needs to show state of mind, or simply gets bored with a straightforward narrative and plays at being creative, so the storyteller recounts a dream.

Since I hate dreams, my own included, I usually skip those parts of a book, so I won't bore you with the details of my dream. Suffice to say that early Wednesday morning, long before the sun gave any indication of wanting to rise, I dreamed I was Grace grieving the death of Pat. I carried the belief I was Grace into the first moments of waking, and for a second I didn't know if I were Grace grieving for Pat or Pat grieving for Grace.

In the aftermath of that strange duality, when I came fully awake, I lay there wondering about my connection to Grace, wondering if somehow my talking about her death had brought it about. I no longer thought Grace existed in some sort of quantum state, both alive and dead, and all we had to do was find a way to observe her and she'd magically appear back in the studio, smiling up at us, asking why she reclined on the floor.

I do know that anything is possible, that at our most infinitesimal level, way beneath cellular construction and even atomic configurations, we are created from discrete patterns of nothingness held together by a force of energy that could destroy—or build—the universe. Our senses, and ultimately our brains, translate those waveforms into what we see, hear, taste, feel, know.

That is what we have to contend with in our daily lives—what we know. And I know Grace is dead.

(Grief is not always so conciliatory. I know Jay is dead, but I also know he is at home waiting for me. It's why I continue to hang around this California desert town though I have no real reason to stay now that my father is gone—I'm reluctant to return to Colorado and confront the foolishness of my belief.)

What do I know other than that Grace is dead? Not much, to be honest, though I do believe someone else was involved with her death. There have been times when one or another of us students slipped on a slick patch of the studio floor, so a fall would not be particularly mysterious, but if Grace had hit her head on the barre hard enough to knock herself out, she would not have been able to arrange herself in the position we found her.

So that left me with three conclusions: someone killed her and arranged the scene; someone killed her and Grace managed to drag herself into position during her final moments; or someone found Grace unconscious, moved her, and left her to die.

But why? How could Grace's death have made a difference to anyone's life? I've heard it said that there are three main motives for murder—sex, power, and money. I suppose sex could be a motive for the murder of a long-married seventy-five year old woman, but it seemed farfetched to me, especially since she appeared to be devoted to her husband. Whatever money Grace had belonged to both her and Charlie so I didn't see financial gain as a possibility for a motive, either. And power? What sort of power could Grace have exerted on anyone, or someone exerted on her? I thought of Deb eagerly slipping into Grace's spot at the front of the class, and I wondered if the desire for that sort of power, so insignificant to the rest of the world, could have made Deb want to do away with a woman she might have considered a competitor.

Knowledge, of course, is power. Perhaps Grace had discovered a secret, but among our assorted classmates, who could have a secret so powerful that only murder would protect it?

I hoped the police would find the truth soon, because the dream made me uneasy. If I couldn't distinguish between myself and Grace, is it possible others saw the same connection? Could I be next on the murderer's list?

I got out of bed and dressed for the day, vowing to protect myself. But against whom? Margot, the woman Buffy had picked out as the perfect murderer? Or maybe Buffy herself, a woman who knew too much about the ways and means of murdering?

***

When I first came to the high desert to look after my father, I was in so much emotional turmoil, the harsh environment barely registered. What did manage to seep beneath the armor of my grief fit the way I felt—arid, bleak, lifeless. Enough years had now passed since Jay's death that I felt more connected to the world, more present, and now the desert sun tortured me. Before I'd walked a quarter of a mile, the heat had burned through my meager clothes— the black cotton leggings and over-sized tee shirt, the hat that was supposed to protect my head, the walking shoes and cushioned socks that were supposed to protect my feet.

By the time I neared the studio for my afternoon class, perspiration dripped off my body and drenched my clothes. The physical discomfort as well as the social discomfort of having to deal with the large group of women waiting outside the studio made me want to turn back, but I plowed ahead.

Luckily, Madame ZeeZee pulled into her parking space before I reached the door, saving me from the chore of having to introduce myself and make polite conversation with the women I didn't know.

I went to the back of the studio with Rhett and Michaela, a Liza Minnelli lookalike who only took Hawaiian classes. While we pulled on our pau skirts, the new women gathered around Madame ZeeZee's small counter to pay for their lessons.

One woman, who looked about fifty, bounced on the balls of her feet with excitement, like a kid waiting for a treat. "I used to take my kids to a Hawaiian class, so I know a lot of the steps." She hugged herself. "They're grown up, and now it's my turn."

"I never even knew this studio was here," another woman said, sounding more annoyed than thrilled.

A third woman spoke in a tired voice. "I read about it on Facebook. My doctor says I need to exercise, and this sounds like less work than going to a gym."

I waited for someone to ask about Grace, but no one mentioned her. Maybe they had forgotten why they'd heard about the studio. Or perhaps they were embarrassed at taking a dead woman's place.

Madame ZeeZee didn't seem to give a thought to how these women had discovered her, but then, she wouldn't. She had a practical bent, and new students—however they'd found her—would help pay the rent.

By the time Madame ZeeZee had taken payment from the women and handed out receipts, there were only forty minutes left for class. She had us form three lines for warm-ups. There were so many people in class we had no choice but to spread out and use the entire length of the dance floor. It wasn't until we were in the midst of practicing arm movements and the basic hula steps—vamping, *helas, amis, kalākaua*—that I realized I was standing where Grace's body had lain. I froze for a second, then offered a quick, silent "I'm sorry, Grace," and gave myself up to the island rhythms.

Later, while Madame ZeeZee taught the new students the first verses of a chant, the advanced class began to arrive, and suddenly order devolved into chaos. The new students milled about, talking to each other and the teacher. Rhett twirled toward the recent arrivals, shouting with laughter, high on adrenaline, and explained about the influx of dancers. The advanced class pulled on skirts or tied sarongs around their waists, gathered up their instruments and set them out on the dance floor, darting around anyone who stood in their way.

I leaned against the barre so I wouldn't add to the commotion. Gradually, the two groups sorted themselves out, one batch of women leaving, the others gathering in the middle of the studio to chat.

Rose told about a friend of hers who had just broken up with her boyfriend, and Lena sidled up next to her. "I am so glad I'm married. I wouldn't want to be out there at my age."

Allie nodded. "It's good to be settled."

"And not married to an asshole," Rhett added.

"I'm lucky. I found the last good man," Deb said then launched into a tale of the wondrous thing her husband had done the previous night. It sounded to me as if he'd merely changed a light bulb, but it was hard to tell because all the women were prattling at once. Rhett listed what she'd fed her husband, Buffy mentioned an off road trip she and her husband had planned for the weekend. Allie bragged about the huge bouquet her husband had sent her that morning for their anniversary, and Lena chimed in, adding a story of her own.

Standing at the barre by myself, I felt bleak and shunted aside by their complacency.

Michaela came and stood next to me. "Are you okay?" Although Michaela was married, she hadn't taken part in the smug chorus, so I felt kindly toward her.

I gave her a sad smile. "Sometimes it seems as if all they talk about is their husbands."

"It's what they know." She sounded sympathetic, but I didn't know if the sympathy were for me or the other women.

I sighed. "I suppose. But it's hard for me."

"That's not their problem, is it?"

Michaela had always seemed wise to me, able to see both sides in any disagreement, but her words sounded accusatory and made me feel more alone than ever. I knew not having a husband anymore was my problem, and I wasn't blaming the wives for leaving me out of the conversation, but didn't friendship mean that you sometimes took another person's situation into consideration? But then, these women were not my friends. We were merely dance mates.

Maybe I was spending too much time in the company of married women. Maybe I needed to seek out other widows as I did in my first year of grief. They, at least, would know how I was feeling.

Madame ZeeZee tried to say something, but she couldn't make herself heard over the din. Finally, she clapped her hands. "Girls, girls!"

In the sudden cessation of chatter, the music for warm-ups sounded louder than usual. Everyone scattered to their places, raised their arms, and began bending at the waist.

At the count of six, Lena gasped. "Oh, My God," she said, "Pat's standing on Grace."

Rhett laughed. "Frankly, my dear . . ."

I stopped and fixed my gaze on Lena. "How do you know I'm standing on Grace? You weren't here when we found her."

Lena's voice sounded as sharp as her spiked hair. "Everyone said she was found the same way you took the photo of her."

"Where were you the morning she died?" I asked. "Why didn't you come to class?"

She looked around the studio, as if searching for support. The others continued to do their warm-ups, though they looked at her in the mirror, apparently waiting for her response.

"This isn't the place for playing detective, Pat."

Resentment lodged in my chest at Madame ZeeZee's reproach—she was the one who'd urged me to find out what happened to Grace—but I kept my mouth shut, even when Deb snickered.

Normally, Madame ZeeZee allowed some conversation in this particular class since most of the women had been with her for more than a decade, but she kept us working, going over and over each dance, correcting the smallest misstep.

When Rose and Lena commiserated *sotto voce* with each other about the teacher's strictness, Madame Zee stopped the music.

"We're dancing at a luau tonight, and we have to be perfect. When you dance on stage, small mistakes aren't noticeable, but when the audience is just a few feet away from you, they notice everything."

"Yeah," Deb said. "And some of you are doing it wrong."

It amazed me that Madame ZeeZee didn't respond to the comment since Deb made more mistakes than anyone, but the teacher ignored her. She turned on the music and said, "Begin again."

"What luau?" Allie asked Lena.

Madame ZeeZee responded. "A bereavement group. When you learn the dances, you can start doing luaus with us. Now that Grace is gone, we need someone to take her place."

"The show must go on. Neither rain nor snow nor death of a classmate . . ." Deb chuckled at her joke, but no one else laughed.

***

Only four of us went to the luau—Madame ZeeZee, Rhett, Lena, and I. The light and easy laughter I heard inside the house as we waited for someone to answer our knock told me these people had not experienced an immediate death. They'd had time to become accustomed, at least in part, to their grief, and to be able to put it aside at times.

We were welcomed by the host, a widower, shown to a bedroom where we could change into our vibrant red flowered pau skirts, red tops, greenery around our wrists and ankles, and yellow plumeria leis and heis. We went outside and sat in a white gazebo, a perfect setting for us in our beautiful costumes, until it was time to perform. We danced using a variety of instruments, *Pu`ili, uliuli*, and *ipu*. And, as always, despite what Madame ZeeZee had claimed in class, any minor missteps were hidden beneath our swishing skirts.

Afterward, the audience gathered around us for photos. A few women who had lost their husbands stayed to talk to us.

"We're bereaved, too," Madame ZeeZee said. "One of my

students just died. She'd been with me for twelve years."

The women expressed sympathy, and we nodded solemnly at their condolences, though I was aware of the vast difference between our loss and theirs. I remembered vividly those first traumatic years after Jay's death, the shock and bewilderment, the unbelievable pain that only screaming could mitigate. I'd gone to a grief support group the first year of my own bereavement to try to make sense of the emotional whirlwind, and now I seemed to be slipping back into sorrow. Wondering if I would benefit from a bit of support, I asked about their group. They looked at me a bit strangely, as if they couldn't figure out why the loss of a friend would prompt my question, so I explained that my husband was dead, though I hastened to add that it's been five years.

"Then you know what it's like to cry at any moment," an older dark haired woman said, tears in her eyes.

I nodded.

"We've just celebrated our first anniversary." The tearful woman pointed to herself then to the tall blonde woman standing next to her. "It's hard, harder than I thought it would be."

"The second year is often worse than the first," I said. I still couldn't believe the fact of those words, and yet I had experienced the phenomenon myself. I had clung to that first anniversary as some sort of goal, a turning point, but after the day had passed, I spiraled back into the grief maelstrom as the truth, that he was never coming back, set in.

"It can't be," the blonde said. "I won't let it happen."

They urged us to stay for the buffet they'd laid out. After changing out of our dancing costumes into our travel costumes of white clam diggers and Hawaiian shirts, we went into the kitchen for a snack. I could hear the two women I'd spoken to discuss what I'd said about the second year.

"I'm afraid I'm going to have another bad year," the tearful woman said.

The blonde woman leaned against the counter, plate in hand. "Not me. Now that I'm out of the first-year widow's fog, I'm done with grief."

A gray-haired woman sitting at the table, her face severe in sorrow, looked down at her still full plate of chicken and fruit salad.

"It's because the widow's fog is gone that the second year is so much more difficult. There's nothing to soften the reality."

I could feel her pain, could even feel the sadness beneath the blonde's bravado. Their grief was still so new that it made my intermittent sorrow seem like nothing worse than a cloudy day. I felt a terrible pang of loneliness. I didn't belong with the women in my class, so smugly married. Nor did I belong with these widows. Would there ever be a place for me again? Would I always feel so set apart?

When I'd started taking classes with Madame ZeeZee, dancing gave me the feeling of belonging, if not to a group, then to a group effort, but Grace's death had changed that. Maybe when the truth was finally known, when we could lay her to rest in our minds, I wouldn't feel so bereft.

But how I could find the truth about Grace? There were no amateur detectives in real life. At least, I'd never heard of any. Fictional plots often demand that an amateur solve the crime, but life does not guarantee neat solutions. Besides, so much of what fictional sleuths do would be considered criminal, such as spying on people, breaking and entering, harassment, and trespassing. If nothing else, an amateur in real life could be arrested for interfering with an investigation.

I often fret about my future and how I'm going to survive on my meager social security check when my savings are gone, but jail time is not a good retirement plan.

Still, I suppose, it wouldn't hurt to ask a few questions. No one had any obligation to respond, though there was a chance at least some of my classmates would like to unburden themselves of angst or regret over Grace's death.

But what if someone confessed to being the murderer? That could be dangerous.

Maybe I should continue to do what any smart amateur would be well advised to do: leave the detecting to the professionals.

Chapter 8

The first thing you learn when you set out to write a novel is that you need a strong protagonist. No ditherers. No brooders.

And I am both.

In an effort to appear strong, at least to myself, I called the police station before I headed to class and asked for Detective Arsalee Morales. The man who answered the phone took my name and number and said he'd give her the information.

Torn between relief and disappointment that I didn't get to talk to the detective, I trudged to the studio. Seeing Margot and Jackie chatting outside the door, I quickened my steps. We said our hello-how-are-yous, then I turned to Margot.

"On Tuesday, you said you thought Lena was here the day Grace died. Do you remember why you thought that?"

Margot's long blonde ponytail swished when she shook her head no. "I just remember seeing her that morning."

"I didn't see her," Jackie said. "She wasn't in the studio when we found Grace."

"Who all was here beside us?" I asked. "Rhett and Deb were. I remember them because I looked over when I heard the door, and both of them were leaving."

"They left?" Margot sounded shocked. "Before the cops came?"

"Yeah." At the time, I thought they were being cowardly, but now I wondered if they'd snuck out because they had something to hide.

Jackie held up two fingers. "Nancy was here. And Buffy."

"They left?" Margot stared across the parking lot, as if unable to fathom such behavior. And then her mouth opened in a silent *oh*. "Now I remember! Lena was over there." She pointed to the gas station at the opposite side of the parking lot. "I was paying for my gas, and she was having coffee. At first I didn't recognize her because she wasn't wearing one of her wigs and she didn't have any makeup on, but it was her. There was a bruise on her cheek, and her eyes were red as if she'd been crying."

"Could she have . . .?" I let my voice trail off, unwilling to say the words out loud.

Jackie narrowed her eyes at me. "Are you thinking she killed Grace?"

"No."

I must have sounded as doubtful as I felt, because Jackie cocked her head and said, "But . . .?"

"But maybe they got in a fight. You know how Lena air boxes when she's agitated. I bet she could do some damage."

"And then what," Jackie said. "Lena leaves her there, cuts across the parking lot for coffee before she goes home to clean up?"

"It's not how I would have written it, but life doesn't follow genre conventions."

"But why would she have fought with Grace?" Margot said. "Lena had enough real violence at home."

Now it was my turn to be shocked. "What? Violence? Who?"

"Her husband."

I thought of yesterday and how Lena had said complacently, *I am so glad I'm married. I wouldn't want to be out there at my age.* Did she really think that being married to an abusive husband was better than not being married at all? Could she have made the comment in an effort to make herself feel better? Or was the black-haired Lena so dissociated from her blonde persona that she didn't know about the abuse?

"How long as this been going on?" I asked.

"A year or two. He was always demanding, but now that he has Alzheimer's, he's gotten angry and abusive. He treats her okay as long as he takes his meds, but sometimes he refuses to take them."

Jackie looked at me and shrugged, then turned to Margot. "How come we didn't know about this?"

"She doesn't want us to feel sorry for her, but she let it slip at Bunco one day. My mother is in the same Bunco group as she is."

And suddenly something that had been bothering me made sense. "Does Madame ZeeZee know?"

Jackie laughed. "I think it would be hard to hide anything from Madame ZeeZee."

So Madame ZeeZee let Lena sleep in the studio to escape her abusive husband.

My feeling of satisfaction at solving that little mystery faded as I realized it only created more questions. Had Grace shown up when

Lena was still there? Did Lena know what happened to Grace? Did Lena have a key and the ability to slip in and out of the studio at will, or had Madame ZeeZee come to let her in?

Rhett sauntered up to us.

"Hey, how're you doing?" Jackie asked.

Rhett grinned broadly. "Super good, but I'll get better."

That was the outrageously upbeat Rhett's way of saying things weren't going well.

"Why did you leave that day?" I spoke more harshly than I intended, but I didn't care. I was fed up with unanswered questions and people who pretended to be other than they were.

Rhett's grin faded, and she shivered. "Dead bodies give me the creeps."

Her tone and the simplicity of her answer rang true. Could all the little mysteries surrounding Grace's death be as easily explained?

We watched Madame ZeeZee drive up, climb out of her Kia, and struggle to open the door while balancing CDs, purse, and carryall.

"Sorry I'm late. Deb and Lena called. They can't come today. Deb is sick and Lena's husband has a doctor's appointment. Since there will be so few of you for beginning tap, I'm cancelling class. I hope you don't mind."

"Good," Rhett said. "My feet hurt. My arthritis is acting up."

We traipsed into the studio, took off our street shoes, and put on our ballet slippers. Margot went into the bathroom to change out of her denim skirt and into her leotard and tights. The rest of us had worn our ballet clothes to the studio, leggings and ballet skirts and leotards. Well, except for me. I wore a tee shirt instead of a leotard.

It felt good to concentrate on the discipline of the steps, to stretch, and even to do the combinations that are often too hard for me.

One combination we practiced over and over: *sissone right, sissone left, pas de bourree, arabesque, glissade, tour jeté*, and ending with a *soutenou* turn. I got frustrated because *tour jetés* are almost impossible for me. Still, after several clumsy attempts at making the turn, Madame ZeeZee said, "Good."

I gave her a sideways glance of disbelief.

"You've got it," she explained. "You just can't do it."

For some reason, her comment made me laugh, but at that

moment, the door crashed open, and my amusement fled.

Detective Arsalee Morales stood in the open doorway, legs wide, hands on hips like Wonder Woman.

"Can I help you?" Madame ZeeZee asked.

The detective crooked a finger at me. "I need to talk to Pat."

I slunk across the floor, and went outside.

"I got the message that you called," Detective Morales said.

Relief washed over me. "Oh, is *that* why you're here?"

"I'm having lunch at the restaurant." She pointed to the Italian place a few doors down from the studio. "I thought I'd drop in and see what you're up to."

What I'm up to. What does that mean?

I tried to keep my tone neutral. "I called to see if you had any news about Grace."

"Is there anything you want to tell me?"

I felt like banging my head with my fists to relieve the frustration of talking to her, but I looked her in the eye. "No. I . . . I." Her bright gaze disconcerted me, and embarrassment kept me from admitting I'd been asking questions. Besides, if she didn't know about Madame ZeeZee letting Lena stay at the studio, which was probably against the law, I certainly wasn't going to tattle.

"You are aware that investigating on your own is dangerous, don't you?" she said.

I nodded without looking at her.

"But you're curious. You need to know if you killed Grace."

"I didn't—"

"Look. If you think your book had anything to do with her death, why don't you write a killer into being? Save us both a lot of trouble."

"So she was killed?"

"We don't have the autopsy results." Without any word of farewell, she strode to the restaurant.

I stared after her, wondering what had happened. Detectives weren't supposed to play games like that, were they? But then, how would I know—the only detectives I knew were fictional ones, and they were created by authors who might be as unfamiliar with the way detectives worked as I am.

Maybe I should create a detective of my own, one who would be more understanding and more understandable.

Too exhausted to do any more jumping around in class, I watched through the glass door until Jackie, Margot, and Rhett finished the sautés that ended the session.

When I reentered the studio, all four women looked at me, perhaps surprised that I hadn't been arrested.

"What was that about?" Margot sounded suspicious, as if she thought I might have betrayed her confidence about Lena.

"The police still don't know how Grace died," I said. "They don't seem all that concerned." I gave a humorless laugh. "She said I should write a killer into being. What sort of detective says that?"

"She seemed straightforward to me," Rhett said. "Just asked a few questions is all."

Madame ZeeZee, Margot, and Jackie nodded their "me too"s.

I shouldn't have been surprised that the cops had talked to Rhett, but I was, not so much that they had tracked her down, but because it showed they had more of an interest in the case than I'd suspected.

Maybe it was just me Arsalee Morales had a problem with. Or maybe she overestimated my influence as an author and was auditioning for a part in my as-yet-unwritten book.

Madame ZeeZee went to her office alcove to gather up her belongings..

"I didn't tell the detective about Lena." I whispered the words to Margot so softly they were barely more than lip movements.

Madame ZeeZee called out, "What did you say?"

"Nothing. Just asking if anyone is going to lunch." I cringed at the lie, but I wasn't ready to admit I knew about Lena. Let Madame ZeeZee keep her secret a bit longer.

Margot declined the lunch invitation, but after Madame ZeeZee locked the door, the rest of us wandered across the parking lot.

"Are you going to write a killer into being?" Jackie asked.

"How can I? If I were to choose one of the women I'm not fond of, it would be like playing favorites—or unfavorites—and that might make my relationship with them even more uncomfortable than it is now. And if I chose someone I liked, that definitely would make our relationship uncomfortable."

"What about someone you don't know?" Madame ZeeZee asked.

"I probably will have to make the killer someone I don't know, but if I don't know someone, how can I write about them?"

Rhett laughed. "So make someone up. I'm having the taquito special."

Except for vegan Jackie, who ordered beans, guacamole, and rice, we all ordered the special.

When we sat down to eat, talk rolled around to husbands, houses, diets, elderly parents. Not having anything to offer on any of those subjects, I munched my food and thought about villains.

Should I create a muscular square-jawed fellow, such as Fearless Fosdick? Or maybe a Hannibal Lector type, who set his fancies on older women? Or what about a Black Widow who killed wives instead of husbands?

All at once I realized what Detective Morales had done—gotten me to think of fictional killers instead of real ones. Cripes, the woman really was playing with me.

Hmmm. Maybe I should write her as the villain. Wouldn't that be an interesting twist?

Chapter 9

If I had become caught in a blockbuster thriller instead of this cozy little mystery, by now a dozen bodies would have been strewn across the desert landscape in an effort to prove both how vile the villain and how heroic the hero.

But there has been only one death, and I have encountered neither villain nor hero, just cops doing their job and women trying to maintain normalcy in the face of tragedy.

On the three day hiatus from class, as I finished emptying my father's house, taking what remained of his effects to a thrift shop and stowing my possessions into a storage unit, I contemplated villainy.

I thought the detective would make a lovely perpetrator because she would be even less obvious than Margot, Jackie, or Buffy. She might have known Charlie, Grace's criminalist husband, since she could have worked for the police department before he retired. The problem with making the cop the evildoer is that if she were as smart as I suspected, her chance of getting caught would be minimal. She would know all about trace evidence and would be able to plant enough extraneous material to confuse even the most astute lab technician. The only way I would know she did it is if she told me, and I sincerely doubted she would unburden herself to me at the end as villains in thrillers do, explaining herself interminably and waving a gun until I managed to escape her final desperate act.

Besides, Grace's death seemed more a matter of opportunity than preparation. The timeline was simply too tight. Grace had died shortly before we found her, so the detective could not have known ahead of time if she'd have privacy to do the deed.

Reluctantly I abandoned the fun of making Arsalee Morales the villain, and considered Lena. I shied away from picturing her as a murderer, mostly because I didn't want to heap more horror onto her thin sad shoulders. But still, she might be involved in some way, might have seen something to shed light on the mystery. I knew I needed to tell the detective about Lena—I'm no lone wolf, at least not when it comes to matters of my safety—but I would have to talk to Madame ZeeZee first, and I didn't quite know how to broach the subject.

Could anyone else have seen something? I should have asked Margot and Jackie if they knew who had arrived at the studio first and how long people had been waiting so I'd have an idea who might have been involved in the crime. I didn't chastise myself for the oversight because knowing who came first wouldn't help much—a killer could have slipped out before any of us arrived.

I thought of the women who had been at the studio that day and wondered if there could have been some sort of conspiracy, with all of them having a hand in the matter. Margot, Jackie, Rhett and Deb, Buffy, Nancy.

Oh my gosh! Nancy! Nancy hadn't been to class since Grace had died, and I hadn't even noticed.

I grabbed my phone off the empty counter where I'd set it while I finished packing the kitchenware, and called Nancy. The phone rang four times, then went to voice mail.

"Hi, Nancy. This is Pat. We missed you in class. Are you okay? Call me."

I set the phone down and wondered if Eddie could have killed Grace, thinking he'd agreed to murder for real, not as a literary game, and now the two of them were hiding out.

Sickened by the direction of my thoughts, sickened even more by my treatment of Grace's death as some sort of puzzle to play with, I grabbed my hat, house key, and a bottle of water, and went for a hike in the desert, but the heat and exertion did nothing to burn away my distaste.

By Monday, the four-bedroom house echoed emptily. Besides personal items and a bit of food, the only things in the house were a pan, a plate, a cup, a set of flatware, a mattress made up as a bed, a bedside lamp, my computer on the counter, and a stool to sit on. I was exhausted from all the work and eager to escape to the studio where I hoped no more bodies were lying in wait.

When I arrived for class, the women were clustered inside by the door. They were chatting excitedly, so immersed in their conversation they didn't seem to notice I had entered the studio.

Kim was back for jazz class. She only took two classes, Arabic and jazz, though lately her attendance at jazz class was sporadic. I stood immobile, trying to make sense of the women's chatter. It sounded as if they were bringing Kim up to date. I distinguished a few words. Grace . . . cops . . . investigation . . . accident. *Accident?*

I angled closer. "What happened?".

"I talked to Charlie this morning," Madame ZeeZee said. "They ruled Grace's death an accident. She fell, banged her head and bled into her brain. The funeral will be held this Saturday."

"Such good news," Allie said. "No one killed her."

"Good news?" Tears blurred my vision. "However it happened, Grace is still dead. She will always be dead."

I felt like a hypocrite, shedding tears that weren't so much for Grace as for my own dead. Would I ever be able to think of death without crying, without being reminded that Jay was gone?

"But aren't you glad you're off the hook?" Deb's sneer belied the friendly-sounding words. "Now no one thinks you're a murderer."

Madame ZeeZee glared at her. "What are you talking about? Nobody thought Pat killed anyone."

I looked at each of the women in turn. Madame ZeeZee. Deb. Allie. Buffy. Lena. Rose. Rhett. Kim. Except for the teacher, none of them looked back at me with the same familiarity they had regarded me before Grace died. Even if they hadn't considered me a murderer, I bet they believed I had brought about her death with all the talk of my book. I sure believed it. The coincidence of Grace being found in the same position as in the photo I'd taken was simply too much to overlook. But apparently the cops didn't think it important.

"So the investigation is closed?" I asked.

"I guess." Madame ZeeZee held out her hands, palms up. Even in a gesture meant to show disbelief tempered with resignation, her hands moved gracefully. I wondered how many years it took to become so unconsciously steeped in dance.

I felt glad I still had time to learn, but then the guilt descended. Because of me, Grace no longer did.

"Stop that, Pat. You have nothing to feel guilty about."

I jerked my head up. Had Madame ZeeZee read my thoughts? No, probably just my body language.

Madame ZeeZee softened her tone. "We all feel bad, but it's time to go on with our lives. We can't live in the past."

She was right. There was nothing I could do about the past. If the disposition of the case was in error, then Charlie needed to follow through, not me. I had my own problems to deal with. Where to go when the new owners took possession of the house. How to get on with my life.

I vowed to put Grace out of my mind. Vowed never again to drag real people into a book. Vowed to stop brooding and questioning and to live in the moment.

The music started. I took a deep breath and let it out slowly. *This moment is my life. This moment, poised on the brink of dance. And it is good. So very good.*

***

The wonderful mood lasted through the two Monday classes. When I asked Madame ZeeZee to explain a step and Deb answered at the same time, as if being in the front row gave her the right to tell us what to do, I waved away the annoying intervention, and concentrated on the teacher's instruction. I ignored black-haired Lena moving too fast for the beat, Rose slouching through the routine, Rhett overdramatizing her lindys. Instead, I danced between Kim and Buffy, who made me feel I was a much better dancer than the mirror showed, and I moved serenely through the dances.

I walked home, still feeling good. Entering the empty house added to my tranquility instead of subtracting from it as I'd expected. I wandered through the rooms, feeling nothing of my parents' presence, feeling not even the ghost of my grief for Jay. I didn't think about what I would do when I lost the only home I'd known the past five years. I simply enjoyed the feeling of a job well done.

And then, the phone rang.

I shouldn't have been surprised—in mysteries, phones always seem to ring when a character needs a change of direction.

But I should have been forewarned. Such calls never bring good news. That I didn't have the person's number in my phone should have been another warning, but even if I had heeded the omens, I would still have taken the call. I am not one of those who can ignore a ringing phone. It presents a mystery, and I don't like mysteries. Not the little mysteries of who is on the other end of a line or whodunit in a whodunit. Not the big mysteries of the meaning of life or what happens when we are dead. I have an insatiable need to know, and mysteries—especially unknowable ones—taunt me.

Luckily, this mystery was easily solved. I answered the phone.

"It's Lena."

Lena? What does she want? I didn't have to wait long to find out, though it took a few seconds to make sense of the breathless words that tumbled over one another.

"Grace wasn't the only one there that morning. What if she knows I saw her? I'm scared. I need to talk to you. Meet me at the gas station by the studio. I'll be there in fifteen minutes."

"Who was there that morning? Look, I'm tired. I don't want to go out. Why can't you tell me now?"

I heard sounds in the background, like someone shouting and things breaking.

"Gotta go. See you in fifteen minutes."

Like a fool in a bad drama, I stared at my phone. *Huh? She expects me to drop everything and drive over there so she can tell me something she could just as easily have told me over the phone?* With a shudder, I realized what had just happened. The worst cliché of all. So often in mysteries, someone makes such a call, and when the recipient arrives at the rendezvous, they find the person dead.

Fear for Lena rippled through me.

Should I notify the police? They would laugh at me. I could ask for Officer Ephraim Ungar, the writer—he would take me seriously—but I didn't feel up to coping with his zeal. Should I stay home? Let Lena handle her fate by herself? Let a stranger find her?

But, as always, my need to know got the best of me. I climbed into my ancient VW bug (no, I am not plagiarizing a well known fictional detective, I really do own such a car—bought it new when I was young and never got another auto) and drove to the gas station.

Lena's white Subaru was parked in front of the gas station. I went inside and looked around. I didn't see anyone but a jeans-wearing woman with pewter-gray hair sitting at a small table, drinking coffee. She waved at me, and I realized it was Lena without either of her wigs. Not raucous. Not babyish. Just tired. And old.

As the fear of finding her dead body left me, I felt like throttling her for putting me through such anxiety. *Alive is good*, I reminded myself.

Lena looked up at me. "Sit down. I can't talk with you hovering over me."

I sat. She didn't talk.

When the silence dragged beyond my patience, I said, "What's going on?"

"Rose says not to tell you anything because you blab."

"What the . . .? When did I . . .?"

She brushed a speck off her pink tee shirt. "She said someone told you something in confidence and you told Madame ZeeZee."

"Huh? I have never spoken to Rose outside of class, so anything she ever said to me, everyone could have heard."

Lena drained her cup and set it down with more force than my question had warranted. "That's all she said, that you blabbed."

I sat shaking my head, wondering if I knew myself so little. Did I really blab? And how elementary school this conversation seemed. I remember sitting in class in fourth grade, waiting for the teacher to come. Each kid whispered to the one behind. All I could hear as the message was passed around the class was, "Spspspsps. And don't tell Pat." When the girl in front of me got the message, she rose, walked around me, and whispered to the kid behind me.

At recess, I finally talked someone into telling me the secret that was so horrible they couldn't tell me. Apparently, our teacher was sick that day, and the other students were afraid I would tell the principal and a substitute would be assigned.

I was flummoxed. I knew that if the students had found out about the teacher's absence, the principal would also know. Were they that stupid they weren't aware of how the system worked? But mostly, I couldn't understand why they thought I would tell. The only time I had ever spoken to the principal, she had taken me aside after an assembly and told me I'd been seen jaywalking. I still remember quaking while she chastised me.

"I'm just repeating what I heard," Lena said.

"I get it. Rose thinks I blab. Is that what you wanted to talk about?"

"I know something, but I don't want you to tell anyone. I don't want to get Madame ZeeZee in trouble."

"Is this about you spending the night in the studio?"

"Who told you?"

64

"No one had to tell me. I figured it out myself."

She fiddled with her Styrofoam cup, turning it this way and that, as if it were the most interesting thing she'd ever seen. "So you know about my husband?"

"I'm very sorry. It must be difficult for you."

Lena rubbed her wrists as if they hurt. "I had no place to go. He was out of control. I couldn't stay at the house with him, my daughter was out of town, and all the motels were filled because of the evacuations."

I nodded to show her I understood. A brush fire had burned out of control in the nearby hills for days, and people close to the burn areas had been told to evacuate. I'd heard that local motels had tripled and quadrupled their rates but so many people had been evacuated, they rented all the rooms at those inflated prices.

"I called Madame ZeeZee. She said I could stay at the studio, so I stopped by her house for a key. I think she regretted the offer because she made me promise not to tell anyone."

Tears rolled down her wrinkled cheeks. "I did something terrible."

My heart pounded. *Oh, no. Please don't tell me you killed Grace.*

"I couldn't stop crying all night. He was so angry at me, I don't know who he is any more or who I am. I felt as if my life was over. I called Grace in the morning. She always said the right thing, and I needed to talk to someone. She thought I was suicidal, so she said she'd stop by on her way to her line-dance class."

Lena looked up at me with sad puppy dog eyes. "I had to tell her where I was. She came. I unlocked the door for her. She hugged me, and we talked. I finally felt able to go back home and deal with my husband."

"I understand all that, but how did Grace end up dead? What did you do?"

"Not me! I didn't do anything. She was my friend." She put her hands on the table, hoisted herself out of the chair, fetched a wad of napkins, and plopped back onto the seat. She wiped her eyes, and blew her nose.

"I think Deb killed her."

The evening had been filled with so many shocks, this one barely seemed to register. Still, when I spoke, my voice shook.

"Deb killed Grace? Why didn't you tell the cops?"

"I couldn't. I lied. I said I was never there."

"I'm guessing you don't want me to talk to them, either."

"You can't say anything to anyone. Promise me you won't."

"I'm lost. Why am I here? Why are you telling me this?"

"Because Deb is blaming you. She says Grace died because you're so disdainful."

I laughed, then caught myself. "I'm sorry. I don't mean to make light of the situation, but it doesn't make any sense. I do know that people think I brought on Grace's death because of the book. The whole 'thoughts create the reality' scenario. But to kill her with disdain? How is that possible."

The hangdog look disappeared from her face, and her voice sounded accusatory. "You come across as arrogant. You stand off by yourself in class and look superior."

I didn't know whether to laugh or cry. Or scream.

I remember feeling sad and lonely and shunted aside by their talk of things that no longer pertained to my life, and they thought me arrogant for not joining in? Cripes. How could they not see the truth?

Did anyone ever see the truth of another person?

I took a deep breath. *This moment is my life.* My new mantra didn't comfort me as it had earlier in the afternoon. If this was my life, I was in big trouble.

"Okay. Tell me. How did my disdain kill Grace?"

"Back when you first started to talk about your book, it upset Deb because you always make everything about you. No matter what she says, you act disdainful and say something to prove how much better you are than her. She says when she told us about her book, you interrupted and told about the book you were going to write about our class."

I laughed unapologetically. "I don't believe this. You were there—don't you remember?—it was the other way around."

She shrugged her shoulders. "Whatever. The thing is, she said that anyone can write a murder. The hard part is doing it, making it look like an accident, and not getting caught. She said that murder, at least, was something you could not do better than her."

Horror blazed through me as understanding dawned. "Are you saying that Deb killed Grace to prove that she's better than me? To prove that she doesn't deserve my disdain? What . . . is she crazy?"

"Maybe. She told me once she had killed her ex-husband, but I don't know if she really had killed him, or if she just pretended she had done it to make herself seem important. You know how she is."

The remembered sound of Deb's laughter echoed in my ear. I didn't know why she had laughed when she'd suggested herself as the victim, but if she had killed her ex-husband, she might have enjoyed the irony of being on the other end of the murder weapon.

"Either way, it seems crazy to me. When did this conversation with Deb take place?"

"A few days before Grace passed away."

"How do you know she killed Grace? Did you see her do it?"

"Grace was alive after we left the studio that morning, but I saw Deb pull into the parking lot when I was going to get my coffee."

She looked at me as if waiting for a verdict.

I looked back at her. "And?"

"And what? That's all there is. I had to tell someone because I saw Deb that day and now that Grace's death has been ruled an accident, it's proof that Deb did it. I don't want to be next. I figure if someone else knows, she won't kill me because it won't gain her anything."

I felt my face go blank. "Are you setting me up to be the next victim?"

"I can't die. I have to take care of my husband and you don't have anyone." She looked at her watch and jumped out of her chair. "Oh, no. I have to go. The caregiver's time is up."

"Wait! How did Deb get into the studio?"

"I forgot to lock the door."

She hurried out of the convenience store, leaving me with more questions than my poor befuddled brain could handle.

Could Deb be a murderer? Did I have to add disdain to the list of my guilts? Was anything Lena told me the truth? Thinking over our conversation, I realized I had brought up the subject of Lena staying at the studio, not her. Could she be such an accomplished liar she had built an entire scenario on that one comment?

Is it possible Lena herself killed Grace?

I dragged myself upright, went outside, climbed into my car. And screamed.

Chapter 10

In the early months after Jay's death, when I couldn't bear my agony any longer, I'd go out in the desert and scream. Sometimes I'd scream for him. "Jay? Jay? Where are you?" Sometimes I would scream mindlessly, in too much pain to form words.

Screaming still worked for me.

After screaming intermittently on the way back to my dad's place, I let myself in the house and fell onto the mattress fully clothed. Although my years of grief had turned me into a fitful sleeper, that night I slept without moving, without dreaming, without once getting up to relieve my bladder.

In the morning, fortified by a protein drink and a handful of supplements, I strode to the studio. Deb stood alone outside the door.

Sometimes when I noticed Deb by herself, I'd steal out of sight and wait for someone else to show up so I wouldn't have to cope with her supercilious attitude, but I marched right up to her and invaded her space.

She stepped back as if afraid I'd attack her.

I shot my words at her. "What happened to Grace?"

She jutted out her chin. "Aren't you getting things mixed up? Shouldn't you be asking yourself that question?"

"You know very well I didn't touch her." She opened her mouth, but I didn't let her get out a single sound. "What did you do to her? I know you were here that morning."

"Are you forgetting her death was ruled an accident?"

"I did not forget. Someone else was here. The police might have dismissed our testimony that Grace lay exactly how she'd posed for the photo. Maybe they thought it dramatic hyperbole. But I know the truth. And so do you." I punctuated each of the last four words with a poke to her chest.

She swung her arm back.

I leaned toward her. "What, are you going to hit *me* now?"

She let her arm drop, seemingly defeated. "I didn't hit her. She fell. You've got to believe me."

I didn't trust this new role of hers, and I remained wary, ready to dance out of her way if she dropped the aggrieved manner and turned aggressive.

I narrowed my eyes at her. "Whenever anyone says, 'you've got to believe me,' I know they are lying."

"It's the truth. When I came to the studio that day, I saw Grace walking to her SUV. It looked as if she tried reaching into her purse for her keys, but the bag wasn't hanging off her shoulder the way it normally did. She hurried back to the studio. She tried the door, and it opened. She went inside. I followed her. She must have heard me, because she whipped around to look and somehow tripped herself up. She fell. Banged her head on the barre. Knocked herself out. That's what happened. I swear it."

My breath caught in my throat as I visualized what came next. "Oh. My. God. You arranged her body and left her there to die." *Because of me. Because of my disdain.*

"I didn't leave her to die. I left her for everyone to see what you'd done. I thought Madame ZeeZee would get there soon and we could call an ambulance. If she hadn't been late that day, everything would have been fine. It's your fault, you and that stupid book of yours. You're the one who killed her."

I dropped to the sidewalk and sat crosslegged. I cradled my midriff with my arms, and rocked forward and back to ease the pain. I told myself the agony would dissipate, but I didn't know how it could. Never before had someone died because of me. I could not forgive myself for that. Nor would I forget it. Tears seeped beneath my closed lids.

"What now?" Deb taunted me. "Are you going to call the cops and blab? Blab to Madame ZeeZee?"

I shook my head more in disbelief than in answer to her question. I didn't know what I was going to do. Would telling the cops bring Grace back to life? Would it ease Charlie's pain? It would be hard enough for him to accept that his beloved wife died accidentally. It would be almost impossible for him to accept that she'd died because someone counted coup.

And what about the class? As nightmarish a class as we were, we still functioned as a group. Would knowing the truth of Grace's demise make any difference to how we danced or interacted? Did I have an obligation to tell Lena her fears were unfounded? That Deb hadn't even known she had a part in setting up the tragedy?

I'd spent so much of my life dithering over minor matters, now that I had to deal with a serious dilemma, I felt paralyzed.

I heard footsteps. "What's with Pat?" Madame ZeeZee asked.

"I don't know." Deb sounded worried. "She was like that when I got here."

Maybe I should tell the cops. Such a lying narcissistic sociopath shouldn't be left on the streets. But what could the cops do? It would be her word against mine. She might have wanted me to know what she'd done—it's no fun winning a sick game of one-upmanship if the loser didn't know about it—but I doubted she would ever admit her part in Grace's death to anyone else.

Slowly and awkwardly, I got to my feet.

"Are you okay?" Deb asked, still pretending to care.

"I'm fine." I all but spit the words at her.

Madame ZeeZee gave me a furrowed brow look of concern.

I softened my tone and added a weak smile for her benefit. "I'm okay, really. Felt sick to my stomach for a few minutes is all."

"Do you want to skip class today?"

I was about say yes to the teacher's question when I caught Deb's smirk. Afraid of what other mischief she might get up to in my absence, I decided to stay. By then, Buffy, Jackie, and Rhett had arrived. Although all five women gathered around me with murmured words of empathy, I felt more alone that ever.

As it happened, I could have left. Deb was on her best behavior, or at least no more pompous than usual. Maybe she felt she'd vanquished her villain, teddy bear though I might be. Or maybe . . . oh, hell. What difference did it make why anyone did anything?

Sometimes you do your best, and everything turns out wrong. Sometimes you do your worst, and everything turns out okay. And who's to say which is which?

I stumbled through ballet, though oddly, perhaps because I wasn't concentrating overly hard, I managed to do six *chaine* turns in a row, a record for me, and I did an acceptable *tour jeté*.

After our Arabic class, Madame ZeeZee offered to drive me back to the house, and I accepted.

We talked of small matters—the belly dance we were learning, Nancy's continued absence, the new students and if any of them would show up for Hawaiian class the next day.

Madame ZeeZee pulled into the circular driveway and turned off the engine. "You can't let anything Deb says bother you."

Even when she turns me into a murderer? "I'll try. I wish I knew how to be less sensitive. But I'm a writer. Being sensitive is part of who I am." I opened the car door. "Do you want to come in? You haven't seen the house since I finished emptying it."

"I'd love to!" She responded so rapidly, I knew she'd been waiting for the invitation.

We wandered around the house. Lately, because of all the work I'd done to get the residence ready for the new owners, I'd come to hate the house, but seeing the place through Madame ZeeZee's eyes, I noticed how lovely it was. Huge great room with vaulted ceiling and a stone wall with a fireplace; a fabulous kitchen with granite counters; formal dining room; media room; two small bedrooms with a connecting bath; a vast master bedroom with a fireplace, built-in bookshelves and a bathroom big enough to dance in. On the other side of the kitchen were my living quarters. A small bedroom and bath, and a large living room.

"It looks brand new," Madame ZeeZee said in amazement.

She was right. My elderly parents lived lightly, as did I. After the rugs were cleaned, the windows washed, and a few smudges on the corners from my father's oxygen tubing wiped away, the place looked as if it had never been lived in.

I felt a sudden pang of nostalgia for the house. Although much of my stay hadn't been fun—I had my grief to live with and my father's too-frequent hospital visits and recuperations to handle—it now seemed as if this interval had been a sinecure, a time out of time. I would soon be dropped back into the real world, a widow and an orphan, left to make my way as best as I could.

"I know it's hard, but you'll be okay." Madame ZeeZee hugged me. "See you tomorrow."

I watched until she got into her car and drove away. The house suddenly felt lonely.

This moment is my life. And it is good. I stood still, breathing in and breathing out. For that span, I actually believed in the goodness of my life, then I remembered Grace and Deb and disdain, and the good feeling crashed.

I went to my computer and Googled "Is it illegal not to report a crime?" I discovered that a citizen has no obligation to report a crime except in the case of child endangerment. You can be charged with a crime if you aided and abetted in any way, but I doubt "disdain" would be considered aiding or abetting. It is against Federal law to conceal a felony if you are directly asked about the wrongdoing during the course of a criminal investigation.

I Googled "Is it a felony to let someone die?" And found out that no, it isn't a felony. It isn't even a crime. There is no "duty to rescue." If you didn't put the person in their predicament, if you have no special relationship to the person, such as parent and child or hotel keeper and guest, then you have no responsibility to help. Deb did more than not help by repositioning Grace, but that probably isn't a crime, either.

I didn't know whether to feel good that I had no obligation to say anything to the cops about Deb's confession or appalled that she could get away with allowing Grace to die. It might not be murder in the eyes of the law, but it sure seemed like murder to me. That Deb could be so coldblooded made my own blood run hot.

Even after finding out what I needed to know, I continued to read various articles about reporting crimes and talking to the police, and I came across two chilling bits of information. One, that if the police call you in to the station wanting you to clarify your statement or if they stop by just to chat, they consider you a suspect or a possible suspect. And two, that you should never talk to the police even if you are innocent because anything you say can and will be used against you. If they haven't Mirandized you, they couldn't use the information in a trial, but they could use it to trip you up further, to take any misstatement or contradiction as a means to further implicate you, to confuse you so much you land in a jail cell. On the other hand, refusing to answer questions other than basic information such as name, address, phone number, would for sure land you on their list of suspects.

I worried about what I might have divulged to Detective Morales that could be used against me in some way, but I barely remembered anything I said. The interrogation seemed far away as if it had happened in another country and to a different person.

But none of that mattered now. Grace's fall had been ruled an accident, and according to Deb, it really had been an accident.

According to Deb. I knew Deb for a liar. I knew Lena for a conniver. It's possible that between the two of them, they had cooked up the story of Grace's fall to hide a deliberate crime, but I had no reason not to believe the story Deb dished out to me.

I just had to learn to accept my part in the tragedy, and go on from there.

And I had to learn to keep my mouth shut.

Apparently, I do have a tendency to blab. Keeping my mouth shut was hard to do, not so much in the beginning Hawaiian class since I didn't know many of the women, but in the advanced class where I knew everyone. As we worked on our dances, I fought the urge to talk about Grace, stifled the need to repeat what Deb had said. I had to keep reminding myself that no good would come of assuaging my pain by spreading it around.

I also found myself freezing instead of reacting to anything or anyone. If an honest, though not admirable reaction such as disdain, caused someone's death, I feared creating some other form of chaos all unknowingly. Telling myself I hadn't killed Grace didn't help, especially when Deb kept sending me conspiratorial glances.

"What's with Pat," Allie whispered to Lena.

Lena, the conniving coward, whispered back, "Just being standoffish."

I managed to get through the classes on Thursday without telling anyone the truth. Despite the heat, I wandered through the desert for hours on Friday as I had done when I first came to look after my father. The long treks that had helped me get through the worst of my grief now offered me a respite from my guilt and sorrow over Grace's demise, but as soon as I showered away grime and sweat, the pain returned.

I did not go to the funeral. Instead, I again walked in the desert and asked Grace to forgive me. I told her I forgave her for her part in the horror. Forgave Jay, too, because if he hadn't died, I would never have come to this hellish place.

If. A small word to carry such a ponderous load.

On Sunday, I turned on my computer and opened a document to begin writing the dance class book. Nothing I wrote now could hurt Grace—the story had already done its damage—and I hoped setting down my feelings about the dancer's death would help me put everything that had happened in perspective.

I got as far as: *I didn't want to kill Grace—it was her idea.*

Then I broke down into tears.

On Monday, no one said anything about my absence at the funeral, and both Deb and Lena seemed to have forgotten they'd ever revealed themselves to me.

Deb planted herself in the front row as if she belonged there. It irritated me because—well, because Deb always irritated me, but mostly because I knew that Buffy had earned the spot.

I made a point of looking away from Deb as we danced. The woman made so many small errors I feared getting mixed up and forgetting the right way to do things, but the others, especially Rose and Lena, watched her as they'd watched Grace. I sometimes caught Allie staring at Deb as if she couldn't forget how the woman had pushed her out of the way to claim the coveted spot, but Allie never said anything, and oddly, neither did Madame ZeeZee.

During Arabic on Tuesday, Madame ZeeZee stood off to the side and watched while we practiced our dances.

I turned right to begin a series of four *ronde de jambs,* right, left, right, left, while Deb and all the others turned left. I stopped and stood there confused. Had I really gotten the steps wrong? But no. I pictured Grace turning right, and knew I'd done it correctly.

"Let's start over," MadameZeeZee said. "Pay attention, Pat. When you dance in a group, you all have to move as one."

But you also have to do the dances right, I wanted to cry out. I tried not to let the dismay at the injustice show on my face. When Madame ZeeZee led us in the dance, and she turned right to begin the *ronde de jambs*, I also tried to hide my feeling of vindication.

Between dances, Madame ZeeZee shuffled through her CD collection, looking for a particular number. She took so long, Rhett got restive and started making up her own dance. Deb and Lena whispered to each other, but the rest of us stood in place waiting for the music to start.

"I can't find it," Madame ZeeZee said, sounding frazzled. "Let's do 'Dola Dola' without the music."

Rhett laughed. "We don't deserve the music."

I remained after class. I wanted to ask Madame ZeeZee what was wrong, but Rose talked to the teacher and didn't give me a chance to say anything. I found it interesting that although Rose seemed to have a hard time speaking up in a group, she found no such constraints when it came to chatting one on one.

When I got tired of listening to Rose catalog her ills, I left.

Later, Madame ZeeZee called me. "Rose said you don't like her talking to me."

"Huh?" What had I ever done to the sickly woman to make her think I harbored such envy? "I don't care who talks to you. I got tired of waiting is all."

"I know. That's what I told her."

"I'm glad you called," I said. "How are you doing? I've been worried about you. You seem distracted lately."

"It's my mother. She's started falling, and she refuses to use the LifeAlert button. Yesterday she sat on the floor for five hours until the caregiver came, and then she screamed at the girl. I am at my wit's end. I can't do anything because she refuses to give me her medical power of attorney. Ninety-eight years old, and she wants to do everything herself. She won't even sign a DNR."

I empathized with my teacher, but I felt a spurt of gladness that the troubles with my parents were over. Dealing with the elderly, especially independent-minded elderly is not easy.

"She's so nasty." Madame ZeeZee said. "I worry that I'm going to be as horrid as she is when I am old."

"You'll be fine. Unless something happens to change your personality, like some kind of disease or a side effect from drugs, your core personality magnifies in old age. I can see us in twenty years. You'll still be teaching dancing, and you'll still be telling me to point my toes."

Madame ZeeZee laughed. The laughter faded into the distance, and I knew she had pulled the phone away from her mouth to talk to her husband. "I have to go," she said. "Rico rented a movie for us to watch. Talk to you later."

***

I looked forward to the beginning Hawaiian class because I felt no pressure, no need to worry about inadvertently saying the wrong thing and creating more chaos. I felt comfortable being around so many women I didn't know, and I thought they felt comfortable with me.

"Where's Maria?" Madame ZeeZee asked. We were milling around, waiting for everyone to arrive, and Maria, the woman who was so thrilled to be taking Hawaiian now that her kids were grown hadn't yet showed up.

Another woman, the one who thought Hawaiian dance was preferable to any other form of exercise, looked sideways at me, then tiptoed up to Madame ZeeZee. She spoke softly, but still I heard.

"Pat hurt her feelings."

I turned my back to hide my mortification. I couldn't remember a single thing I had ever said to the woman besides general civilities. Maybe she had taken my silence personally?

I didn't speak during class. I tried to keep my attention focused on the dances, but I couldn't concentrate. I kept obsessing about saying the wrong thing.

Would I ever feel comfortable saying anything to anyone again, no matter how benign the comment?

After the beginning class left, Madame ZeeZee watched the advanced class practice a dance we should have known well because we had performed it a year previously in a concert at the local college.

We'd been working on new dances recently and hadn't practiced that particular dance in several months, but we did okay without either Grace or Madame ZeeZee dancing in front of us. Until the final verse.

In Hawaiian, each verse is repeated twice in exactly the same way, but in this particular dance—"Green Rose"—when the last verse repeated, we did different steps than we had the first time the verse played. Deb did something I knew was wrong for that last verse and the rest of us foundered. I stood there while the music died out, trying to recall the right steps, but I had absolutely no memory of that final sequence.

I've always prided myself on having a good memory, and I believed everything it fed me. Whenever I've become party to a he said/she said or she said/she said argument about something that had happened, I could often find some sort of corroboration for my side, such as in a text or an email, which added credence to my belief. Also, in dance class, I often remember steps when others don't. It seemed inconceivable that when it came to those missing steps, my mind was a complete blank.

We danced "Green Rose" a second time, with Madame ZeeZee leading us. I did the dance perfectly, but only because I watched her. I still didn't remember ever having done those final steps before. It was as if the memory had been completely erased.

Walking home after class, I pondered the mystery of the missing memory. Could this be the beginning of Alzheimers? Or could I always have had blank spots in my memory? If so, how would I know? I only knew what I remembered.

I did remember telling Jackie once that I was an unreliable narrator, but I'd been talking about my lack of attention to details, not my memory. But now I wondered about Grace's death.

Could I have done something besides play the book game that got her killed? Did Deb know what I had done, and that's why she claimed the death was my fault? Not remembering a casual slight to another woman, seemed normal. Even erasing a few steps of a dance wasn't all that traumatic. But losing the memory of a murder was something completely different, and I refused to believe the ghastly thought.

Still, I hardly slept at all that night, and when I did, I dreamed of shadowy beings I should have remembered, but didn't.

Chapter 11

I woke from the nightmare and suddenly remembered dancing the final steps of "Green Rose." Taking the restored memory as a sign my memory banks were intact, I searched my mind for further remembrances of Grace's death. When I couldn't find any trace of lost memories, I decided not to torment myself further about having had an actual hand in Grace's death. I carried a heavy enough burden of guilt as it was.

Too exhausted to walk, I drove to the studio. Apparently, I wasn't the only one who had a bad night's sleep. Rhett didn't display her usual exuberance, and the deep lines etched on Deb's face made it seem as if she were folding in on herself.

Madame ZeeZee arrived, looking as tired as I felt. "I have to leave early to go look after my mom. Her caretaker can't come today." She opened the door to let us in. "Where is everyone?"

"Didn't Buffy say she was going to the beach for a long weekend?" Rhett asked me.

I shook my head in a noncommittal response, not wanting to admit I'd been too self-centered lately to pay attention to what people talked about in class.

"I'm sure that's what she said." Rhett looked at herself in the mirror, pulled her red top down over her zebra-patterned leggings, and grimaced. "I don't know where everyone else is."

Allie, dressed in dirty pink tights with a black leotard and wrinkled ballet skirt, wandered into the studio fifteen minutes late. She offered no apology to Madame ZeeZee, no word of greeting to the rest of us. She'd always been quiet—and immaculately dressed— but she'd never been rude, and I couldn't help wondering if Grace's death had grieved her even though she hadn't known the woman long. At our age—at any age, actually—the reminder of life's end could be disillusioning.

After we spent an hour on ballet, doing simple moves and combinations, Madame ZeeZee's cell phone rang. She tensed as she picked it up and said hello, but after a second, her shoulders relaxed. "Thanks for letting me know. See you next week." She snapped the phone shut. "That was Rose. She won't be here for tap. Let's put on our tap shoes and run through 'New York, New York.'"

To my embarrassment, I dropped the cane when we were supposed to flip it. Lena's titter stopped abruptly when her cane too clattered to the floor. Rhett accidentally threw her cane across the room. Or maybe it wasn't an accident. With Rhett, you never knew.

Madame ZeeZee finally dismissed us for the week. Rhett's whoop, subdued though it was, drowned out my sigh of relief.

I spent two or three hours each day of my danceless weekend hiking in the desert, trying to walk off my stress. I could feel the wonder of the desert ambience creeping over me, and I gave in to the wilderness experience, tame though it might be.

It seems strange now, but when I first moved in with my father, I hadn't realized the Mojave Desert was a mere twenty minute walk from the house. I'd seen the knolls in the near distance, of course, but I never gave a thought to what lay beyond them.

People say you never forget your first time, and that is true. I will never forget the first time I found myself in the desert. I'd been taking my usual walk around the upscale neighborhood, and I came to a gully as wide as an alley between two custom-built stucco houses. I tramped through the gully to a narrow trail that ultimately led to a dirt road. I walked along the road, stopping every once in a while to snap a photo. Finally, tired and thirsty, I turned around to walk back, and I saw nothing but desert. Long stretches of sandy soil, rocks, and creosote bushes framed by craggy knolls. No people. No cars. No houses.

Awe filled me, and I realized then that eventually I would be okay, that I would come to accept Jay's death and my lonely life. I might not like that he was gone, might always miss him, but I would be okay.

After that, I'd walked in the desert every day, taking myriad photos. Despite the desert revelation that I would be okay, I had a lot of grief to work through, and I found it easier to accept life through a camera lens rather than taking it raw. (Though come to think of it, I haven't seen life raw since the fourth grade when I got my first pair of eyeglasses, and now that I have to wear photochromic lenses to protect my eyes from cataracts, I never get to see life's true colors.)

Now, once again, I found comfort seeing life at one remove. I lost myself behind my camera, shooting creosote bushes, prickly pear, cholla, and yucca.

I hiked out to the spot that had so inspired me the first time I'd come to the desert. Stopped and looked around. A jackrabbit loped by, but other than that, no creature made itself known. I felt the breeze cooling my sweat, heard the air whistling faintly as it passed my ears. I stilled my thoughts and simply stood there in the middle of the desert, deep blue skies above, sun-heated soil beneath the soles of my shoes, desert knolls surrounding me.

I took a deep breath, let it out.

This moment is my life. And it is good.

I had no sense of longing for something or someone, no sense of waiting. No guilt. No regret. My entire life—all the joys and pains, the learning and creating, the loves and losses—had led to that very moment, and I felt as if I had arrived where I was supposed to be. There was no reason for me to be there, nothing for me to do, no task to accomplish. All I had to do was . . . be.

One cannot stand in the middle of the desert forever, so after a few minutes, I continued my walk, still feeling the effects of that one perfect moment.

I knew then that no matter how I felt about Grace's death, I would get over my guilt, might even forget my part in the tragedy. I couldn't change the past, but I could change the future by trying to kinder and more conciliatory to those who irritated me.

Luckily, I did not have to put this more saintly me to the test right away. Deb did not show up for class on Monday.

Madame ZeeZee, who'd spent the weekend getting more help for her mom, seemed happier and more focused. She solved the matter of who should dance in the front row by assigning Kim to that spot for jazz and forming us into a single line for tap.

We did well. No great mistakes in our steps. Just effortless dancing, as if our group, amoeba-like, had flowed around where Grace used to be and formed into a new shape.

Apparently, life really did go on.

And so did death.

Chapter 12

Children streamed out of the stopped school bus, crossed the street, and climbed into the cars waiting to whisk them home.

In no hurry to get back to the empty house, and still feeling mellow after the weekend's revelation and today's pleasant dance sessions, I sat patiently, watching but not watching the parade. Then the implication of what I was seeing struck me. School bus. School kids. *September?* Where had August gone?

I checked my phone for the date, and pressed my free palm to my heart. *Whew.* I hadn't lost a whole month, just part of it. September didn't start for another ten days.

In Colorado where I'd spent most of my life, by now I would already be able to detect the first tendrils of autumn reaching out for its starring role in the dance of the seasons, but here in the desert, I hadn't noticed any lessening of the summer heat. It's possible there were changes, perhaps a touch of cool brought down from the mountains by the ever-present wind, but self-absorption because of the book, my waning grief, and my uncertain future might have kept me from noticing.

A honk startled me, and I realized the road ahead of me had cleared. Apparently, my bug didn't pick up speed fast enough, because as I accelerated, the honker swerved around me in her Hummer, narrowly missing an oncoming car. I shook my head like a tut-tutting old woman and proceeded cautiously to my father's house.

A white SUV similar to those my neighbors drove sat in front of the house. I wondered briefly who had visitors, but by the time I entered the garage, the matter had already been chased out of my mind by a new thought.

The realtors called this cavernous space a three-car garage, but it could easily house six Volkswagen bugs, especially now that all my stuff had been removed. My brother told me once that our dad had fallen in love with the garage, which is why our parents had bought the house. It amused me that my unhandy aged father had so loved the garage, he kept it empty except for his Lexus. He must have enjoyed driving into the cavernous space as much as I did, and it saddened me to think of how hard it had been for him when he could no longer operate a vehicle.

I unlocked the connecting door to the house, dropped my dance bag, hat, and purse on the mattress in my bedroom, then meandered out to the kitchen and opened my computer.

The doorbell rang, making me jump.

I didn't answer the strident summons. I'd had my fill of talking to solar representatives. They couldn't seem to understand that I didn't own the house, that the new residents hadn't yet taken possession.

The bell rang again. And again.

Cripes. Don't they ever give up?

I went to the door and yanked it open.

Detective Arsalee Morales stood there, finger poised to ring the bell again.

I opened my mouth, but not a single word came out.

The detective had no such problem. "I'd like to ask you a few questions," she said. "Can I come in?"

I stepped out of the house and began to close the door behind me. I knew that once inside a dwelling, cops could tell a lot about a person, and I wasn't sure I trusted this woman.

But then my sense of humor kicked in. I opened the door wide and stepped aside to let her enter the empty house.

Her lips quirked. "I like what you've done with the place."

"Took me a long time to get the right look." Maybe exchanging not-so-witty witticisms with the detective was a bad idea, but it helped put me at ease. I had done nothing wrong, and I didn't want to act as if I had.

"Have you started writing your book yet?"

I laughed, thinking of the single line I had written. "Yes."

"Did you write the beginning?"

"Is this why you're here? To talk about my book?"

She looked around the living room as if searching for a place to sit, then she focused her dark eyes on my face.

"Tell me the story again."

I inclined my head toward her briefcase. "You already have the story. I told it several times."

"Well, can I see what you've written?"

I glanced over at my laptop, the screen bright and welcoming. I knew a lawyer would want me to demand a search warrant, but I couldn't see what harm it would do to indulge the woman.

I sauntered to the machine, opened my work in progress, and stepped back so Detective Morales could see the manuscript. A hint of citrus that wasn't strong enough to be perfume scented the air when she took a step forward. Maybe the fragrance of her shampoo.

She looked at the single line of words then at me.

"That's all you have? *'I didn't want to kill Grace—it was her idea.'*"

"We've been through this. It's not a confession. It's the first line of the book." I emitted a single humph of unamused laughter. "As you can see, the novel is going badly."

"Maybe you felt as if you needed more inspiration?"

All of a sudden it struck home that I was being interrogated. "Wait a minute. What's going on?"

"You don't know?"

"Am I some kind of suspect?" *But a suspect in what?*

Her gaze burned through me like a laser. "Should you be?"

"I don't want to go through this again. You'll have to leave." I moved toward the door to let her out.

"Please. Tell me the story once more. You might remember something new."

I heaved a theatrical sigh to show her how put upon I felt, and thought back to the beginning.

I told her about having lunch after the ballet performance, and I repeated those same deadly words. *"You should write a book about us. I'll volunteer to be the murder victim."*

"Then what?"

"We talked about the book for several days before I decided to write the story because I didn't want to hurt anyone. Some of the things I like about them are things they hate about themselves."

"How did you decide on the means of death?"

"The other dancers offered suggestions for weapons, such as blunt force trauma, poison and insulin."

"Had you decided how to administer the insulin?"

"Not really. Maybe an EpiPen."

"Who was going to be the perp?"

"A couple of people volunteered to be the killer, but . . ." I clamped my mouth shut. Lena was right. I really did blab and I didn't want the detective to think that Madame ZeeZee or Nancy's Eddie had anything to do with Grace's death.

"What victims did you consider?"

"No one but Grace. Well, except for Madame ZeeZee. I told you about her and her connection to Ruth St. Denis."

Detective Morales said nothing. Just looked at me.

And wouldn't you know—that interrogation technique really does work. I scrabbled around in my brain for something to say to break the ominous silence.

"Deb volunteered to be the victim. Well sort of. She said, '*Maybe I should be the victim*.' She laughed when she said it, so I didn't take her seriously."

"Who was there the day she volunteered to be the victim?"

"All of us, I imagine."

"Do you have an outline for the book?"

I shook my head. I fall somewhere between a plotter and pantster, the ludicrous term for someone who writes by the seat of her pants, so my outlining is more a mental exercise than a formal structure.

"Did you take notes?"

"Some." I went to the computer, opened my OneNote program and skimmed through the files. I found the one I wanted, and opened it. "I only made note of the people with interesting comments that day. In a book, you can't introduce a dozen or more characters all at once. That's a good way of losing a reader before you hook her. So I don't know everyone who was there. I think it was a Monday. It was after lunch, and not everyone went out with us."

"Who do you remember?"

I shook my head. I really did not want to mention names.

She hefted her briefcase onto the counter. The snap of the latches sounded like pops from a silenced gun. She riffled through a few pages. "You said Buffy, Lena, Deb, and Grace were there."

"I did? I don't remember telling you that." But then, the entire interview seemed a blurred spot in my memory.

"Could others have been there with you?"

"I'm sure there were. I remember we were a big group. The waitress had to put two large tables together." And Buffy had made a joke about not having volunteered to be the victim.

As if the detective had heard my unspoken words, she said, "Buffy is the science teacher, right?"

I nodded, feeling as if I were betraying a friend, but I wasn't telling the detective anything she didn't already know.

"And Buffy suggested the insulin."

Had I told the detective that? Had someone else told her? Or was she guessing?

"I can't say," I whispered, though Buffy's words rose to the surface of my mind with glowing urgency. *"She can still die if she gets more insulin than her body can handle, and almost all of us have access to insulin. Most of us are either diabetic or are married to a diabetic."*

A heavy feeling settled in my stomach, as if I'd swallowed a boulder instead of an unpalatable possibility.

"Someone else died, didn't they?" The words sounded so soft and halting I didn't recognize my own voice.

"Are you allergic to anything? Bee stings? Peanut butter?"

"Just environmental allergies like smog and dust."

"Have you ever bought an EpiPen?"

"No."

"Are you diabetic?"

"I don't think so."

"You don't know? Who's your doctor?"

"I don't go to the doctor. Haven't been for ten years."

"What happened ten years ago?"

I felt so frazzled by her change of pace and the rapid-fire questions, I no longer had the ability to debate the advisability of answering. I told her the truth, though I couldn't see what it had to do with my book. "I broke my ankle when I went to Carlsbad for my mother's funeral. I spent the viewing in the emergency room and the funeral with the orthopedic surgeon."

"Was it a bad break?"

"He called it a super sprain. He took off the cast the emergency people had put on and replaced it with a removable cast. If I'd been home, I probably wouldn't have gone to the doctor."

"When was the last time you had a physical?"

"I don't know. When I was twenty-five, I think."

"So you really don't know if you're diabetic."

"That's what I said."

The detective gathered her papers and stashed them in her briefcase. "I'll be in touch."

I held out a shaky hand. "You can't go yet."

She looked at my hand as if I were holding a gun on her. I dropped my arm and gripped the counter with my fingers to hold myself up.

"Who died? Deb?"

The detective abruptly halted in her march to the door, as if I'd said something wrong—or right—then she resumed her implacable retreat.

Tears sprang to my eyes. *I killed her. I killed Deb.*

I propped myself on the stool, buried my face in my arms, and wept for a woman I didn't even like.

When I got hold of myself, I went outside to see if Detective Morales was still around, but I saw no sign of her or the white SUV except a dime-sized spot of oil where the vehicle had been parked.

I went to the bedroom for my phone. I wanted to call Madame ZeeZee to see if she knew what was going on, but my hands shook so badly, I dropped the device. I decided to wait to talk to her until I calmed down.

I paced the house, feeling as if I were moving on fast forward. One frantic step after the other, around and around the living room. Questions tumbled in my mind so quickly I couldn't find the words to lasso them into docility.

Gradually, my steps slowed.

My mind slowed.

I reviewed the interrogation, trying to make sense of it, and at the end of my deliberations, I concluded that I only knew something had happened to bring myself to the detective's attention. Anything else was a matter of my jumping to conclusions. Had someone died? Maybe. Had someone suffered an overdose of insulin. Possible. Was I a suspect? Could be.

All conjecture.

I perched on the stool in front of my computer. The screen showed my notes for the beginning of the book. I'd listed a few quirks for the women, such as Rhett's don't-give-a-damn attitude and Deb's penchant for topping whatever anyone said with an anecdote of her own.

And I'd made a note to try to give everyone a different voice. The trouble I had with trying to make everyone sound different is that while everyone's voice had a different timbre, we all spoke General American, an accentless form of English often employed by newscasters because it offered no hint of regional origins or colloquialisms. None of us were given to using profanities, about half the women had been teachers, and all were educated. The only difference I'd ever noticed in word usage was an occasional ya'll from Rose.

Madame ZeeZee insisted that we dance as one. Had any differences faded during our years of acting as a single being?

When I'd first started taking dance classes, there'd been women with accents—a woman born in Taiwan, a woman from Japan, a Latina whose accent came and went depending on her mood, but they'd dropped out sometime during the past year.

When I realized what I was doing—distracting myself from having to think of death—I decided to go with the flow, and opened my manuscript. I sat for a few minutes thinking what I wanted to say, then typed a couple more lines.

I've literally massacred hundreds of thousands of people, so it shouldn't have been difficult to do away with one petite older woman, but the truth is I couldn't think of a single reason why I—or anyone—would want Grace dead.

I still couldn't think of why anyone would want Grace dead. I don't think Deb meant for her to die. She'd become caught up in some sort of crazed *pas de deux* with me and the perceived rivalry had taken her too far.

Did she regret what she had done when she'd come back to herself? Is that why she'd looked so awful on Friday? Or was she still playing the game with me, giving herself an insulin injection, not to kill, but to make herself sick and lay the blame on me to prove once again how vile I was?

I'd been ready to accept the idea I was no hero, but equally, I could not accept the role of villain. I simply was not that powerful.

A tiny voice deep inside me whispered, "But what if you are?"

Chapter 13

I know only three things about my paternal great-grandfather. He was a German-American inventor who had worked with Thomas Edison and maybe even Tesla. He invented the postmarking machine that was in use for decades until the electronic age—the only reason my family is not rich is because he sold the patent to an investor, who did get rich off it, for funds to invent a new subway sweeper. And he had two wives. We didn't know which was our great-grandmother— the one he committed to the infamous Blackwell insane asylum, or the one he threw down the stairs.

His son was an embezzler who spent time in prison, and ended up as an alcoholic.

And *his* son, my father, kept himself to a very strict and narrow life, filled with minutia and prayer, in order not to succumb to the chaos that had been his heritage.

In a rare moment of camaraderie, my siblings and I admitted that we too had felt something not quite sane living inside of us.

My sister tried to find out if the incarcerated woman was our great-grandmother but it didn't matter to me. I knew any inherited instability had come from our great-grandfather.

I remember as a teenager being terrified of therapists and people with insights because I feared what they would see. Oddly, it was only after falling into the chaotic and insane state we call grief that I realized I was completely sane.

But, then, did any insane person ever think she was crazy? Didn't we all think we were the norm, and everyone else weird?

I'd been so deep in my musings that I reached the studio without any clear concept of how I got there. I must have dragged my feet the whole way because I arrived late. Jackie, Buffy, Margot, Rhett, Lena, and Allie were already doing the *grande reverence* that signified the beginning of class.

A smile or two as I changed into ballet shoes heartened me and made me think nothing had happened to reinstigate the hostility toward me. I slipped into my place at the bar for *pliés* and *cambrés*.

When Madame ZeeZee went to put on different music, I

whispered to Buffy, "Did Deb call in sick?"

"I don't know. Madame ZeeZee didn't say."

I nodded my thanks, thinking that yesterday's visit from Detective Morales could have been nothing more than a matter of putting the finishing touches on Grace's case before filing it away for good, and stress coupled with my overactive imagination had blown the whole thing out of proportion.

I did not look in the mirror as we did our barre work, not even when we moved to the middle of the floor for combinations. I felt light and ballerina-ish and didn't want to see the truth.

Kim arrived for Arabic long before ballet class ended—she didn't have much control over when her bus would pick her up or drop her off. Rose arrived early, too. She'd stopped taking ballet when her health issues got the better of her, but she tried to keep up with the less strenuous classes.

Nancy, of course, didn't come. She hadn't returned my call. She was probably on a beach somewhere having fun with Eddie, but I couldn't help wondering if she had been the reason for the detective's visit. I dismissed the idea. Nancy really had no part in the book except for offering Eddie's services for the murderer and for her suggestion that I unravel everyone's secret.

I looked around at each of the women in turn. Did they have secrets they would do anything to protect? If so, they were probably buried far in the past. They chatted so openly about their lives, they seemed transparent, or semi-transparent, anyway.

During the bustle between classes, Madame ZeeZee's phone rang.

At first, none of us paid attention, then one by one, we stopped to listen to her side of the obviously painful conversation.

"Oh, no . . . I'm so sorry . . . when . . . how did it . . ."

"Her mother?" Margot asked.

"It had to happen sometime," Rhett said.

Oh, poor Madame ZeeZee. With as much trouble as she was having with the old woman's care, it would still be hard for her to lose her mother.

After several more long pauses and exclamations of disbelief, Madame ZeeZee snapped her phone shut. She didn't say anything. We gathered around her.

"Is your mom okay?" Buffy asked.

Madame ZeeZee shook her head, not slowly to signify a negative answer, but quickly, as if to clear her mind.

"That was Emmett. Deb's husband. She's gone."

Allie drew in a sharp breath.

Lena looked confused. "Gone where?"

Madame ZeeZee's shoulders sagged. She must have felt her unnatural posture because she immediately straightened. "Deb passed away yesterday morning. Insulin overdose."

"But she wasn't diabetic," Rose said.

Madame ZeeZee held out her hands. "All I know is Emmett said her hypoglycemia got really bad. She was so dizzy and disoriented, she thought she was going into shock from a bad allergic reaction. Instead of eating something, she used the EpiPen. She fell into a coma Saturday. He took her to the hospital, but they couldn't reverse the damage."

"No," Lena rubbed her wrists. "It's not possible. An EpiPen wouldn't have killed her."

Madame ZeeZee said quietly, "It would if it were filled with insulin."

I froze. I didn't just go rigid, I also got chilled, as if my internal temperature had dropped about twenty degrees.

As one, Rose, Kim, Buffy, Rhett, Lena, and Allie turned to stare at me. If Madame ZeeZee noticed, she would have been pleased to see their acting as a single entity. Margot and Jackie followed the other women's example and glanced my way, but the two ballet dancers didn't seem to know what was going on. And maybe they didn't know. They hadn't been at the lunch where we'd discussed ways of killing Grace.

Deep inside my arctic body, I found my voice. "Why are you looking at me? I'm not the one who came up with the insulin scenario."

"But you're the one killing us," Allie said.

I went from ice to fire in an instant. "What the hell is wrong with you people? Do you really think I'm so powerful that my thinking of writing a story about murder will kill you? If so, you'd better be damn good to me, or I'll write you off next."

Jackie laughed. "You tell them, Pat."

"Grace's death was your fault," Lena said.

I whipped off the belly dance skirt I'd donned a few minutes before. "I can't do this. I'm sorry Grace is gone, but I'm not the one who initiated some insane pissing contest and left her to die. And I'm sorry Deb is gone, but I didn't do anything to her, either. Quite frankly, I'm not going to miss Deb. She wasn't a nice person, but whatever crimes she committed, whatever she did to Grace or to anyone else, it's over." I grabbed my street shoes, and opened the door. "I'm going home to put all of you in my book. Goodbye."

The door closed slowly, as if their silence were a physical presence so great it couldn't be contained. Right before the door completely shut, Rose's words drifted out. "Did ya'll hear that? Did she really say 'pissing contest'?"

Chapter 14

Jackie pulled her black Mini convertible next to me a couple of blocks from the studio, and opened the door. "I'll give you a ride home."

"Thank you." I climbed into the tiny space and fastened the seatbelt.

Jackie laughed. "That certainly was an interesting show you put on."

I couldn't help smiling at her cheery comment. "I don't know what got into me. Lately, I'm not playing nicely with the other children in my class."

"The other children in your class seem to think you're a witch."

"Witch with a 'b'?"

"That, too. But mostly witch with a 'w'. They really believe you're killing off the class. Maybe Buffy and Madame ZeeZee don't, but the rest of them do."

"Oh, for cripes sake. It goes to show how one crazy apple can spoil the whole barrel."

"Who's the crazy apple? You?"

I surprised myself with a genuine laugh. "I've been tormenting myself with such thoughts. I probably spend too much time alone. But no, not me."

"What did you mean about an insane pissing contest and leaving someone to die?" Jackie chuckled. "I think they were more shocked by those words than what you said."

"Did you know about the insulin?"

If she were surprised by the change of topic, she didn't let her feelings show.

"Lena explained. Sort of. Something about your suggesting it as a means of murder?"

"It wasn't me who suggested it. Were you there that day we talked about ways of killing Grace?" I felt sure she hadn't been, but I could no longer rely on my memory.

"It must have been a Monday because I remember people talking about it the next day at ballet class."

Then she probably hadn't killed Deb. So it should be safe to talk to her.

Squelching the internal voice that taunted, "blabber," I told Jackie about Lena and Deb and how Grace had died. I didn't spare myself, and luckily, Jackie seemed to understand how my disdain could have set the whole sorry affair into motion without my having to go into long explanations.

"So you think Deb killed herself accidentally to continue making you look like a murderer?"

"It sounds nuts, doesn't it? I didn't know she hated me so much to put herself in that position."

"I don't think she did it to herself."

I jerked my head sideways to look at her. "You don't?"

"If she wanted to make herself sick, she would have used the altered EpiPen when her blood sugar levels were up to give herself some control over the situation."

I chewed on my lower lip as I considered the possibility. "But what if she used it by mistake?"

"Diabetics live in fear of dying from low blood sugar while they are asleep. I imagine hypoglycemics feel the same way. If she had tampered with the EpiPen, she would have made damn sure she kept it separate from her emergency supplies."

"So you're saying . . ." I couldn't bring myself to finish my thought, but Jackie finished it for me.

"Someone murdered Deb." For once Jackie's words weren't tinged with laughter.

"But not because of me."

"I doubt it. She might have borrowed the idea of the EpiPen from you, but she murdered for reasons of her own."

"You said 'she murdered.' It had to be someone from class, didn't it?" I almost whispered the words.

"Yeah, scary." And this time Jackie did laugh, though I couldn't join her. I didn't see the humor in dancing with a murderer.

"But who could have done it?"

"Could have?" Jackie echoed. "Any of us *could* have done it if we had access to an EpiPen and insulin. It would be easy enough to slip the weapon into Deb's purse when no one was looking. But who *would* have done it? I don't know. It had to have been someone who didn't mind the expense. An EpiPen can cost as much as six hundred dollars. And it couldn't have been easy to empty the pen and fill it with insulin. But to do all that and wait for death to happen takes someone with a long standing grudge. I couldn't have done it, could you?"

Jackie drove into the curved driveway, and left her engine running while I clambered out.

"See you Tuesday." With a laugh she added a few sinister-sounding words. "At least I hope I will."

A white SUV that might have been the same one I saw the previous day sat in front of the house. I decided, with a little shiver, I wouldn't answer the door for anyone, so if the vehicle belonged to the detective, she was out of luck.

The doorbell didn't ring.

***

I Googled my classmates but found out little. Jackie belonged to a March of Dimes team that raised more money than anyone else one year, but that wasn't news to me—our ballet class had gone on one of the marches with her. Buffy was not, as she claimed, the most boring person in the world, but the mentions I found did make her seem completely normal and wholesome—a college biology paper that had been included in a now out of print anthology, a decade-old commendation for being a good teacher, photos of quilts that had been featured in quilt shows. I checked her Facebook page—nothing there but pictures of her family, especially her grandchildren, and talk of vacations with her husband in their RV.

The rest of the class seemed to be ciphers, at least according to Google, but I did find a bit of information on Facebook. Rhett listed her academic credentials and her work history as a special ed teacher, most of which I already knew. She also shared religious sayings, which surprised me because in offline life, she didn't seem like a proselytizer. Allie posted photos of the presents her husband gave her, such as the lovely bouquet she mentioned in class recently, and links to the places they went. Apparently, last Friday, they'd gone to a concert and dinner in Los Angeles. Not surprisingly, most of what Madame ZeeZee posted had to do with dance.

Of the others—Lena, Margo, Rose, Kim, Nancy—I could find no trace.

I paced the floor, wishing I could talk to Jay, wishing he really were back home in Colorado, as my subconscious believed, so I could call him. But if he were home, I wouldn't need to call. I would be there with him instead of dealing with this murderous mess.

I used to have friends, but during his long illness, they drifted away. People like things unambiguous. A person gets sick, then the person gets well. But years of his getting a bit better and a bit worse, coupled with my inability to offer a jolly "Oh, he's doing fine. So much better!" as people seemed to expect, left me with one friend— Jay. When he died, I was left with . . . me.

During these years without Jay, I tried to find friends, but I didn't seem to click with married women, and everyone else I met eventually moved on while I seemed to be standing in place.

I wished I knew someone who could help me find out the truth, help me find out about my classmates's early lives, and then I realized I did know someone.

I might not have friends, but do I have fans, and Wanda Hughes was one of my first.

In our dealings online, she had always come across as wise, witty, and wonderful, but when I finally got a chance to meet her in person, I discovered that was all true, but that she had a silly side as well as the serious one. And I discovered she was a prodigious genealogical researcher. Her husband had been adopted as a baby, and he'd spent a life time wondering about his family. Wanda found his family for him, brothers he didn't know he had, and they were all delighted with her success.

I sent Wanda an email telling her my woeful story, and asked for her help. After my lonesome late lunch of tuna salad and a glass of water, I played computer solitaire until time for bed, but I didn't hear back from her.

***

I'm not a natural writer. I can't sit down, rest my fingers on the keyboard, and let my subconscious type out a story for me. I have to do the work. And I had to learn to do the work. I used to read as many

95

books on writing I could get my hands on to help me to find my way to being an accomplished storyteller. One thing that sticks out in my mind from all those instructions is that heroines should never cry. If the character cries, the writing instructors said, the reader won't. It could be true, but so what? People cry. Characters cry. It's not the lack of tears that determines strength, but what happens after the tears.

Do you give up? Do you get up?

Me . . . I do both. Give up and then get up. And once up, I keep going.

I cried myself to sleep, thinking of how I'd never see Jay again. Why did the women I danced with still get to be with their husbands, and I didn't? How come I couldn't see him one last time? Have one more talk with him? Feel the warmth of his smile once again? Jay has been gone for five years, but sometimes it's the being gone that matters and not how long it's been. And that night, I felt his goneness as if it were a recent occurrence.

In the morning, I dragged myself out of bed, washed my face in cold water to try to shrink the puffiness around my eyes, and went for a walk in the desert. I came back, took a shower, ate lunch, pulled on my basic dance clothes—black leggings and oversized black tee shirt—then headed for Hawaiian class.

I did not want to go to the studio. Did not want to see any of those women ever again. But I feared that if I got in the habit of walking away from something I loved because of people I didn't particularly care for, I'd end up living a stagnant life. The crazy cat lady sans cats.

Despite my resolve, I dawdled. What could I possibly say to anyone to make them feel better about their chances of surviving the class? How could I get them to understand I was no witch, just a sad and lonely woman who had a tendency to self-pity?

Excited chatter filled the studio. A couple of new students had enrolled, and they seemed thrilled to be there. One heavyset woman with sympathetic eyes trotted toward me, arm outstretched. She was dressed like me, though her tee shirt was blue.

"I'm Maggie," she said, a huge smile lighting her face.

I shook her hand. The warmth of her greeting melted my reluctance at being there, and I couldn't help smiling in return.

"Maggie. I like that. I'll remember."

"Maggie's been telling us about her bariatric surgery," Rhett said. "I wonder if it would work for me."

I shook my head, perplexed. Why did Rhett continue to think herself fat? Just one of the small mysteries of life that shouldn't matter now that more fatal mysteries plagued me.

The woman who'd come to class instead of going to the gym asked Maggie, "Didn't the surgery take?"

I felt appalled by her crassness, but Maggie just smiled. "The surgery went fine. I lost a hundred pounds. Then I broke my leg and felt so sorry for myself, I ate M&Ms. One after another. Day after day. By the time I got back on my feet, I'd regained the weight."

"Can't you get the surgery again?" the gymless lady asked.

"No. All I have is a pouch instead of a stomach. If they take that out, I'll die."

A couple of women drew in their breaths as if the word "die" reminded them of the truth inherent in our real life murder mystery. The others seemed to be contemplating the consequences of radical surgery.

In the silence, the first strains of music sounded.

Madame ZeeZee lined us up in three rows.

"Since there are so many in the class, would you rather I didn't stay?" I asked.

"We'll be fine. I don't want you to leave."

The two women who had gasped at the mention of dying, looked around surreptitiously, as if searching for the killer. Did they think this was some sort of mystery weekend, and once the class was over, the murderer would be discovered and the victims brought back to life, gleeful smiles lighting up their faces?

Maggie did well in class. When Madame ZeeZee complimented her, Maggie explained that in her slim youth, she had been a gymnast, and had taken dance classes as part of her training.

She still had rhythm, and she was still light on her feet.

After the first session was over, she asked Madame ZeeZee if she could stay to watch the more advanced class, and the teacher agreed. It made me feel good that Maggie remained. Her aura seemed as large as her person, and she pulled everyone into her orbit with her charm. Because of her, I felt no stress at being in class with potential murderers, no need to obsess over who done it.

After class, several women gathered around Maggie. I didn't know if the surgery fascinated them, or if Maggie's presence drew them to her, but I too felt the pull of her charisma. I hung around for a few minutes, wanting to tell her how much her being there had meant to me, but I couldn't manage to make myself heard.

Maggie caught my eye and waved, not with a palm up to say goodbye, but with a palm down and her fingers flicking as if motioning me away.

I nodded at her, showing I didn't take offense.

A dark blue Chevy Suburban in need of a wash was parked in my dad's driveway.

Wanda leaned against the cab, arms crossed, waiting for me. I ran the last few steps, and hugged the heavyset woman. I hadn't realized how starved for human touch I'd been, and I let her envelop me for a few seconds before my rush of questions pulled me away.

"What are you doing here? Did you drive all night? How did you find Madame ZeeZee's studio? And why did you use the name Maggie?"

She laughed, a lovely contralto. "I couldn't let one of my favorite authors have all the fun!"

I nodded my head toward her vehicle. "Does that thing fly? You live almost eight hundred miles north of here."

"I was only about four hours away. We were visiting friends of my husband's in Fresno." She wrinkled her nose to show what she thought of the friends. "When I got your email last night, I used it as an excuse to leave him there by himself. I didn't plan to go to your class, but I wanted to see who everyone was. And I wanted to surprise you."

I sighed happily. "It was such a lovely surprise. You have no idea how much I dreaded going to the studio today."

"Why did you go? Anyone else would have walked away."

"You know. The whole crazy cat lady thing."

She nodded in understanding. "I remember. You told me you're afraid of stagnating."

"But why call yourself Maggie?"

"Why not Maggie? I always liked the name. We know at least one person there is not who she pretends to be, so what's one more?"

"How long can you stay?" I asked.

"Just tonight. I thought I'd join your classes tomorrow to see if I can learn anything more, and then leave after that."

I folded my arms around my midriff and steeled myself. "Did you learn something already?

She laughed. "I sure did. I learned you're a real witch."

I dropped my arms to my side. "Oh. That's nothing new."

She yanked a duffle bag out of the back of the vehicle. "You don't mind if I spend the night, do you?"

"I'd love it, but you might mind. There's no furniture."

She handed me the duffle bag and pulled out a box with a picture of an air mattress on the side. "Instant bed."

I looked up at the clear blue sky. Though the sun was behind me, the glare made me squint. I breathed in. Breathed out. Smelled sun-warmed earth and the unmistakable odor of laundry detergent wafting from a nearby house.

This moment is my life. And it is so very, very good.

"I almost forgot." Wanda opened the passenger door and held aloft a bag from a local chicken place. "Dinner!"

I laughed at the huge bag. "You don't eat enough to keep a kitten alive."

Wanda leaned back and tilted her head to look me up and down. "What I thought. You're not eating, either."

I don't know how she could tell. Whether I ate more or less, my extra-large size seldom fluctuated, but maybe she'd detected a bit of gauntness in my face.

She'd brought everything for a picnic—plates, napkins, bottles of water, and several side dishes to go with the chicken. We sat on the floor, our backs against the breakfast bar, and ate and talked.

She kept me laughing with stories of her cats. She'd adopted a blue Maine coon cat and so loved the gray beast with the white bib, she'd said she'd never get another cat unless it was like Buddy. And wouldn't you know, one morning, a gray cat with a white bib showed up at her back door. The cat was not a blue Maine coon, but it was like Buddy, just what she'd asked for.

Because of Buddy and his brother, I knew Wanda would understand about words creating reality and that you needed to be careful how you used them.

When we'd eaten our fill and stowed the copious leftovers in the refrigerator, Wanda pulled her tablet computer out of the duffle bag. She'd started a list of suspects, and now she added Michaela.

"Michaela?" I queried. "You think she's a suspect?"

"I think everyone's a suspect." She smiled beatifically at me. "Even you."

I laughed ruefully. "You got me there."

But she didn't have my name on her list of suspects, though she had included two women I'd ruled out. "You're considering Jackie and Margot?"

"That they didn't turn to look at you when Madame ZeeZee announced Deb's passing doesn't mean they're innocent. A guilty person might not look because she would know for sure you didn't have anything to do with Deb's death. You also said the women talked about means of murdering Grace even after that luncheon. Margot or Jackie could have overheard about putting insulin in the EpiPen."

I nodded slowly, unwilling to admit that women who were so self-disciplined they'd spent years at the ballet barre would be willing to resort to murder. But then, wouldn't a dancer also be a person who could forgo immediate satisfaction and wait patiently until her enemy needed the EpiPen?

"I'm not considering any of the new women," I said. "I don't know them, and they didn't show up until after Grace died."

"I suppose it's possible that Grace's death gave someone the idea of killing Deb," Wanda said, "but I won't check the new women out except as a last resort. I looked online, and found no mention of Grace's death or possible murder except in local Peach Valley Facebook groups. It was not exactly a media event."

What a sad epitaph for Grace. *Not exactly a media event.* As if the death of a sports figure or a musician meant so much more than hers.

I focused my gaze on Wanda's list, though the names were etched in my brain. "It seems impossible that one of the women I dance with is a murderer, but given the circumstances, it also seems impossible that one of them isn't."

"A real conundrum," Wanda said. "What I've been able to find out so far only shows your classmates in a good light. No murderous impulses. While I waited for you to get home, I checked out Michaela online. She seems to be devout. She's often mentioned in diocesan newsletters, and has been honored several times for her services. There is one thing." She paused and looked around as if to make sure others weren't around to overhear, then whispered, "Her daughter is a showgirl in Vegas."

I laughed. "I know. Ironic, isn't it? It's not really a secret though. She mentioned it once. She's very proud of her daughter."

"And Jackie is rather a heroine."

"The March of Dimes thing?"

"No. Better. She and her husband were on an aerial tour of the Hudson River basin, and the pilot passed out. A heart attack. Jackie landed the plane, saving the lives of all ten passengers and the pilot."

I laughed. "Can you see Sherlock Holmes or Hercule Poirot or Nero Wolfe going through the trouble of looking for devils and finding only saints?

Wanda said softly. "And yet, a woman is dead."

I could feel the humor leaving my body, seeping out through my pores. "I hate death."

"It's a fact of life. There's nothing you can do about it."

Tears sprang to my eyes. Angrily, I brushed them away. "I can do something. I can find out who killed Deb."

Wanda smiled sadly at me. "And then?"

I had no answer for her.

Chapter 15

Wanda and I sauntered along the sidewalk that fronted the strip shopping center where Madame ZeeZee's studio was located. Wanda wanted to get a feel for the area, to put what she would learn online into perspective. We reached the last store, then turned back.

The man who owned the nail salon stepped out of his door and lit a cigarette. He stood in front of the studio and smoked.

Wanda stopped in her tracks. "Who's that?"

"Someone who hates Madame ZeeZee, though he shouldn't. Several of the women in class get their nails done there. I considered him as the villain of the book, but couldn't make it work."

"Why not?"

"Motive, for one. I couldn't figure out why he would kill Grace. If he killed anyone, it would be Rhett because she used to run him off. Yelled at him to smoke in front of his own damn place. He seems scared of her now."

Wanda kept her eyes focused on the dark little man. "I bet he hears a lot of what goes on in the studio."

"I hadn't thought of that, but he could have heard everything Deb told me about why Grace died."

Wanda touched a finger to her chin. "And then what? He killed Deb as some sort of revenge because of his secret infatuation with Grace?"

The man glanced at us, stubbed out his cigarette, and disappeared back into his shop.

We giggled like schoolgirls, and headed back down the sidewalk.

"I would prefer him to be the killer rather than someone I know and like, but I just don't see it. If Deb had been shot, then taken out to the desert and buried, he'd be my first suspect, but the whole EpiPen thing? No. How would he have been able to check to see what EpiPen Deb carried, then later switch it with the insulin filled pen?"

"It does sound more like a woman's crime. I wish I could have met your Detective Morales. I'd have liked to know what she's thinking."

I laughed. "*My* detective? She's not mine. You can have her."

By the time we reached the studio door, the rest of my classmates had begun congregating.

I stood a few feet away from the group, as had now become my habit, and listened to Wanda—Maggie—draw the women out. She asked seemingly casual questions—last names, maiden names, where they were from, how many children they had, how long they'd been married, what work they had done, if their parents were still living—but I knew she was filing the information in her prodigious memory.

Instead of listening to their words, I watched how the women responded, looking for tells, but no one seemed to resent Wanda's questions, no one acted guilty. I didn't sense any hesitation or holding back, but then, if one of these women were hiding a deadly secret of long standing, by now her cover story would be solidly in place, might even feel like the truth to her.

I had to laugh at my pretensions from the night before. I'd declared my determination to find out who killed Deb, but standing in the bright morning sun it seemed an impossible task.

Even worse, the little voice inside me that seemed to be making itself heard with increasing frequency asked, *Do you really want to know the truth?*

Madame ZeeZee arrived, and we all trooped inside. Wanda went with her to the small office nook to pay for her classes, and in a moment, she had the teacher laughing and talking about her years as part of a dance troupe.

After we performed our *grande reverence,* Madame ZeeZee got serious, almost schoolmarmish, as she often did when we had a new class member. I used to wonder if she were playing a part, but I think it's more that a new student gives her a fresh start, a way to reclaim control over her adult classes, which, unlike her children's classes, sometimes devolve into a social club.

To temper her sternness and to accommodate Maggie, Madame ZeeZee kept the steps and stretching and combinations simple.

After ballet, Margot and Jackie left. So did Buffy and Allie, who were too advanced for beginning tap. Except for Maggie, who kept on her ballet-type slippers, we changed into our tap shoes, and worked on techniques—easy steps like windshield wipers, and more complicated ones like On Broadway and time steps. After class,

Maggie asked if anyone would like to go to lunch. All of us, Madame ZeeZee, Rhett, Lena, Rose, Maggie, and me, ambled across the parking lot to the Mexican restaurant. Madame ZeeZee and I split a taquito special, and then I split my half with Maggie.

For the first time in a long while, I enjoyed being part of a group. It seemed so normal—a cluster of women out for lunch. No one mentioned Deb's absence, but then, there would be no reason to. As older women, all with multiple calls on our time, we were rather a changeable group, and Deb had not often gone to lunch with us. Besides, Maggie made us all feel comfortable with one another, and I'm sure no one wanted to think of the problems tearing us apart.

Without any sort of signal, we all rose at the same time, and tossed our garbage in the trash receptacle.

"Can I give you a ride home?" Maggie asked me.

"Thank you." I wanted a final word in private with her before she left and hadn't been sure how to arrange it.

"I envy you your dance classes," Wanda said, buckling up. "It's such a great opportunity." She paused at a stop sign and turned her head to look at me. "Is Madame ZeeZee really almost eighty?"

I laughed. "Hard to believe, isn't it?"

"I would have guessed fifty. And she's still teaching physical fitness at the college?"

"Yep."

She shook her head. "Amazing. You don't think . . ."

"What? That she has a deep secret she's hiding? No, I don't. I could be wrong, of course, but she doesn't seem to be the type to murder anyone over something that happened long ago. She'd tell us. Or me, anyway, since we're friends. She's been such a great teacher, not just dance, but life. She never holds grudges, and so I'm learning not to hold grudges, either. To just let things go."

"Well, she does have one secret."

Dread curled in the pit of my stomach. "What?"

"She's not Russian. I looked her up. She was born in Los Angeles. She's a mixture of Hispanic, Greek, and a touch of Italian."

"Oh, cripes. You scared the hell out of me. She's my lynchpin right now. Without dance classes, I'm afraid I'll just disappear."

"We can't have that. Not until I read your next book. Who didn't I meet?"

"Kim Saunderling. She's the blind woman. Takes only Arabic and jazz. And Nancy Pahrump. She used to take all the beginning classes, but she doesn't come any more."

"When was the last time you saw Nancy?"

I blew out my cheeks as I contemplated Wanda's question. "I think the day we found Grace's body. She was being escorted to a police car." I stared at her, jaw gaping. "Could she . . . No, she couldn't."

Wanda kept her gaze on the road, but the distant look in her eye told me she was seeing more than the traffic ahead of her. "If Deb is right, Nancy didn't kill Grace. No one did, really. And there's no indication Nancy is a victim, right?"

"Right. You know what bothers me about all this?" I didn't wait for a response, but kept charging ahead. "Nothing seems to be happening."

"Women died. That's something. And all the grief they are leaving behind, that's something, too."

"I know, but . . . Well, in a mystery story, something is always happening. There are chases and fights and break-ins and all sorts of things going on. It's not that I want to deal with any of that stuff, but all I do is think. It's like everything is happening in my head. As if it's not real. Just one long waking nightmare."

"Like it's being written in your head rather than happening for real?"

I nodded. "Yeah, like that."

"And you need it to be real?"

Again my nod.

"Why?"

I slumped as far as the seat belt would allow me. "I don't know."

"Could it be that if it's real, and if you make sense of it, then you make sense of death?"

"Maybe."

"And if you make sense of death, perhaps Jay really is home in Colorado waiting for you?"

I had never put the thought in so many words, but Wanda seemed to understand the way I felt. "It doesn't make sense, does it?"

"Grief doesn't make sense."

"What's weird is that I hadn't really cried much the last couple of years. I thought I'd moved past the worst of my grief, but now I cry all the time."

"Well, your dad did just die."

I sat up straight. "Oh. Of course. Grief for him. For my mother, too. She died shortly before Jay got really bad, so I never had time to mourn her."

"Grace's and Deb's murders seem to have brought back all your unresolved feelings about death." Wanda pulled into the driveway. "So, let's suppose you do find out who killed Deb. Let's suppose you really do put death in its place, and by some miraculous sleight of hand, Jay really is back in Colorado. Would you go home to him?"

Tears stung my eyes and rolled down my cheeks. "Don't ask me that." I sobbed. "Please don't ask."

We got out of her vehicle, and she held me while I cried.

"I loved him with my whole soul from the moment I met him." I pulled away from her. Averted my gaze so she couldn't see my eyes. "But I hated his being sick. I wanted it over. I didn't want him to die. I just wanted him not sick." I choked out the words. "I'm different now. More like I was before I met him. What if I go back and I feel trapped? What if I hate him? What if I've changed too much? What if he has changed?" Then, very softly, "What if he dies again?"

She shifted her weight from one foot to the other. I could feel her conflict. She wanted to stay and comfort me, but she needed to leave.

I fumbled in my purse for a tissue, wiped my eyes, and blew my nose. I stuffed the wad back into the bag, and drew in a shaky breath.

"I'll be okay. Thank you. Thank you for coming. Thank you for listening."

Wanda still seemed torn, but she headed back around the Suburban to the driver's side. "You don't need to thank me. Just put me in your book."

I laughed. "You got it. Who do you want to be? Wanda or Maggie?"

"Both." She gave me one last hug, hopped into the vehicle, and slowly drove off.

I stood alone on the driveway and watched her leave, ghosts of the dead fogging my mind.

Chapter 16

Verde Ranchero, a gated community for people over fifty-five, resembled no ranch I had ever seen, and the only green seemed to be the golf course that meandered around the small lots with their large houses. Luckily for me, security was lax. All I had to do was sit in my VW bug, wait for a resident to open the gate, and drive in right behind them.

My phone has a built-in GPS, otherwise I might still be driving around, trying to find Deb's house on Juvenal Street. But the robotic voice directed me to the right place, a sprawling red-tiled stucco house with narrow strips of rose-colored rocks separating the domicile from its neighbors.

As I walked up to the front door, I rehearsed silently what I intended to say. *Hi, Emmett. I'm Pat, a friend of Deb's from dance class. I wanted to extend my condolences for your loss.* Once I got those few words out, I hoped to find a way to lead the conversation around to Deb's past.

I rang the bell. Someone yanked open the door partway, but I couldn't see who did it—my photochromic lenses were too dark and the interior of the house too dim. I barely got out, "Hi, Emmett," when the door slammed shut.

I rang the bell again.

A deep voice from inside the house shouted, "Go away. Go away I don't want your food. I don't need my house cleaned. I don't want you to do my laundry."

"I'm a friend of Deb's."

"A widow, right? Or are you divorced?"

I couldn't imagine what I had done to inspire such enmity. If I had told him my name, perhaps, but being a widow? What did that have to do with anything? And then I remembered a guy in my grief group who had been chased constantly by desperate women who wanted a husband. They all had different reasons for hounding him—some wanted him to assuage their loneliness, some wanted him to massage their itch, some wanted a meal ticket. And some, maybe most, wanted to feel needed. What I found most appalling about his situation is that a lot of the women had tracked him down through his wife's obituary. He didn't seem to mind, and in fact, he married one of the women almost right away because he wanted to be looked after, but judging by Emmett's fury, he did not seem interested in taking up with anyone quite yet.

"Please, Emmett. I'd like to talk about Deb."

"Go away." This time the voice sounded tired, as if the anger had burned out.

"I took dance classes with Deb. My name is Pat."

The door opened wide, and a frail, stooped man with sparse white hair peered at me. "Pat? The writer?"

"Ye-es."

He leaned on a cane with his left hand and held out his right arm to indicate the interior of the house. "Come in. Come in. Debbie often talked about you. She so admired you."

I gulped. *Admired me? What sort of insane situation had I gotten myself into now?*

"She was excited about being a part of your book and so thrilled when you asked her advice about writing." He hobbled from the small entry way into the living room. "Sit down. Sit down."

I looked from one piece of overly ornate furniture to another. The sofa and chairs seemed buried in wildly vibrant pillows, and the tables and shelves stuffed with small framed photos and figurines of animals in dance costumes. The pale turquoise walls were strangely devoid of ornament. I lowered myself to the edge of a chair. The place must have been decorated by Deb. It didn't at all mesh with the drab raggy sweater, ancient sweat pants, and duct-tape-wrapped slippers her husband wore.

He plopped onto the couch and stared at me, eyes bright with tears. I remembered Deb talking about his changing a light bulb once as if it were the most marvelous thing in the world, and now that I saw the man in all his frailty, I could see why the ordinary task could have seemed so wondrous.

"We miss Deb. She added so much to the class." I told myself the words weren't really a lie. She had added drama, and one way or another, her absence would be felt.

Emmett picked up a photo from the ranks on the table next to him and stared at it. "She was always a joy. A joy. But you know that."

The door bell rang. "Go away," he bellowed. "Go away." He struggled to his feet. "I want to show you something." He led me into the next room. It looked like a modern version of an old fashioned kitchen with a huge amount of counter space, copper pots and pans hanging from a rack, stainless steel appliances, glass fronted cabinets, and six chairs arranged around an oval table with all its leaves inserted. The kitchen would have been lovely if every available space had not been filled with covered dishes.

I stared, speechless, at the largess. One or two dishes would be indicative of neighbors helping a neighbor, but this seemed more like an onslaught. Were women alone really so desperate? Would I too one day comb the obituaries to find my next husband?

"What am I going to do with all this food?" Emmett wailed. "What am I going to do?"

"What about a homeless shelter?"

"The one I talked to didn't want any of it."

"Call around to the churches. I'm sure they know people who would love to have some food."

He smiled at me. "You really are as smart as Debbie said you were."

Suddenly, I felt bad about my deception. "I didn't really—"

"You didn't really think she liked you, did you? Did you? My Debbie was like that. Hard to understand. But she had a heart of gold. A heart of gold."

"I cried for her," I said. That, at least, was the truth.

"Thank you." He took a few steps back toward the living room then stopped. "Are you hungry? I have plenty of food. Plenty of food." He laughed, a shrill sound that hinted at how close grief had nudged him to the edge of sanity

"Thank you. But no, I'm fine."

We went back to the living room. He picked up Deb's photo and held it to his chest. She'd seemed truly devoted to him, and he to her. What had they seen in each other? They both had strange idiosyncrasies, her with her need to top everyone's story, he with his repetitions, but other than that, they seemed opposites. But maybe the opposites attracted. His drabness, her color. His vacuity, her imperiousness.

"How did you meet?" I asked

He fixed his gaze on the photo. "At her husband's funeral."

I reminded myself not to be surprised at any discrepancies since Deb seldom seemed to tell the truth. "I thought they were divorced."

"They were. I guess I should have said ex-husband. I guess I should have."

"Okay, that makes sense."

He shook his head sadly, and continued shaking it. "Nothing makes sense. Nothing does."

"Why would anyone . . .?" I let my voice trail off, not knowing how to voice the question without bringing him more pain, but he understood.

"No one would want to . . . to . . ." He touched a finger lightly to Deb's face in the photo. "I told the police it had to have been tampering, like that Tylenol case a long time ago. Everyone loved my Debbie. Loved my sweet Debbie."

"Did her ex-husband love her?"

"Yes, of course. But he wanted children. So did Debbie. More than anything. But the children never came."

"Is that why he divorced her?"

"He kept hoping she'd get pregnant, so he waited until after she went through menopause. They'd been married thirty-two years."

"What a prince," I muttered.

"Thirty-two years. She was so hurt. Thought they'd be married forever. She didn't know how to handle it." He whispered to the photo, "Oh, Debbie, I'm so sorry, I didn't understand. Now I do. Now I do."

"It's hard losing someone," I said.

He jerked his head up as if suddenly remembering he wasn't alone. "You lost someone?"

"Just about everyone. My mom. My dad. My husband."

"I was an orphan. Never married until I met Debbie."

My stomach clenched against a feeling of nausea. I thought I'd gotten a bum deal lately, but this poor fellow had been served a whole lifetime of not belonging.

I stood up to leave, but he motioned for me to sit down again.

"Don't go. Don't go. Talking to one of Debbie's friends makes her more real."

"I know." I held my midriff, still feeling nauseous. "Sometimes it feels as if you've made it up and it was never real at all."

"Never real at all," he whispered.

"I don't know much about Deb's early life," I said. "What was she like?" *Did she really do all those things she'd claimed to have done?*

"We've only been married nine years. She was sixty. I was eighty. Jim, her ex-husband started working for me after the divorce. I owned a car dealership. But I'd never met her before his funeral. His funeral. She was so vibrant and colorful! Everyone else wore black, but she wore electric blue. I couldn't take my eyes off her." He touched the photo, and whispered, "Couldn't take my eyes off her."

I didn't feel as if I should interrupt his grief, so I waited.

After a minute, he looked up and gave a start. "I didn't know her before, but she told me how wild she'd been after the divorce. She couldn't bear to spend a second alone. Went to bars. Picked up guys. Couldn't stand the pain. The pain. But I never saw any of that. After the funeral, she was so happy. It's like she buried her grief with him. Buried her grief with him."

"Did you know any of her friends?"

"She dumped them when we got married. Said she only needed me. I'm glad. I had her all to myself. Had her all to myself."

"Did her ex-husband ever have kids?"

"No." He laughed. "He was seeing some young thing. They were going to get married and have a bunch of kids. But then he died. He died."

"How did he die?"

"Drowned in the Jacuzzi. An accident."

My heart beat so hard, I felt as if I were shaking. I clasped my hands together to keep them still. *So she had killed her ex-husband and made it look like an accident.*

He put the photo on the seat next to him. "That's what the cops said. That it was an accident. I kept after them, telling them there is no way a big guy like that could have drowned in a Jacuzzi, but they said he'd been drinking, fell when he tried to get out and . . . drowned. Drowned."

"What did Deb think?"

"She said it was an accident. Said it had almost happened

before." He looked at me, pale eyes magnified by tears. "She's gone. Gone. What am I going to do now?"

What am I going to do now? The refrain of the newly bereaved and the not so newly bereaved.

"I don't know, Emmett. All I know is what I did. Get up in the morning. Put one foot in front of the other. Breathe in and out."

"Not much of an answer."

"I'm sorry, it's the only answer I have. The years pass. That I know."

And they would pass for him, too. Though at eighty-nine, he might not have many years left. The stress of grief is hard on the relatively young, and for the elderly, it can be a killer. But then, my father was about Emmett's age when my mother died, and he'd lived for almost seven years afterward so it's hard to tell what will happen.

"Do you know who Jim was going to marry?" I asked.

"Is she someone I need to notify about Debbie? About Debbie?"

"I'm sure she wouldn't expect it. I was just curious."

"I don't remember her name. It was so long ago."

I stood and edged toward the door. "Thank you for talking to me."

He picked up the photo again, and caressed it with the back of his hand. "Take some food with you when you leave."

I fled Verde Ranchero as if I were escaping a prison, but I could not escape my horrifying thoughts. Deb had once said, with her usual know-it-all attitude, that divorce was worse than death. And apparently, for her, it had been. Had she killed her ex-husband to stop the pain? Or had she killed him to stop the marriage and the cessation of pain came as a welcome side effect? If so, had the fiancée killed Deb for revenge?

For just a moment, I felt relieved that someone other than a dance mate had killed Deb, but then I realized the women at Madame ZeeZee's dance studio weren't off the hook. Even if the fiancée had waited nine years to exact retribution, she couldn't have known about Buffy's idea of putting insulin in an EpiPen.

And anyway, despite what Lena had told me about Deb saying she killed her ex-husband, Jim might really have died accidentally. Sometimes an accident is just an accident.

But I didn't believe it.

Chapter 17

What is the measure of a woman's life? Is it what other people think of her? What she thinks of herself? What she does? What she imagines she's done?

I couldn't figure out the truth of Deb. Her husband's "Sweet Debbie" seemed so at odds with the woman I thought her to be. I could now see why she needed to be first, though, to have others think her special. With a husband like Jim, her deceased ex, how could she not have developed a desperate need for acceptance? Maybe she hadn't wanted to make me out to be a villain or to punish me for my disdain by rearranging Grace's body. Maybe she simply wanted to make sure she had a part in my book.

That damn book.

I felt bad that I would never know the real Deb. I felt bad that her death removed all possibility of my making amends for my part in her tragedy, even though, in my heart, I knew nothing would have changed. A few kind words from me would not put her world back together, would not give her the children she had so desperately needed. And although I felt sorry for her, maybe even understood her a bit better, I could not bring myself to like her.

And for that, I felt bad, too.

I'd gone to see Emmett on Friday, and Friday night I barely slept. I couldn't stop thinking of Deb. Couldn't get the image of all those covered dishes of food out of my mind. I knew I'd inherited my tendency to brood from my father, and his father, and his father's father, but that knowledge, like so much knowledge, didn't help me.

Nor did walking in the desert.

Shortly after I returned from my walk on Saturday, Madame ZeeZee called and asked if I wanted to go to lunch. She'd had a bad day on Friday with her mother, and needed to talk.

I jumped at the chance to exchange thoughts of one tragedy with another. At least whatever Madame ZeeZee's mother suffered had nothing to do with me. We agreed to meet at the Mexican restaurant by the studio and share our usual taquito special.

As Madame ZeeZee and I ate, we talked about the horrors of

growing to a great old age. We compared my father's experiences with her mother's, and I couldn't help thinking of Grace's gentle death. Although I'm sure she had plenty of ills to contend with, at seventy-five, Grace had been a long way from the problems of a person slowly returning to dust while still alive—the dryness no amount of liquid could soothe, the floods of mucus that never seemed to end, the anxieties created by a body that had lost the ability to repair itself.

Was Grace pleased to have been spared all that misery or was she saddened to have lost out on a bit more life?

We ate everything on our plates. I'm sure the taquitos were as good as they always were and the guacamole and cheese topping as fresh, but I barely tasted the food. Although life is for the living, thoughts of death and dying so overwhelmed me, I had a hard time focusing on the small enjoyment of eating.

While Madame ZeeZee went to fill our drink cups, I cleared the trash off our two-person table to give us more room, but I left the red basket of chips for us to nibble on.

Housekeeping chores done, we settled back to continue our conversation. I put one elbow on the now accessible table, hand cupped around my face. "I'm sorry you have to go through this," I said. "I wish I could help."

"I don't know what you could do for my mother. There's nothing *I* can do. Did I tell you she refused to accept hospice? She's afraid they will kill her."

"I'm lucky. My dad wanted hospice. It certainly helped me. When he fell, I had someone to call."

"My mother still won't call anyone when she falls. She just waits until the caregiver arrives."

"Do you think people choose how they die?"

Madame ZeeZee's eyes opened wide. "Don't talk like that!"

"I don't mean suicide. I mean, subconsciously. My dad said he was ready to go, but he seemed terrified of dying, as if he couldn't choose. But then there's Grace. I wonder sometimes if Grace had some sort of debilitating illness and had volunteered to be the victim in my book out of a subconscious desire to have it all over with."

"It was a joke," Madame ZeeZee said. "I remember her laughing. You have to stop questioning everything, Pat. Things happen for a reason, even if we don't know what the reason is."

"You're right." I meant she was right about my having to stop questioning. I still didn't know if anything happened for a reason or if meaning was something we carved out of the eternal chaos.

"I'm glad you came back to class. When you left on Tuesday, I didn't know if you ever would." Madame ZeeZee smiled. "You certainly caused a commotion! No one knew what you meant about Deb and Grace."

She paused as if waiting for me to volunteer the information. When I remained silent, she said, "What *did* you mean? What happened the day of Grace's accident?"

"Do you really want to know?" I traded her gaze for gaze. "It's not pretty."

Her eyes grew wide. Interest? Fright? I couldn't tell.

Then she nodded. "It happened at my studio. I should know."

So once again I told the story, beginning with Lena's revelation and ending with Deb's confession.

Madame ZeeZee's shoulders sagged, and several seconds went by before she straightened them again. "Rico was mad at me for giving Lena the keys, but I couldn't let her spend the night with us. He said I could lose the studio if anyone ever found out she was there. You won't tell the cops, will you?"

"Not without your permission."

Madame ZeeZee put the straw of her drink in her mouth She didn't take a sip, but seemed to use the moment to reflect. "Do you think Deb told the truth?"

"I believe so, but I don't know for sure. I talked to her husband yesterday, and he mentioned how much she wanted to be a part of the book. Maybe she really didn't consider the possibility that there could be consequences."

"I was late that day."

I shook an admonishing finger at her. "If I can't think it was my fault, then you can't either. It was a horrible sequence of events, but in the end, it was Deb's fault. She's the one who made the final decision to wait and not call an ambulance."

"It's a nightmare, isn't it? And now Deb's passed, too." After a suitable grave pause, she giggled. "Rhett and those girls really think you're killing us off."

"If so, then *I* am your nightmare, aren't I? But if I had that sort of power, I would use it for life, not death." I laughed. "Maybe I should have given the story a different title. Madame ZeeZee's Treasure—then we could have all gotten rich."

"Have you figured out yet who killed Deb?"

"No. I'm afraid to."

"Afraid that it's someone you especially like?" Madame ZeeZee spoke so softly, I knew she feared the same thing.

I nodded my acquiescence. "One thing that is so very difficult about grief is that it turns everything upside down. What you think you would feel, you don't. What you feel, you couldn't even have imagined. I know it seems as if I am still grieving, but it's not like the way it was in the beginning. Life has settled down again to where it's understandable. But I'm afraid of my life turning upside down again." Tears stung my eyes. "I can't deal with that sort of internal chaos, and I'm afraid if it turned out to be someone I like . . ."

"But you have to find out. I don't want to be known as the death studio."

I'd bowed my head to hide my tears, but now I jerked my head up. "What? Who said that?"

"One of the new girls in beginning Hawaiian. She didn't say it in a bad way, either. Almost like it was . . . fun."

"A couple of those women seem to think you're running some sort of murder weekend. I don't know what's wrong with people."

"I've worked too hard to end up a laughingstock." She tapped a wine-colored fingernail on the table in front of me. "You have to stop this. Now."

I focused on the nail as if it were a miniature dagger ready to plunge into my heart. "Then I need your help. I don't know the women in class all that well."

"I don't either. We're friends. But not really."

"Still, you must know something about their backgrounds. Some of them have been with you for many years"

"Buffy started around the same time you did. Maybe a month or so before. You know her better than I do."

"I like Buffy." I laughed. "And I need her. I dance so much better when I am next to her. I know the dances, but I have a hard time finding the beat. She has such a great sense of rhythm and timing, it helps keep me on track. Some dances, like "I Love the Night Life," I have no problem with—the beat is obvious even to me, but in other dances, I have a hard time fitting the steps to the music."

Madame ZeeZee pulled her brows together. "You need to be able to do the dances on your own."

"I'm amazed I can dance at all. I'm not tone deaf exactly, but the melody, harmonies, and beat all mesh into a single sound. I can't always hear the notes I need to pay attention to."

"You'll learn." She spoke so matter-of-factly, I paused to savor the idea.

"It's funny," I said when the moment passed. "Buffy and I used to do things together—went to the fair, saw a local production of *The Music Man* in the park, went to a quilt show. I even house sat for her and her husband once, but then ... I don't know what happened. Maybe she became afraid I'd want to move in with her when I have to leave my dad's house."

Madame ZeeZee picked up an uneaten chip, broke it in half, and dropped both pieces back into the bowl. "Do you think Buffy had anything to do with Deb passing?"

"She came up with the idea of the insulin and the EpiPen, but no, I don't think she did anything to Deb. If she'd wanted to kill her, she'd just do it. She taught science. I'm sure she could have found a way that would have seemed an accident without implicating her."

"But maybe that's what she wants you to think. Could she be playing games with you like Deb did?"

I thought back to the conversation where Buffy had explained why Jackie and Margot would have made good suspects. She did seem to know a lot about mysteries, but such knowledge spoke more of being a reader than a doer.

"I don't see her playing mind games, but I think she sees and understands more of the undercurrents than she lets on."

Madame ZeeZee leaned back as if to get a better look at me. "What kind of undercurrents?"

"You know. Like Buffy not wanting to be in the front row in dance class, Allie wanting it desperately, and Deb claiming the spot for herself."

"I don't remember that."

"You were sorting through your CDs, I think."

She tapped her nails on the table in front of herself. "So not Buffy. What about Jackie? She came to class because of you."

"Oh, right." I had forgotten that. For a while, I had belonged to a walking club. I figured that if I were going to walk anyway, I could turn it into a social outing. Jackie and I often walked together. We were both taking care of our fathers, and we had a lot to discuss. When I found out about her love of dancing, I told her about Madame ZeeZee's studio. Both our fathers are gone now, neither of us walk with the club any more, but the dancing endures.

"I don't see Jackie doing it. She wouldn't be subtle the way Buffy would. She used to own a concrete business, and her sons own it now, so if she wanted to do away with someone, she could make the person disappear forever and no one would know. Or she would fly out over the ocean and dump the body. Jackie is straightforward. The EpiPen scenario seems too . . . convoluted."

"A lot of you girls started around the same time. Kim was there when you came, right?"

"Yes. She was so natural, I didn't know she couldn't see for about a month."

"So she must have started dancing with us right before you did. Nancy came the same day Kim did."

"I signed up about two years ago. What happened then to attract so many students?"

"I moved the studio. It used to be hidden behind another store, and I thought this was a better location."

"It seems to have worked out."

Madame ZeeZee picked up a piece of the chip she had broken, and chewed it slowly. "I lost a lot of dancers when I moved. Either they didn't want to drive that far or they thought they were too old and stopped coming. One eighty year old quit because she said that no one had any business dancing after eighty." She laughed. "I guess I'll have to close the studio next year when I turn eighty."

"Grace and Deb were with you a long time, weren't they?"

"From the beginning." Her eyebrows shot up. "Could someone be removing the rest of the original group?"

I leaned back in the hard wooden chair and folded my arms. "Interesting possibility. But why?"

Madame ZeeZee gave a short laugh. "Because the killer's crazy?"

"That, too. But there would have to be reason for the craziness to focus on those particular students."

One more tap of the fingernail. "If Allie wanted to be in the front, maybe she thought Grace and Deb were her rivals."

I sat tall as I remembered the dirty looks Allie had been giving Deb. "What do you know about Allie?"

"Not much." Madame ZeeZee picked up another chip and broke it absentmindedly. "She's a lot older than she claims to be."

"She says she's fifty. How old is she?"

"Seventy at least. She said she saw me in a production at Radio City Music Hall. We only danced there once. Fifty-two years ago."

"Yeah, it would be hard to see a performance before one is born. But maybe she lied about being there to butter you up?"

"She remembered the number. The same one I'm teaching you. 'Flying Home.'"

"She looks amazing for her age. Still so beautiful."

Madame ZeeZee smiled a bit cattily. "Compliments of her plastic surgeon. Apparently she liked his work so much, she married him."

No wonder the woman had such unlined skin! And eyes pulled to an exotic slant. "It's funny. I never considered she'd had plastic surgery. I thought rearranging your face was only for celebrities." I shook my head in a futile effort to erase the last few words. "That's not true. I knew regular people got plastic surgery, I just never met anyone before."

"Allie wasn't regular people. She was a star on Broadway."

I leaned forward. "Really?"

"That's what she said."

"She could be the doer. She wants the limelight and will stop anyone who gets in her way." Then I slumped in my seat when I thought it out. "But Allie didn't kill Grace. Deb did."

"What about Deb? Could Allie have done it to Deb?"

"I suppose. But really, killing a rival so you can be in the first row of dancers instead of the second? Seems a bit much, especially since we're not exactly a professional dance troupe. Besides, you told us that anyone who knows the dances can be up front."

"Allie is a good dancer," Madame ZeeZee said. "I have to give her that. She's only been with me a couple of months. When she learns the dances, I'll take her with us to performances. I worry about Rose. I don't think she can dance much longer."

"How long has Rose been with you?"

"As long as Deb and Grace. About twelve years."

I felt my jaw drop. "I thought she was newer. She's . . ."

Madame ZeeZee's mouth twisted as if she were in pain. "She's getting way too skinny. And now that Grace is gone, Rose seems to have lost whatever ability she had for dancing."

Would the same thing happen to me if Buffy were to quit? But no, she absented herself often on various trips, and I did okay without relying on her timing. Not great, but okay.

I took a long pull on my straw. "What's Rose like? Could she have done away with Deb out of some sort of frustration or rivalry?"

"She's a country girl. A good mother. A devoted wife, even though her husband doesn't deserve it. He tends to be mean."

I gave a humph of laughter. "There seems to be a lot of that going around. I sometimes envy these women for still having someone, but I think I am better off. At least I don't have to worry about being stuck with a husband who treats me badly."

"Did Jay ever treat you bad?"

"Never. He was the kindest man I ever knew. I remember once in the grocery store we were talking about how disappointing it is to live in a world where everyone is out for themselves. He said he wouldn't do anything for anyone ever again. As he was saying that, we passed a little old lady who couldn't reach something on the top shelf. He handed it down to her, then continued talking about only looking out for himself. I don't know if he ever realized how deeply ingrained his kindness is. Was."

I could feel the tears welling up as they always did when I talked about Jay. I brushed the wetness away and said briskly, "Lena. You haven't told me about Lena."

"You know her story now. Her husband started getting ill a long time ago. That's why she took dance classes. She needed to find a life for herself. It's only lately he got so angry at her." She sighed. "Poor girl. She's needs to admit him to an Alzheimer's unit, but she won't listen to reason. Just like my mother."

I put my elbows on the table and propped my chin in one hand. "Do you think Lena could have been so . . . distraught . . . that she wanted to hurt Deb? The EpiPen thing was such a long shot, it might have been more to disable Deb than to kill her. Lena seemed afraid of Deb, as if she thought she was next on Deb's hit list."

"You mentioned envy." Madame ZeeZee narrowed her eyes at me. I steeled myself for a rebuke. "Both Deb and Grace were happily married. Could Lena or Rose have killed them out of envy or spite?

I let out my breath, and contemplated the possibility. "Maybe after Grace died, someone was so pleased that one of the smug marrieds was dead that she tried to remove another."

"Smug marrieds?" Madame ZeeZee queried.

I shifted in my seat. "I'm sorry. I shouldn't have said that, but when all the married women get together they sound smug as they talk about the care and feeding of their husbands or how good their husbands are to them."

Her mouth dropped open. "Is that how you think of me?"

Remorse snaked through me. "No. Of course not. You have always been good to me. So has Rico."

Madame ZeeZee nodded. "He's a good man."

"It's weird to discover that much of the married women's talk is more about pumping themselves up to accept their situation than because they're self-satisfied. You never know about people. I did know Rhett's situation more or less."

"She was a mess after the divorce, but dancing helped, and so did meeting her new husband."

I folded my arms on the table. "I really don't understand any of this. These women have lived a total of about seven hundred years, and in all those years, until now, nothing out of the ordinary seems to have happened. We've all suffered tragedies and been dealt challenges, of course. After a certain age, it's to be expected. But I haven't found anything so awful it's worth killing over."

Madame ZeeZee slowly ate a chip and followed it with a long drink. "Do you really think learning about these girl's lives will help you find the truth and keep someone else from being slain?"

I shrugged my shoulders. "It can't hurt."

"Okay." Madame ZeeZee gave a single nod as if making a decision. "I do know something. I promised to keep it to myself, but since it's important, I'll tell you."

Chapter 18

"Madame ZeeZee rose, grabbed her purse from the floor beside her chair, and started to walk away.

"Hey!"

She jerked around to look at me.

I held out a hand to stay her retreat. "You can't drop a bombshell like that and just leave!"

"I'm not leaving." She giggled. "I'm going to the restroom."

"Oh." I slumped in my chair, feeling foolish. This amateur detective gig was not exactly easy.

I went to get a refill for my diet cola and a handful of lime wedges from the salsa bar, figuring the limes would offer some nutrition to offset the chemicals that would accumulate in my brain. I squeezed the limes into the drink and inhaled the clean scent. I was wiping my hands with a napkin when Madame ZeeZee returned.

She settled herself in her chair, took a sip of her drink, and drew in a breath. "It was a dark and stormy night."

I laughed. I thought she'd set me up for a joke, but when her face darkened and she shook an admonishing finger at me, I instantly sobered, feeling sure she was about to tell me something I would just as soon not hear. But, as always, my need to know overrode the urge to flee.

"Kim was driving home from her mother's house. Her mom had urged her to stay since the driving conditions were so dangerous, but her husband wanted to leave. Kim agreed. She had an early shift at the hospital the next morning. She was a nurse, did you know that? And her seven-year-old son had school."

I could feel the dread tightening my stomach. Kim didn't have children, at least none she ever talked about.

Madame ZeeZee's voice thickened. "Her son was in the back seat, but he wanted to sit up front with his mom and dad. He took off his seat belt. She turned around to scold him, and that's when it happened. A truck ran a red light. She didn't see it."

"That's how she lost her sight? In a traffic accident?"

"No. She was fine. Just a broken shoulder." She took a slow sip from her drink, as if she didn't want to tell me the next part.

"Something happened to the boy?"

"He didn't make it. Neither did her husband."

Although I'd known what Madame ZeeZee would say, it didn't mitigate the shock and horror that slammed into me and stole my breath. That poor woman. I couldn't even imagine how she must have felt. To have the pain of their deaths as well as the guilt that must have assailed her would have been too much to bear. But she always seemed so . . . serene.

"How long ago did this happen?"

"Twenty years maybe."

Long enough to have found some sort of acceptance, but still, from what I have heard, losing a child is even worse than losing a husband. They say you never get over the death of your child. You feel the loss, the absence, for the rest of your life. But to lose both her husband and her child at the same time?

I put my elbows on the table and covered my face with my hands. How do people ever deal with the horrors life throws around with such abandon? But people survived and even thrived. I pictured Kim so casually coping with her blindness, going out of her way to make sure people were as comfortable with her situation as she was.

"How did she lose her sight?"

"That came much later. For the first year, she put all her effort into her work, but it wasn't enough. She felt that nothing would ever fill the emptiness."

"What she must have gone through." I shook my head, thinking not just of the pain but of her courage. And yet, what other choice did she have? No matter how horrendous an experience, you found a way to reorganize your brain to encompass the unimaginable. And life went on.

Or maybe it didn't. Maybe you keep the pain inside you, and one day, listening to your fellow students talk about a life—marriage, husband, children, grandchildren—that had been denied you, you snap, and . . .

But putting insulin in an EpiPen didn't sound like someone snapping. It sounded like someone with a long-time grudge.

"What happened to the driver of the truck?" I asked.

"Nothing. Just a ticket, I think. He hadn't been drinking or texting or anything. He tried to stop in time, but he hydroplaned into the intersection. Kim refused to sue. He had kids, and she didn't want to destroy their lives."

If Kim didn't hold a grudge for the man who killed her husband and child, why would she begrudge Deb the happiness she'd found? It would have made more sense, in a senseless sort of way, for her to have gone after one of the women in class who had it all.

But Deb had been so very annoying.

"What are you thinking?" Madame ZeeZee's voice broke into my musings.

"Just wondering if Kim could have wanted Deb dead, but I don't believe she solves her problems in such a lethal way. And I don't think she could have tampered with the EpiPen. She would have needed an accomplice." I shook my head. "I don't see it."

"I've been blessed. I never felt the grief that you and Kim did. I have two sons that grew to manhood. My first husband was selfish, but he never laid a hand on me or the boys, and Rico is good to me."

I laughed ruefully. "One thing your nightmare is teaching me is to be grateful for what I had then and what I have now. But I can't handle hearing about any more pain."

"There's more to Kim's story."

Oh, please, no.

I pulled in a deep breath and let it out slowly. "Okay."

"She survived the first year somehow but her grief got worse. She looked around for a way to make a difference. She thought she should do something where her sorrow was an asset. She said people in extreme emotional pain deserved someone who understood how they felt. She became a hospice nurse for a while, then she met a minister who was trying to put together a medical team to help out at a mission in Nigeria."

Madame ZeeZee sipped through her straw, and I felt she was gathering strength to tell the rest of the tale. I finished my drink, sucked on a piece of ice, and waited.

"She said the place was truly appalling," Madame ZeezZee continued. "She'd been told most of the people had Hansen's disease, but she hadn't realized how bad off they were. Hansen's disease is curable, but in Nigeria at that time, the villagers still cast out the afflicted. And many didn't get the antibiotics they needed."

"A leper colony? Kim worked at a leper colony?" I pictured the stylish woman I thought had been a model, living in a mud hut and toiling under the hot African sun. "How long was she there?"

"About three years. She came back, worked as an ER nurse, and eventually remarried. Five years ago, she started losing her sight. It wasn't until she mentioned her stay in Africa that the doctors found the problem. She'd contracted leprosy."

"It took that long for anyone to realize she had the disease?"

"Kim says it has a lengthy incubation period. She was cured of the disease, but never regained her sight. Her husband couldn't stand the stigma of being married to a leper, so he left."

"But if she was cured, then she no longer has the disease."

Madame ZeeZee shrugged. "He told her he would never be able to think of her the same way. He said it gave him the willies to touch her."

I bowed my head under the weight of all that sorrow. And then I jerked my head up. "This is a secret worth killing over. Do you think Deb could have found out about the Hansen's disease?"

"Kim might have told her, but if Deb knew about the Hansen's disease, for sure she'd have been telling us about her own bout with leprosy."

I laughed, but cut it short when I heard a trill of hysteria in the high note. "And I still don't see Kim killing with insulin. Killing with kindness, maybe, but that's all. No one who's endured what she has and come out on the side of the saints would hurt anyone."

"But someone killed Deb, and I might be next." Madame ZeeZee tapped a fingernail on the table in front of me. "You have to stop it."

"How?"

"You're the writer. You'll figure it out."

***

I spend so much time online with other writers—discussing various aspects of the writing life, responding to their comments on my blogs, deleting their promos from my Facebook feed—that I tend to forget not everyone is a writer. Not everyone dismisses authors as just one of an annoying herd.

I suppose it seems to readers and non-readers alike that writers have special powers. We create worlds and people out of our imaginings and make those worlds available for other people to experience as if the worlds were real.

But life is not something we create out of our imaginations. Or maybe it is. Maybe life is what we collectively have imagined. Even so, what does one voice matter? How could I possibly figure out the truth of anything?

I thought of the mystery novels I had read, and how often I had tossed aside a book when the amateur detective gathered all the suspects together and forced the murderer to confess. I used to think it a phony—and an oh so trite—ending. But on the way home from my lunch with Madame ZeeZee, I wondered how else an amateur could find out the truth. Without a confession or a witness, there is no way to know what someone has done. No way to prove it.

Cops can rely on circumstantial evidence, of course, on the minutiae of the crime scene, and on the inferences they draw from the interrogations, but those of us with only a pen and our imaginings are at a disadvantage.

Back at the house, I threw my bag and my hat on the makeshift bed and went out to the kitchen to turn on my computer. I opened a document and rested my fingers on the keyboard as if it were a Ouija board planchette. No truth appeared on the page. No untruths, either. The screen remained blank.

I'd ruled out all the women for one reason or another. Jackie too forthright, Kim too serene, Buffy too nice, Nancy too removed, Margot too disciplined. And the others all seemed to be what they purported to be.

But one of the women was living a lie.

I thought of gathering them all together for a finale, and imagined that after a few pointed questions, the murderer would scream, "No more. No more questions. I confess." And the cops, like clowns out of a Volkswagen bug, would pour out of the tiny bathroom, the only place in the studio to hide, and would place the woman under arrest.

It could happen.

Chapter 19

Before the end of jazz class on Monday, I realized the traditional ending to Deb's murder mystery story could never happen. Would never happen.

Not everyone took all the classes. The only time we all would be in the studio at the same time was between ballet class and Arabic class on Tuesday. (Well, except for Michaela who only took Hawaiian classes but, unlike Wanda, I did not consider her for the villain. No matter how devout a person's reputation, a showgirl daughter you are proud of would in no way be a reason to murder.)

And on most class days, someone was absent.

Monday turned out to be a day when few women showed up. Buffy, Allie, Kim, and I came to class. The studio seemed so empty, it shocked me to realize only three people were absent—Rose, Rhett, and Lena. Margo and Jackie did not take jazz. Nancy seemed to have quit. And Grace and Deb were dead.

Would Madame ZeeZee be able to keep the studio open? She did have her children's classes and the new students for Hawaiian, but what if they weren't enough? What would I do without dance?

If my dancing days were coming to an end, I better learn what I could while I had a chance.

But Monday did not seem to be a day for learning. Even though for once we all dressed the way we were supposed to in black leggings and red shirts with black "Jazz/Tappers" emblazoned on the back above a silhouette of a jazz dancer, each of us danced to a different beat, even the two women who usually kept perfect time. Allie seemed to have appointed herself to count aloud the sets of eight, but from the pained look on Buffy's face and her own emphatic count, "*One*, two, three, four, *five*, six, seven, eight," I presumed Allie, uncharacteristically, was as out of sync with the music as I tend to be.

I smiled at their battle of the beats, but it wasn't really funny. I think I have it bad that I can't hear what I am supposed to hear, but how much worse it must be for Buffy who knows the beat and has to suffer through our crude interpretation.

Buffy caught me smiling and smiled in return, but no one else seemed to see the humor in the discordance or even to notice it. Allie acted as if she were the only dancer in the room. And Madame ZeeZee worked with Kim, arranging the woman's hands and arms in the proper gestures, and explaining the positioning of the feet.

I paused to watch Kim, who'd added a buckle-like fastener to gather the shirt at her hip, turning our practice uniform into a chic outfit, and I marveled at the life this stylish woman had led and with what grace she dealt with her circumstances.

Then I started moving to the beat again. Well, sort of.

I heard Allie's, "Onetwothreefourfivesixseveneight," on one side of me and Buffy's "*One*, two, three, four, *five*, six, seven, eight," on the other side. And suddenly, I got the giggles.

Madame ZeeZee fixed me with a stare. "What's so funny?"

As fast as the giggles had risen in my throat, they subsided. "Just trying not to cry," I said. Which was the truth. I'd spent most of Sunday in tears. I'd found no other way to relieve the stress of the second-hand sorrow that had been dumped on me, and I was as sick of tears as I was of the pain that instigated them.

"There's no crying in dance class," Buffy said, misquoting a famous line from a movie, which elicited a chuckle from me but no one else.

"Let's start again." Madame ZeeZee turned to face the mirrored wall, then made eye contact with my reflection. "And this time, Pat, keep in step with Buffy and Allie."

I couldn't help it. I giggled again.

Madame ZeeZee gave me a pained look. "You girls have no discipline."

When it became apparent that we could not get through a whole dance without devolving into chaos, Madame ZeeZee had us concentrate on one small fast-paced sequence. Walk, walk, step ball change, step forward, touch, step back, touch, pivot, step ball change, pivot, pose. And so the hour passed.

"How is the book coming," Kim asked when Madame ZeeZee finally turned off the music.

"About as well as you'd expect," I said.

"Are you any closer to figuring out who did it?"

I couldn't tell if Kim referred to the real-life deaths in the studio or my as-yet-unwritten fictional ones. Either way, my answer was the same: a rueful shake of my head. When I realized she couldn't see my response. I said aloud, "I am ruefully shaking my head no."

"I wish you'd tell us who you were going to kill off next," Buffy said, sounding serious. "I need to know if I should get my affairs in order." Then she laughed.

Kim smiled. "Would be handy to know." Kim turned to Madame ZeeZee and asked about her mother. The teacher mentioned her difficulty getting the frail nonagenarian to agree on hospice.

"Would you like me to talk to her?" Kim asked. "I could explain that hospice isn't about keeping you drugged on morphine. It's about keeping you as comfortable and as active as possible during the time you have left."

Madame ZeeZee's eyes lit up with hope, and then the light dimmed. "She won't talk to you. She won't talk to anyone. Stubborn old woman."

"It's a good thing my husband is still healthy," Allie said. "He's already told me that when the time comes, he won't sign up for hospice." She paused a moment, as if hearing the words echo in her mind, then she added, "He's much older than I am. In his seventies."

I scrutinized her, but could see no indication—other than, perhaps, the hesitation— that her words hid a falsehood. Does everyone lie with such ease? If so, discovering which of my classmates murdered Deb would be even more impossible than it already seemed.

But then, what did I know? Allie might have told the truth about her husband being much older than she, and the deceit lay elsewhere, such as in her claim that she'd seen Madame ZeeZee dance in New York.

Did any of this matter? When I found out the truth—if I found out the truth—I would probably do nothing to facilitate an arrest. Having been raised by authoritarian parents, I have no love for authority figures. I could not see myself going to the cops and trying to arrange the classic mystery finale, could not see myself turning in the perp if the cops failed in their job.

Nor did I want to undertake the responsibility of seeing the doer punished. If I were wrong about Buffy's involvement, for example, or Kim's, there is no way I would ever say anything that would result in their incarceration. The uncountable din would drive Buffy mad, and Kim had already suffered enough to pay for a dozen crimes.

Even if the murderer turned out to be someone I didn't like, I wouldn't go to the cops. The months—years—of pretrial depositions and the trial itself would all but destroy my renewed interest in life.

But I couldn't allow someone to keep killing off Madame ZeeZee's students, either. And I needed to know the truth for my own peace of mind.

Kim waited for her bus at the front of the studio. Allie and Madame ZeeZee waited with her. Buffy changed her shoes at the back of the studio in the little waiting room. I stayed in the center of the floor, idly stretching while I mused.

Kim's bus came, and she called out her goodbyes. When Madame ZeeZee and Allie walked Kim outside, I went to change into my tap shoes.

Buffy said, "Well, did you get it all figured out?"

I gave her a questioning look.

"I could hear your mental gears creaking all the way over here."

I laughed. "Sorry. The gears spun, but that's about it. You know as much about all this as I do. Who do *you* think tampered with the EpiPen?"

"The woman who killed Deb."

"Well, duh." It felt good to share a laugh, but I kept after her. "I mean, really, who do you think did it?

"I do what I'm told. I don't get paid to think."

"In other words," I said, "you're as clueless as I am."

"More so." Buffy tilted her head as she regarded me. "I think you know what happened to Grace."

I'd told enough people the story that one more wouldn't hurt. I leaned toward her and spoke softly. "She fell. Deb found her. Instead of calling an ambulance, Deb rearranged her body, and left her there for us to find."

Buffy didn't seem surprised by my revelation. She merely nodded and said, "To prove that the villain creates the hero?"

"Something like that."

"But what was Grace doing here?"

"She came to see Lena."

"So that's who spent the night in the studio. I wondered."

I sighed. "I take dance classes to get away from death, but that wicked old grim reaper seems to be following me everywhere."

Buffy gave me the stern look that must have once quelled rambunctious students. "You don't really think you had anything to do with Grace or Deb dying, do you?"

"No. But . . ."

"What are you girls talking about?" Madame ZeeZee asked.

I gave a start. I hadn't heard the teacher and Allie approach. I hoped they hadn't heard anything but the last couple of exchanges.

"I was trying to think of an answer to Buffy's question. She asked whether I thought I had anything to do with Grace's and Deb's deaths."

"Of course you didn't," Madame ZeeZee said at the same time Allie burst forth with, "Of course you did."

Buffy, Madame ZeeZee, and I jerked around to look at Allie.

She lifted her chin. "Pat killed Grace, and then someone killed Deb, wanting to make it look like Pat did it. That's what everyone is saying."

"Everyone who? I don't think Pat killed those two girls." Madame ZeeZee turned to Buffy. "Do you?"

Buffy looked uncomfortable at being forced to take sides, but she shook her head no.

Madame ZeeZee gave Allie a basilisk stare that would have had me quaking, but Allie didn't even blink.

"You tell everyone that Pat didn't have anything to do with Grace and Deb. She's helping me find out who did it."

Buffy and I exchanged open-mouthed glances.

I sure as hell hoped Allie didn't spread Madame ZeeZee's little tidbit around. I had no interest in being the bucket on someone's kick-the-bucket list. Trying for damage control, I said forcefully, "I'm just a writer. I have no authority to investigate. And I've told the cops less than you people have. You think I blab? Well, I wasn't the one who told the cops that I confessed to killing Grace. I owe someone payback for that, but I am not an avenger. I just want the killing to stop." I poked a finger at Allie. "You tell everyone that."

Allie backed away from me, but I could see she wasn't backing down. She truly seemed to believe I'd killed Grace and that someone killed Deb to make it look like I'd done it. My need-to-know nudged aside the last of my ire, and I realized whoever had come up with that particular motive—or rationale—for Deb's murder was the person I needed to talk to.

"Let's work on our dance," Madame ZeeZee said.

Allie sat down, pulled off her jazz shoes. She put on one tap shoe and dangled the other from her fingers as if she'd suddenly lost all strength or will. And maybe she had. For the first time, I could see signs of age in the dark crescents beneath her eyes and in the pallor of her cheeks. Despite her insistence on blaming me for the dancers's deaths, I felt sorry for her. It must be hard pretending to be so much younger than you are, feigning vigor you might not feel. And the cultural references—how did she ever keep them straight? She'd never be able to reference things she did, but had to refer instead to things she'd never experienced. No wonder she seldom spoke. It would be a much safer alternative than risk becoming muddled.

I used to wonder what it would be like to be beautiful, but if beauty was something a person needed to hold on to at all costs, the price of beauty was too much to pay.

Buffy stood in the center of the dance floor waiting for us. I went to join her, my taps click-clicking as I walked.

Madame ZeeZee headed for her office alcove. Allie slipped off the tap shoe she was wearing and carried both shoes to the front of the studio. She grabbed her purse, dance bag, and street shoes, and disappeared out the door.

Madame ZeeZee put on the music for "Flying Home," and came onto the floor to dance with us. She looked around. "Where's Allie?"

Buffy shrugged. "She left."

I held out my arms, palms up, in entreaty. "I'm sorry. I shouldn't have spoken to her the way I did."

"It's not your fault," Madame ZeeZee said.

Buffy laughed and said to me, "Well, she did call you a murderer."

Madame ZeeZee laughed, too. "Couldn't live like that."

But I didn't manage even a ghost of a smile. Singlehandedly, I seemed to be destroying Madame ZeeZee's studio.

Buffy did a few quick tap steps. "Let's just forget everything and dance."

And so we did—in step and on the beat.

I felt upbeat all the way home. Listening to my stream of consciousness, I even heard myself using the term to describe my mood, and I wondered if the "beat" part of "upbeat" had anything to do with a musical beat. As soon as I walked in the door of my father's house, I opened my computer to check the origin of the word. Apparently, an upbeat is where the conductor raises his/her baton, but is inherently no more positive than a downbeat. Not that I knew exactly what that meant, being musically challenged as I am, but it was still good to know.

I'd been spending most of my non-class, non-walking time on the computer. I pretended to be working on my book, but when I wasn't checking my Facebook feed for interesting posts, I played solitaire and waited for an email from Wanda.

And that night was no exception.

I added a few sentences to my work in progress: *Though most of us humans frown on murder, we do grudgingly admit some folks are so villainous they need to be eliminated, but no one would consider Grace a villain. She is charming, kind, with a smile for everyone, and the ghost of her youthful beauty is still apparent on her lovely face.*

Besides, killing a friend is a good way to lose that friend, and dance class would not be the same without Grace.

I considered revising that last phrase. Dance class hadn't been the same without Grace, but our group had healed itself. Unfortunately, Deb's murder had torn us apart again.

Tired of dithering, I let the phrasing stand, saved my changes, closed the document, and spent the rest of the evening playing solitaire. Finally, when I couldn't stand to look at those virtual cards one more second, I received a brief message from Wanda:

On one of the yearbook sites, I saw a brief reference to Jackie McDerr. This is your Jackie, right? If so, she went to Woodbury University in Los Angeles, but was kicked out for starting a race riot. Could be something.

I leaned back and had to grab the edge of the counter to keep from falling off the stool. *Jackie? Race riots?* Oh, my. Wanda was right, this could be something. But enough to kill over? It was too late to call Jackie, but we had ballet the next day. I could ask her in person if I could only figure out how to finesse the question.

Chapter 20

I left for the studio a little earlier than normal on Tuesday, hoping to talk to Jackie before class, and found her waiting by the door. Alone.

"Hi, Pat," Jackie said.

"You started a race riot?" So much for finesse. Not even a "hi" or "how are you" to smooth the way. Just the naked question.

Jackie took a step back. "You're good. How did you find that out?"

"My researcher saw a comment on an online yearbook site."

"Your researcher?" Jackie grinned broadly. "Wow, you're really taking this whole investigation thing seriously."

"And you're not."

Jackie laughed. "It was nothing, believe me."

"How can it be nothing if you got kicked out of college?"

"That's not what happened."

"So, what did happen?"

"I went to a private college in Los Angeles. Woodbury University. They only had two fields of study, art and business. I majored in art."

"Art as in doing art or art as in appreciating art?"

"Doing. I wasn't great at it, but I did okay."

"I don't know why, but I never would have guessed you were an artist." I smiled to take any sting out of my words.

"I'm more of a collector now. Masks. Mostly wood carvings. Every time my husband and I go on a trip, I look for a special mask. I have one from every continent and most countries."

I studied her, trying to see the artist beneath the cheerful I-am-what-you-see exterior. "How come I don't know this?"

Another laugh. "I don't like boring people."

"What's with all this 'boring' stuff? You don't want to bore people. Buffy says she's the most boring person in the world."

"I am."

I whipped my head around at the sound of Buffy's voice. "How long have you been standing there?"

Buffy readjusted the shoulder strap of her quilted dance bag. "Just got here."

"You really aren't observant, are you?" Jackie said with a laugh.

My cantankerous, "I told you I wasn't," elicited amusement from both Jackie and Buffy.

I tried to catch Jackie's eye to let her know I wouldn't give away her secret about the riots, but she'd looked away from me and spoke to Buffy.

"I was telling Pat about causing a race riot in college."

"So I guess it's not a secret?" I said, still feeling tetchy.

"I told you it wasn't," Jackie responded, echoing my words. "This is what happened. When I went to Woodbury, the dorm was in an old apartment building about five miles from campus. It was an all white dorm, mostly because the student body was predominantly Caucasian. An African girl enrolled at Woodbury—"

"African or African American?" Buffy asked.

"African. I forget what country. I remember her name. Zalika. Zalika wasn't allowed to stay in the dorm but boarded with a black family. I didn't think that was right. So I talked to everyone in the dorm about how unfair, bigoted, and wrong it was to discriminate against her. I guess I got people pretty riled up because I was called into the administration office. I told them the truth about what I said. Apparently Dorm Daddy—"

"Dorm Daddy?" Buffy queried.

"That's what we called the old guy who ran the dorms. Dorm Daddy. He wanted me out. Not just for that but because a bunch of us and our boyfriends had once dumped a bucket of water on his head for being so . . ."

"Dorm-Daddy-ish?" Buffy said, trying to help Jackie think of an appropriate word.

Jackie laughed. "Yes. They didn't kick me out of college, but they did kick me out of the dorm. When I got the eviction papers, in the blank space for 'reason for eviction,' they'd written, 'inciting race riots.' I find it amusing that my sticking up for Zalika turned into 'inciting race riots.'"

The three of us chuckled at the sad truth, then Jackie continued her story.

"To be fair, that was during the time of the Watts riots, and everyone was overly sensitive. But what's really funny is that the school wasn't discriminating against Zalika. Zalika's family was discriminating against us. They didn't want her living in the dorm. Apparently, she was some sort of princess, and the royal family didn't want her associating with us plebians."

We were still snickering over the irony when Madame ZeeZee pulled up. "What's so funny?"

"Life," Jackie said.

"I wish life were funny," Madame ZeeZee said. "I've about had it with my mom. She fell again. She won't go to assisted living. She won't agree to hospice. Medicare won't pay for more hours for her caregivers. And she insists she wants round-the-clock care. I don't know who she thinks is going to pay for the extra hours. I can't afford it."

Jackie laughed. "Sounds pretty funny to me. My mother is the same way. Stubborn."

A sad-faced older woman wearing tights, trunks and top with butterfly sleeves trudged across the parking lot toward us. When she saw me glancing her way, she flashed a brilliant smile, and I realized the woman was Rhett. Her animation usually made her seem like a much younger woman, but for that second, I had seen the years hanging heavily on her not-fat body. I wondered what had made her look so sad.

Buffy must have wondered the same thing, because she asked, "Are you okay, Rhett?"

Rhett beamed at her. "Super good, but I'll get better."

In class, she stayed as far away from me as possible as if she feared me. Did she have something to hide? Or did she in fact think I was killing everyone as Madame ZeeZee claimed?

We finished our barre work, which had elicited only one halfhearted "point your toes, Pat," from Madame ZeeZee. We stretched, then moved to the center of the floor to practice *port de bras.* After that Madame ZeeZee gave us various combinations to do. One step involved hopping on the ball of the left foot while kicking the right leg out. I could barely do the step flatfooted.

"You're supposed to be on *relevé*, Pat," Madame ZeeZee reminded me

I tried again but could not rise on one foot. "I'm sorry. I can't."

"I hate people who say 'can't'" Rhett muttered.

I turned to her and adopted Detective Morales' Wonder Woman pose—hands on hips, legs in a wide stance. "What did you say?"

"Whenever my special ed kids said 'can't' I'd tell them to go to the grocery story and look for can'ts. I told them they would find lots of cans but no can'ts."

Kim had arrived sometime during class and was sitting watching us out of the corners of her eyes. She turned her head from me to Rhett. "Pat didn't say she wouldn't try or that she'd never be able to do it. But she's right. She can't do it now."

"If there are no can'ts in a grocery store," Buffy said, "then you can't find can'ts there, can you?"

Margot stretched her leg above her head. With her slim body encased in black leotard and pink tights, and hair pulled off her face into a ponytail, she looked like the quintessential ballerina.

I pointed to Margot. "That's something else I can't do."

Kim laughed. "Who can?"

Rhett plastered a smile on her face. "Frankly, my dear . . ."

Madame ZeeZee let out a theatrical sigh. "Sixteen sautés. That's something you can all do. And then you can go get changed."

After the jumps, we scattered. Rhett, Buffy, and I changed into our silk belly dance practice skirts. Kim moved gracefully to the center of the floor, looking like a queen with her hair tucked under a cloche that matched her skirt and top. Margot and Jackie left.

"Has anyone heard from Lena or Rose or Allie?" Madame ZeeZee asked.

We all shook our heads.

"They're probably afraid Pat's going to kill them, too." Rhett laughed when she spoke, but I could detect no humor in her manner. If anything, she seemed angry at me.

Despite her relentless insistence on showing a positive face to the world, whatever strain Rhett lived under continued to bleed through to the surface. Could she have killed Deb and the strain of hiding her involvement overwhelmed her? But no, I remembered seeing signs of stress before the dying began.

Rhett's husband had multiple health problems, including diabetes, which he refused to acknowledge, putting the burden on Rhett to ensure he ate right and got his insulin. That would make anyone tense, especially if financial problems and a greedy ex-husband were added to the mix. Despite my own precarious situation, I felt sorry for Rhett, though I'm sure she wouldn't welcome my pity.

Arabic class didn't seem quite as dysfunctional as the previous day's jazz class, but it wasn't easy, either. We were working on an East Indian dance for a performance later in the year, and the strange beat tested even Buffy's sense of rhythm. Rhett danced to her own peculiar drum. And I kept stopping to think.

I'd always tried to use dance class as a vacation from myself, parking my troubles at the door so I could dance worry-free, but I couldn't stop obsessing long enough to find the freedom dancing usually gave me.

I fretted about everyone's stress levels, though I could not fault anyone for their anxieties. Murder would put pressure on any group, and if group members were plagued by other troubles, such as sick spouses, vicious ex-husbands, aging parents, it's a wonder any of my classmates were functioning halfway normally.

As I thought about the pressures of my dance mates's lives and of the ghastly tricks stress could play on a fragile mind, I realized there was one woman who was living a life of soul-breaking strain, and I felt sure that woman's burden threatened to destroy her, and maybe those in her vicinity.

After class, no one wanted to go to lunch, so I went to the Mexican restaurant alone. I sat at a small table and called the woman.

"Meet me at the taquito place in fifteen minutes." She offered frantic excuses, but I talked over her. "I know what you did. See you in fifteen minutes."

Chapter 21

She came hobbling in twenty minutes later, wearing faded jeans and a western-style chambray shirt with most of the buttons left undone. Her blonde wig tilted toward her right eye, giving her a waifish look.

"What the hell is the matter with you?" she demanded. A catch in her voice belied the autocratic tone

"Just returning the favor," I said. "Did you want anything? A drink? Food?"

She plopped into the plastic chair on the opposite side of the laminated table. "I want you to tell me what you think I did."

"I don't think you did anything."

She scrambled to her feet. "What kind of game are you playing?"

"A nicer one than you played on me, Lena. Sit down and I'll tell you. Or rather, you'll tell me."

Lena sat down gingerly, keeping her bleary eyes on me the whole time. The musky odor of fear emanated from her body.

"You really don't know what you did the morning Grace died, do you?" I spoke softly, trying to calm her.

She sat tall and glared at me, then she slumped, melting into a puddle of skin and bones, but her mouth remained pinched into a thin line.

"No," she managed to say through her clamped lips.

"You didn't kill Grace."

"I didn't?"

I could see hope warring with her distrust of me.

"You didn't kill her. No one did. Grace left with you. Do you remember that?"

She shook her head no.

"As you told me, you forgot to lock the door, but that's all you did. Nothing else was your fault."

Eyes swimming with tears, she looked at me. "Nothing?"

"Grace forgot her purse. She went back inside. Deb followed her. Apparently, she startled Grace. Grace spun around and slipped on a slick spot. She whacked her head on the barre as she fell."

"So it really was an accident like the official report said?"

"Technically."

"But Deb was there, right? Didn't she call an ambulance?"

"Do you remember talking to me and trying to blame me for the whole thing because of my disdain and arrogance?"

She bowed her head and nodded.

"Well, that's basically the truth. Deb arranged Grace's body to look like the photo I took, then she went outside to wait for us to get there. Madame ZeeZee was late, and Deb never said anything."

"So that's how Grace died? You're sure?"

"If you can believe Deb." I continued in the same soft tone. "How long have you had this dissociative disorder?'

"Once when I was young, but not since then until now."

"It's the stress, isn't it?

She massaged her wrists, and nodded.

I held out my arms, wrists up. "Do you want to tell me about that?"

I thought she'd refuse, but she looked at my unscarred wrists and then at the thin white lines on her own wrists, and sighed.

"I don't remember. I'd just gotten pregnant, and . . . I don't know. My husband said he found me in the bathroom with my blood draining into the tub. He had me committed. I had the baby in the institution. Pathetic, huh?"

I gave her a sad little smile. "You were sick."

She sat a little straighter. "I was fine after she was born. She was a wonder. The best thing that ever happened to me and my husband. I never regretted . . ."

"Never regretted having an affair?"

She stared at me. "I told Grace about my suicide attempt when her son tried to kill himself, but I didn't tell her about the affair. I never told anyone. How do you know?"

I shook my head noncommittally, not wanting her to know it had been a guess. I know pregnancy causes its own pressures and hormonal imbalances, but to try to kill yourself over a natural marital state spoke of more than normal stress.

"I was so afraid," Lena whispered. "My husband was sterile. I didn't know what he'd do when he found out. He accepted our daughter as a miracle. Or seemed to. But now . . ."

"Now he's accusing you of being unfaithful."

"Somehow he knows she isn't his. The Alzheimer's makes him confused, but he's sure I had an affair. And it makes him angry." She put her face in her hands and repeated, "So very angry."

"Could he have known all along?" I asked.

She lifted her head. "Maybe. The doctors at the institution might have told him she has a different blood type than he does. Or something. He was a good husband. A great father. He loved us. And now he doesn't love me." Tears spilled down her cheeks. "He doesn't."

"I'm sure he loves you still," I said. My belief in the words must have reached her, because she looked at me beseechingly.

"You think so?"

"I know so. He never said anything all these years. I bet he forgave you a long time ago and took joy in your miracle baby. He's not . . . him . . . anymore. He talks to you through the disease, not his heart."

She nodded slowly, and spoke as if to herself. "He's never angry at our daughter." She gave a little laugh. "Well, except when she doesn't come to see him when he wants her to."

"See? You gave him a daughter. Made him a father."

"I never told her the truth. Never told her birth father, either. I don't want to."

I blew out a breath. "That I can't help you with. All I can say is take everything one step at a time. What I don't understand is why you were so afraid of Deb. If you didn't know what happened to Grace, why would you think Deb had killed her? And why would you think she'd kill you next, or me?"

"I'm not really sure. Lately, I don't remember things clearly, and I have some blank spots. I think I was afraid she'd found out about the affair and would tell my husband."

"But if he already knew?"

She smiled wryly. "It's one thing to know and another to know beyond a doubt. I didn't want him to have to deal with the reality."

"Is there a possibility that you killed Deb to stop her from talking and don't remember?"

She rubbed her wrists. "No," she said.

But I heard the doubt in her voice, and I'm sure she did too.

Chapter 22

There were many things in Lena's tale that didn't make sense. It's possible she was still playing games with me, but it seemed as if she'd told me what she remembered. And her distress over her husband certainly seemed real. Besides, I'd seen evidence of dissociation in her behavior, which had helped me piece the story together.

I didn't fool myself into thinking I had helped Lena—to be honest, curiosity motivated me. I needed to know the truth.

It was as simple—and as compelling—as that.

The first time I noticed curiosity being a powerful motivator came in the months after Jay died. At first, I found absolutely no reason to survive the pain, but one thing kept me going—curiosity about what would happen to me. Never would I have imagined taking dance classes. Never would I have imagined talking to potential murderers.

Had Lena killed Deb? I didn't know. Couldn't know.

But I felt satisfaction—and a whole lot of sorrow—at having solved the mystery of Lena's erratic behavior.

Such thoughts accompanied me on my walk back to my father's neighborhood. As I neared his house, I saw something shiny on the road just past the driveway, and I hurried to see if it could be a coin.

Jay and I had never been too proud to pick up coins, and I still continued the practice, though now every time I saw a coin, I imagine it a sign that Jay thought of me. If I found a penny, it felt like a smile. A dime meant he approved. When I made the decision to take dance classes, I found two dimes a few inches apart. When I actually started classes, I found another two dimes spaced exactly the same as the first two. Such approval!

But apparently, Jay didn't approve of my playing detective. I found no dime but a spot of new oil.

The next door neighbor stood nearby, watering the rose bushes encircling a stone fountain. She wore skinny jeans and a crop-top. At a few years older than me, she seemed too old for such a getup, but then, I shouldn't judge—my dance ensemble also seemed more fitting to the younger generation.

She set the watering can on the waist-high wall connecting the two properties, then hurried up to me, her silver hair as dull as a nickel in the sun. An avid look had replaced the anger she usually offered me, anger because I had forgotten to invite her to my father's funeral. Huh? I didn't know invitations were part of the process. My siblings and I had so much to do in the days after the old man died—following his instructions for the funeral, gathering his important papers, doing all the end of life chores that never seem to end—I'd presumed that putting obituaries in papers in every town he'd ever lived would have served as an invitation. Besides, whatever she'd done for my father to merit special consideration had taken place before my arrival. In the years I'd lived with him, she'd visited him only twice.

But no matter how much I'd apologized, she'd never forgiven me for the unintended slight.

"The cops were here." She held herself importantly, but there was no mistaking the malicious glee that tinged her words.

"How wonderful for you." I edged away from her toward the house.

"They asked all sorts of questions. They wanted to know if your dad was diabetic. If he ever needed an EpiPen."

"That's nice," I said, trying to keep my voice even. I didn't want her to know how much her words had shaken me. The cops really did consider me a suspect!

And suddenly I started to giggle. I thought of the cops chasing after me, me chasing after the murderer, the murderer chasing after her next victim, the victim chasing a hero—a long disappearing line of people chasing people.

"I told them it was possible you killed your father."

My giggles stopped abruptly. "You what?"

"Well, he was fine the last time I saw him. And then he died."

"You saw him three years ago. He went through many hospitalizations since then. He was almost ninety-eight, for cripes sake. Why did you say I killed him?"

She puffed out her bony chest. "Because I think you did kill him. You told me once he hadn't been a good father."

"So what? He was still my father, good or bad."

"I told the cops you were tired of looking after him."

I simply stared at her, amazed at how she had mangled the truth. I'd often been exhausted, as anyone who has ever been the primary care giver of an elderly person would understand, and I might have mentioned being tired to her once, but nothing about being tired of looking after him.

Finally I managed to get out a single word. "So?"

"So I think you could have killed him."

"What did the cops say?"

"They thanked me."

I tilted my head to study her. "You're never going to forgive me for not inviting you to the funeral, are you?"

"No. You might not have loved him, but I did." She turned, picked up her watering can, and tottered on high-heeled slippers toward her garage.

The truth is, I had a rocky relationship with my father. I loved him, but I'd been angry at him for many years. When I was a kid, I knew both he and my mother were doing the best they could, but in my forties, I woke up and thought, whoa! I was the kid. They were the parents. They should have been the ones making allowances for me.

It's that anger, along with having nowhere else to go, that brought me to Peach Valley. I knew there would come a time, after both my parents were gone, after my grief over Jay's death had dissipated, when I would have to go on alone, and I did not want to carry old anger into my new life.

And it worked. When my father died, I didn't feel as if I'd surrendered my unsettling daughterhood, but as if I'd helped him let go of his fatherhood. No regrets, no anger, nothing for either one of us to be sorry for. He died unencumbered—simply a man going to meet his maker. I gave him that, and he gave me peace.

If the cops didn't understand the dynamics of my relationship with my father, they sure as hell would understand the doctor's records, which would show the truth of my care. And then there was the whole hospice thing. Investigators did not request autopsies or exhumations on hospice patients, and even if they did and found morphine in my father's system, there would be a whole lot less than what had been prescribed.

I considered texting my siblings and telling them about the neighbor causing trouble, but I doubted they'd care. They seemed to think that our parent's deaths dissolved the family, and an occasional bland text sufficed to keep us connected.

But if I ran into serious trouble, I'm sure one or both of them would help, as I would help them. Or so I told myself.

I couldn't help wondering, though, what was wrong with me that people were so willing to believe I could murder. But people think what they want to think. I knew the truth, and I could only hope the truth would keep me free.

Would this experience make me a better writer? If nothing else, it would give me a plethora of emotions to draw upon.

After the encounter with the neighbor, I paced the living room until I calmed myself, then turned on the computer and checked my email. A message from Wanda!

I researched Grace Worthington. 75 years old. Nothing in her background is out of the ordinary. Wife, mother, grandmother. And the memorials left on Facebook and the other networking sites all show her as a kind woman, well-loved, and much missed.

Lena Thomas, 68, had once been institutionalized, but I couldn't find out much except that she had a baby while there. Do you want me to pursue this?

Rhett Norris, 71, is divorced. Remarried. Seven kids. I found some public court documents that show an ongoing suit. Apparently her husband accused her of stealing his money. Relevant maybe?

Kim Saunderling, 59, is widowed and divorced. One child, deceased. Nurse. Missionary. Went to Africa as part of a medical team. Could this be something?

I couldn't find anything about Rose Rowland, Alice Shaffer, and Margot Janicks.

The only thing I found out so far about Deb Gillespie is that she was born in Peach Valley. It's strange because Peach Valley seems to be a place people go to not come from.

Another interesting thing: Has Buffy ever told you about her parents? You said Buffy had nothing to hide, but it's possible she is keeping a secret. It turns out that her mother is also her sister.

Chapter 23

"If I found out your secret, would you want to know that I know?"

I'd cornered Buffy during the commotion between the two Hawaiian classes and asked my question softly so as not to be overheard.

Perhaps I spoke too softly, because Buffy didn't even look at me, didn't seem to hear.

"Buffy? Well?"

She started. "You're talking to me? I don't have any secrets. I told you that."

"Yeah, I know." I gave her a wry smile. "Boring. I get it."

"Wait a minute." She searched my face. "You found something?"

"About your mother."

She shook her head, her brow wrinkled in confusion. "What about my mother?"

"Well, that she's your sister."

I'd never known Buffy to get angry, but right then, I could feel her ire striking me as if it were a weapon.

"You're taking this whole detective thing too far. Making a joke out of all of us. Of me. I laughed about being a cracker, but for you to turn me into the spawn of an incestuous relationship is unconscionable."

She'd raised her voice, which made Allie turn her head in our direction, but apparently the din kept her from understanding the words because, without a pause, she continued to talk about the weekend trip she and her husband planned to take.

"Not incest," I said, perplexed by her response. "You didn't know you were adopted?"

She put her hands on her hips. "I'm not adopted."

I held up my palms in surrender. "All right. I'm sorry. I shouldn't have said anything. You're not adopted."

Her tanned face seemed to go pale. "I am?" she whispered.

I nodded.

"Who am I?"

"You're still the same person, but your mother is your sister. You were a late-life baby. Your sister got married about a year after you were born. She and her husband adopted you after your parents died in an accident. You were in the car, but your toddler seat protected you, and you survived."

An uncertain smile flickered on her lips. "Are you making this up?"

"No. I have digital copies of the corroborating paperwork I can send you. An announcement of your birth. Your sister's wedding announcement. The article about the accident. The obituary naming you and your sister as the surviving children."

"Why didn't my mother, I mean my sister, tell me?"

"She's still your mother. She adopted you. I bet she often forgot that you weren't her birth daughter. After all, you did have the tie of blood. When she did remember, she probably couldn't find the words or the right time. And then it was too late."

"I don't know what to think."

"Think that I'm a hagged old witch for springing this on you," I said.

She let out a single laugh, or maybe it was a sob.

"Who's a hagged old witch?" Madame ZeeZee asked, coming across the floor toward us.

"Me," I said. "I seem to be doing more harm than good with my detecting."

By then, everyone but the few advanced students who'd come for class had left, and my words seemed to echo throughout the studio.

"Then give it up," Rhett called out from where she was doing *piqué* turns by the bar.

"No. Don't give it up," Madame ZeeZee said.

"What did you find out?" Rose asked eagerly. Maybe too eagerly? Did she fear I'd discovered something about her?

I put on a self-deprecating smile. "I've learned that everyone has a secret. That everyone here is from somewhere else. That we're all heroes, villains, and victims."

"Not me." Rhett beamed. "I'm an angel. See?" She did half a *piqué* turn so we could view the gold wings imprinted on the back of her fitted red tee shirt.

We lined up across the studio to do the warm-up routine for Hawaiian class. Rose, Rhett, Allie, Buffy, and me. When Madame ZeeZee disappeared into her alcove to start the music, Buffy leaned toward me.

"You'll send me the papers?" she whispered.

"I'll email them. If I'd known you didn't have them, I would have printed them out for you."

The music started. Arms raised, we waited for the introduction to finish and the melody to begin. By then, Madame ZeeZee had moved in front of our line and led us in the comforting sequence of steps.

No one counted aloud. Allie took tiny, almost fearful steps. Rhett danced boisterously. Rose hummed, not quite with the music. Madame ZeeZee and Buffy seemed lost in their thoughts. And me— I tried to ignore everything except the pure joy of movement, but did not succeed.

***

When you set out on a quest, any kind of quest, whether it is a search for adventure, identity, meaning, truth, you can't control what you will find. And once you've found something, you can't unfind it or change the ensuing ripples. If you don't like where the quest is leading you, you can either continue the quest despite your dislike, or you can give up. At least that's what I told myself, but I knew I couldn't quit. I had to see the investigation through to the end. I'd already set so much in motion that quitting was not an option. Perhaps that's the way it always is with a quest.

I don't think Buffy had anything to do with Deb's murder. Her stunned response to my news about her adoption did not seem simulated, and if she didn't know about that particular secret, she'd have no secret to protect.

And anyway, it wasn't much of a secret once you knew the truth—certainly not something worth killing over. I felt glad I could still rule Buffy out as a killer, but sad that I might have ruined whatever friendship we'd found.

But there still lingered the problem of who had killed Deb.

Considering how angry Rhett seemed to be with me, I figured

talking with her would be the logical next step. After tap class on Thursday, when Rhett asked if anyone wanted to go to lunch, I said yes, but no one else did. Buffy had been especially silent in class, and she'd slipped out even before Rhett asked the question. Allie wanted to hurry home to prepare for the weekend getaway with her husband. And Madame ZeeZee needed to check on her mother.

I wouldn't have been surprised if Rhett had reneged on her invitation to lunch when she realized only I would join her, but she didn't raise an objection.

We chatted about minor matters while we hiked across the parking lot—the difficulty of doing *eschappes* in ballet, how her new tap shoes made her tap dancing better, the sequence of steps in the dance we were learning, the heat. Always the heat!

I wasn't especially hungry, and the redolence of spices didn't entice me, so I ordered chips and guacamole. Rhett ordered a full meal—she skipped dinner in an effort to lose weight, so she ate her main meal in the middle of the day.

By the time we got our orders, we'd exhausted our repertory of small talk.

I took a deep breath. Despite the noise of the restaurant—the clinking of pots in the kitchen, the ring of the register, the voice of a woman ordering—my inhalation sounded loud enough to catch Rhett's attention. She leaned back as if to distance her from the question I am sure she expected.

"Why are you so angry at me," I asked.

She laughed. "I'm not angry. I never get angry. It's a waste of my time."

"Well, you certainly don't act very happy with me lately."

"Why do you say that?" She grinned broadly. "I'm super good."

I pushed the guacamole around my plate with a chip. "Something is going on with you. Does it have to do with the money your husband wants?"

Rhett looked at me, then her gaze slid off to the left. "Do you remember Gerda the woman who used to take ballet? About my size but with small boobs? Hennaed hair in braids around the top of her head like a crown?"

I scrunched up my face, trying to recall the woman. "Vaguely."

"She stopped coming to ballet when Madame ZeeZee allowed

Jackie and Margot to take beginning classes with us."

I sat straighter. "Oh, right. It was shortly after I started with ballet. I felt thrilled to be dancing with such accomplished women, and I couldn't understand why Gerda got so peeved. She told me she didn't want to dance with the professionals."

Rhett laughed. "Yep. That's her. When Madame ZeeZee asked us why Gerda didn't come to class anymore, you repeated what Gerda had told you. Madame ZeeZee got annoyed and said, 'There are no professionals here.' Remember?"

I nodded. "Gerda discontinued all dance classes after that. I still don't know why my giving Madame ZeeZee the reason she didn't want to take ballet anymore had offended Gerda so much. She knows that Madame ZeeZee always keeps track of us, and if someone stops coming without explanation, she worries."

Rhett scooped up a forkful of beans and rice. "Gerda was really angry with you. She told me and Rose never to tell you anything, that you blabbed."

All at once I understood where my reputation as a blabber had come from—that one silly, long-forgotten episode. But apparently, it hadn't seemed silly to Gerda. A pang of regret settled in my stomach.

I pushed my plate of guacamole and chips away from me. "Do you have Gerda's phone number? I'd like to call her and tell her I'm sorry. I didn't mean to upset her."

"I had lunch with her and Rose right after she quit and I haven't seen her since. Ask Rose. She might have Gerda's phone number."

"Well, do you have Rose's number?"

"No." Then Rhett laughed. "Gerda wasn't just mad at you for gossiping. It's that you seemed to belittle her, especially since we *are* dancing with a professional."

I folded my arms on the table. "Professional? There aren't any professionals in class. Well, Madame ZeeZee, but no one else."

Rhett covered her mouth with a hand that didn't quite hide a gleeful smile. "Margot."

"Margot went professional?" I thought back to everything Margot had said about herself. Ballet lessons from a very young age. Protégé of her dance teacher. Taught a class of little ones. Planned to take over the studio when her teacher retired but couldn't manage the payments. Got married and had kids. Didn't dance for ten years or so until she found Madame ZeeZee.

"When was this? Where was this?"

Rhett leaned back and grinned. "Lithuania."

I knew Margot had a Lithuanian ancestry, but I got the impression she'd been born in the United States to an immigrant mother, not that she'd been an immigrant herself. Maybe my disbelief showed my insularity. Like the rest of us, Margot spoke General American without a hint of a foreign accent. In fact, she seemed a fifty-something version of the quintessential California girl—tall, beautiful, long blonde hair, trim and fit, perfect white teeth, outgoing, loved all things water. Only the lines on her face and a bit of creasing on her neck showed her age.

I shook my head and kept shaking it. "Let me get this straight. Gerda told you that Margot used to dance professionally in Lithuania? What's Margot doing here in the high desert? What's the big secret? And how does Gerda know?"

Rhett held up a finger and shot it at me. "Now that's a good question. Well . . ." She paused to take a few bites of food, a small smile playing on her lips.

"You're really enjoying this, aren't you?" I asked.

"I want to help." Her voice grew soft and serious, but I didn't know if I should trust this pronouncement or anything else she said. I don't remember ever catching her in a lie, except for the pretense about always feeling great, but since she plastered optimism on her face like a mask, I had no way of gauging anything that came out of her mouth.

"How did Gerda find out about Margot?" I asked.

"A friend of hers visiting from Europe recognized Margot. Margot was rather a sensation in Lithuania and the European dancing community about thirty years ago, but not for dancing. She murdered someone, then disappeared."

"Uh, no."

"Uh, yes," Rhett mimicked me. "Margot isn't her real name. Gerda says it's Margruta something. I don't remember the last name, but it sounded like Yasiks cabbage."

"Why didn't you say anything when I started looking for reasons people might have had to tamper with Deb's EpiPen?"

Rhett grinned. "Not my problem. Not my circus. Not my monkey."

"Didn't it bother you knowing you were dancing with a murderer?"

"Not my problem. Not my—"

"Not your circus. Not your monkey. I get it." I stared at her for a few seconds, long enough for her smile to dim. "Do you know what a red herring is?" I asked.

"Of course I do. A journalist in the early eighteen hundreds said when he was a child he used to drag a smoked herring across the trail to lead the hounds away from a hunt. He claimed that his fellow journalists were as easily led."

That gave me pause. I'd heard a different etymology of the term, but this one made as much sense as any other. And it fit my purpose. I smiled at Rhett. "Well, I smell a red herring."

She opened her eyes wide. "A red herring?"

"You dragged such a great scent across my trail that I almost lost track of the hunt. But I still want to know. Why are you angry with me?"

"It wasn't a false trail. Margot really is this Margruta."

I sniffed. "Do I smell another red herring?"

"Okay, you're right. I am angry at you. My ex-husband keeps coming after some money he says I stole. He hid hundreds of thousands from me in a Philippine bank, and all I took was the household money I'd saved up. It wasn't much, just a few thousand. I'd give it back if I had it, but it's gone. I needed it to live on after he kicked me out of the house."

"Did Deb find out about the law suit? Is that what this is about? You're worried that I think you killed her?"

"You don't get it."

I put my elbows on the table and my chin in my hands. "I'm listening."

She stood, flung her purse over her shoulder, and loomed over me. "All these people are dying, and my husband is still alive. You said you could kill him. And you haven't." Then she stalked from the restaurant.

I watched her go. Realizing the place had become too silent, I looked around. The other patrons, the cook behind the pass-through bar, and the woman at the counter were all staring at me. A couple of women at the next table had their phones in their hands as if they were ready to call the police.

I held up my palms, opened my mouth to explain, then closed it again when I realized I had no explanation.

I ignored the furtive looks they continued to throw at me and finished my guacamole. When I cleared away the debris from my meal as well as Rhett's, I came to one conclusion: I sure was overdoing the whole "dashing out of the restaurant in the middle of a meal" cliché.

Walking back to the house, I tried to figure out what to do next. Call Margot, of course, but what if she didn't want to talk to me? I couldn't pull the same stunt on her that I pulled on Lena—I had no reason to believe the truth of anything Rhett had told me, especially since it came fourth hand.

I planned a whole speech, but in the end, it didn't matter. When I called Margot, I got her voicemail. I left a message asking her to call me. Called Lena and left a message on her machine. Called Nancy, too, but did not leave a message because I'd already left two or three messages for her and I'd begun to feel like a stalker. Called Madame ZeeZee's cell and left a message. Called her house and talked to her husband who said she was with her mother and he'd have her call me when she returned home.

I Googled "Margruta Jasiks Lithuanian ballerina" and found a reference to a Margruta Jasikevičius in an eight-year-old blog about dancers from around the world who had disappeared under mysterious circumstances. According to the blogger, during a thirty-year period, at least twenty-five ballerinas from eight different European countries had gone missing, and the blogger wondered if the aliens were collecting dancers. The picture the blogger posted of Margruta Jasikevičius looked a lot like the Margot I knew, just younger. I Googled "Margruta Jasikevičius Lithuanian ballerina" and got a screen full of hits, but all led back to that single blog.

I emailed Wanda, thanked her for the information about Buffy. I told her about Margot, gave her the name Margruta Jasikevičius and asked her to see what she could find out. I ended my message with *Did I tell you that Madame ZeeZee thinks Allie Shaffer is in her seventies, not fifty as Allie claimed?*

Then, like a dancer backstage ready for the curtain to rise, I waited.

153

Chapter 24

Madame ZeeZee called. She told me about the visit with her mother—the poor old woman still insisted on twenty-four hour care, which was out of the question, but resisted the available help, such as hospice. Although some people advised the teacher to put her mother in a home, I knew she couldn't do it. End of life situations aren't just about the dying. The ones who would be left behind are strongly affected, and they have to make decisions they could live with for the rest of their lives.

After listening to Madame ZeeZee's woes, I hadn't the heart to remind her of the problems at her studio, so I didn't ask what she knew of Margot. Next time we were at lunch, I would broach the subject more gently. Assuming, of course, I could summon up any gentleness and subtlety. The more I delved into the lives of my classmates, the less gentle and subtle I felt.

I suppose it's only human nature (though a bit naïve) to feel betrayed at finding out people weren't as they presented themselves. To be honest, the stories I'd been hearing might only have raised a modicum of interest or curiosity, except for one thing.

Murder.

And more importantly (to me, anyway), murder that bled over into my classes, taking the fun out of dancing.

I wasn't so naïve as to believe things would go back the way they were, but they would go forward to a new way of being. And I desperately wanted to be in that forward place. No more death. No more dying. Just dancing.

When I had all but given up hope of hearing from anyone else that evening, Lena called. She seemed so buoyant, for a moment I didn't recognize her voice. After we said our hi-how-are-yous, I asked if she had Rose's phone number.

A long silence. Then she said hesitantly, "Is this about Deb?"

"Ye-es." Until then, I hadn't made the obvious mental connection between Margot's potential secret and Deb's murder, but if what Rhett had told me was true, Margot had the strongest motive of any of us. Could she have killed Deb to protect her secret?

". . . only an online affair, but she doesn't want her husband to know, and she was afraid Deb would tell him."

Whoa. An online affair? Who? Determined not to miss another important bit of information, I focused my attention on Lena's voice.

"You won't tell the cops, will you?" she asked.

"I promise." An easy promise to make since I didn't know who we were talking about.

"Thank you. I wouldn't have mentioned Rose's affair, but since you already knew . . ."

"I didn't . . ." I'd intended to say I hadn't known about Rose, but decided that prudence at this point would be a good idea. Instead, I tried to erase my false start by quickly introducing a different topic. "Something I don't understand. Everyone feared Deb telling on them. Did she really tattle?"

A sharp intake of breath on the end of the line. Then a slow letting go. "It never got that far."

I felt the gears in my brain whir. "Wait a minute. Are you talking about blackmail?"

"No!" Then, a very quiet "yes."

"I never heard about this."

"Well, you're new."

"I've been taking classes for two years."

"You only started taking the advanced classes with us a few months ago. We've been with Madame ZeeZee twelve years. Me, Grace, Deb, Rose. There were some others who quit after giving Deb what she demanded because they didn't want to deal with her anymore."

"Did Madame ZeeZee know?"

"No."

"Why didn't you tell her?"

"Well, Deb said . . ."

I sighed. "So Deb threatened you about that, too. What sort of things did she want?"

All buoyancy had disappeared from Lena's voice. "You know that pretty ring she wears?"

"Yes," I said, though to be honest, I'd paid as little attention to Deb as possible, and hadn't a clue what jewelry she wore.

"That's mine. A gift from my mother when I went to college."

"You gave it to her so that she wouldn't tell your husband about your daughter? And she wore it as what? A reminder?"

"Something like that. At the beginning, we were all friends, so we talked, you know how women do. After a few years, Deb extorted a token from each of us. That's what she called them, 'good faith tokens.' Then everything went smoothly. Until your book."

I'd been pacing while listening to her, but now I lowered myself to the floor and slumped against the wall of the living room. "That damn book."

"I don't know what Grace was thinking when she suggested you write about us. But then, how could any of us have guessed what you would set in motion. I suppose it was really the suggestion that we share our secrets with you that upset Deb so much. The book itself was a problem, of course, since she felt you were upstaging her, but the secrets thing put her over the edge. She considered herself the keeper of our secrets, and whatever power they gave her would be destroyed if everyone knew what she knew."

I laughed, a full-bodied laugh that went on for several seconds. When I got control of myself, I said, "I'm sorry. I didn't mean to make light of the situation, but it sounds so . . . Machiavellian. Or high school-ish."

"It's the way things were."

"Why didn't you all quit?"

"We like dancing. We like performing. There's no other place up here that offers any classes for seniors except for line dancing. Besides, we all like Madame ZeeZee."

"So you put up with Deb's abuse for twelve years?"

"It wasn't like that."

I let out a hoot of derisive laughter. "It never is."

"No," she protested. "It really wasn't. For the last six or seven years, she's been as sweet as can be until . . ."

'Yeah, I get it. Until my book."

"Can I help you with anything else?" She spoke briskly, as if trying to break the connection.

"As a matter of fact, you can. When we talked that first day, you were concerned about my blabbing. In light of what you told me about Deb, it seems . . . redundant."

She chuckled. "I guess we're a bit sensitive on the matter. You see, we don't really know you very well."

Unfortunately, I'm getting to know you people all too well. I swallowed the words and kept the thought to myself.

"And," she continued, "you're so chummy with that detective, what's her name?"

"Detective Arsalee Morales. Is that the one you mean?"

"Morales. Yes."

Even though I knew she couldn't see me, I shook my head in consternation. "Chummy? You're kidding, right? We're not chummy. From what I can tell, I'm her main suspect."

"Oh." A long silence. "So that's why . . ."

"Why what?"

Again that brisk, off-putting voice. "I really do need to go."

"Please. Tell me what you meant."

"She was here the other day asking about you. If you had access to insulin. If I'd ever taken my insulin to the studio. If you could have stolen it when I did."

"What did you say?"

"I said I hadn't noticed any missing, but that it's possible you could have stolen some."

"Swell. When I'm in prison, will you come visit me?"

"It has to be you. It can't be one of us."

That stung. "Why does it have to be me? You're the ones with motive."

"If we wanted to kill Deb, we'd have done it long ago."

On that inarguable point, she disconnected the call, leaving me feeling uneasy. If everyone, including the cops, considered me the prime suspect, then all the more reason to uncover the truth.

The problem with my finding the murderer continued to be too many suspects. Too much motivation. I felt like a dog walker with an dozen leashes in my hands, each pulling me in a different direction. Margot a possible murderer. Rose and her affair. Lena with the question of her daughter's paternity. Buffy with her sister/mother issue. Rhett and the alleged stolen money. Allie and the lie about her age. Kim with the horror of her now-cured disease. Nancy and her secret, whatever that might be.

It amazed me that Deb had managed to live sixty-nine years. A person with that much need for power and with no compunction how she got the upper hand, must have left a long trail of victims throughout her lifetime. But perhaps she'd learned to keep her sociopathic tendencies under control, exacting only small tokens of power, nothing worth killing over. Unless she had gone too far.

Or could it be that she hadn't gone too far, but that someone's circumstances had changed, making Deb's demise imperative? My circumstances certainly had changed, though I had no secret to protect, no power struggle to win. I had problem enough controlling my own life, I certainly had no desire to control anyone else's. Even if there wasn't a specific cause for a change of circumstances, all of Madame ZeeZee's nightmarish students were getting older, and the problems of age could have dictated a need to be done with Deb.

I continued to sit on the floor of my father's empty house until a full bladder made me struggle to my feet. After taking care of the urgent need, I scrambled a couple of eggs and ate them at the computer, compulsively playing one game of solitaire after another.

***

I went to bed before midnight, but didn't fall asleep until the early morning hours. I awoke in the glare of the sun, with no idea the time or even the day. I groped the floor by my bed until I found my phone, the only clock I had.

Friday. Ten-thirty.

I pulled the covers over my head, but after a few minutes, I gathered my courage and hoisted myself upright. I dressed, dawdled in the bathroom, and fixed a protein drink with a handful of supplements for breakfast, then the road beckoned.

I stood protected from the wind at the top of my father's circular drive, and tried to decide whether to go right or left. Right would take me to the desert. Left would take me to Nancy's house, three miles away. Did I feel like walking that far in the heat?

I patted the pocket of my long-sleeved flowered shirt to make sure I'd grabbed a bottle of water, checked the pocket of my black cotton knit pants for my keys and phone, secured Jay's old cowboy hat under my chin to make sure it didn't blow off. I looked behind me at the door to the house, thinking I had a third option—go back inside. But nothing waited for me indoors, just the empty rooms, three days with no dancing, and a computer that was beginning to bore me.

I took a few tentative steps to the right then, drawing a deep breath of faintly rose-scented air, I picked up speed and determination.

It seemed odd to see so many roses still blooming, but out here, they would continue to bloom until late fall. I stopped to take a photo of a perfect rose, then stooped for a whiff, but detected no scent. Apparently, that particular rose did not add to the ambient fragrance.

Since Peach Valley is a relatively new place, built long after straight streets had become anathema, I wandered from one curvy road to another, never quite knowing what direction I headed at any given moment. I had to check the GPS on my phone twice to make sure I kept on the right track. A little over an hour later, I arrived at Nancy's property, an older house with dark siding and a white picket fence—very un-California-like.

A few sharp yips came in response to my ringing the doorbell. *Well, someone's home.*

Nancy answered the door wearing dark slacks and a man's faded blue shirt. We stared at each other for a moment, then she smiled at me and stepped aside to let me enter.

"What are you doing here?" she asked at the same time I said, "I wasn't sure you'd be home."

We shared a laugh followed by an awkward silence.

Finally, I said, "I got worried about you. I've been calling and not getting any answer. I hope you're okay."

"I'm fine." She gestured to a couch where I could sit. "I've been here. I didn't get your messages."

"I called your cell."

"Have a seat," she said. "Can I get you something to drink?"

I pulled out my water bottle and held it up as if I were toasting her.

She perched on the edge of a chair. "My cell is broken. I haven't been able to get a new one."

"Oh! Well, that explains why you didn't get my messages."

She chuckled, a quick little pitter-patter, then slid her gaze to a car magazine displayed on the coffee table in front of her.

I pushed myself to my feet. "I'm sorry. I shouldn't have barged in. You must be busy. I can come back another time."

"No, that's all right." But she too got to her feet.

"We miss you at dance class."

"I miss class, too."

I felt confused and awkward as if my words were stones dropping onto sand without any ripple of connection or camaraderie. "What's going on?" I asked.

She didn't pretend ignorance. "It's hard. Grace's passing brought back bad memories. I just couldn't face any more death."

"I understand." I stepped forward to hug her, but she folded her arms across her chest.

"It's too much," she murmured.

Tears sprang to my eyes. "I know."

"You don't know," she said with no inflection in her voice.

My husband is gone, too, I wanted to cry out, but I didn't think she'd like the reminder of more death.

We stood there, shifting our feet. I took a few steps away, then stopped. "Remember when you said everyone should tell me their secrets?"

Her eyes looked hard. "No."

I pretended I didn't hear and continued, "I wondered about a secret I can use for your character in the book. It doesn't have to be real."

"I don't have a secret."

I shook my head in frustration, but she misunderstood the gesture, and gave another quick pitter-patter of laughter.

"I really don't."

"Are you sure you're okay? You seem so different."

A spark of her normal impishness flared in her eyes. "Just tired." And then the spark ignited and her voice became animated. "Eddie and I are fixing the DeLorean."

"Really? Wow!"

"Want to see it?"

"Yes! Please."

She led me around to the garage at the back of the house. The last time I'd seen the garage, the DeLorean had all but been buried in boxes, broken furniture, and other storage, but everything had been cleared out and the iconic vehicle held pride of place.

The stainless-steel body looked the same as when I'd seen it, but now the gull-wing doors were open, giving the antique car the eerie look of something from a far-flung future. The interior had been reupholstered in black, and looked inviting.

"Does it work?" I asked unable to take my gaze off the vehicle.

"We need a couple more parts. Eddie and I have been traveling to DeLorean car shows trying to find the necessary components, and I think we've got a lead."

I smiled at the excitement in her voice, at the pride she displayed in both Eddie and the vehicle. "What made you go ahead with the project?"

"We heard they're going to build DeLoreans again. I didn't want to be a me-too, but if we got there first, then . . ." She laughed, not a short pitter-patter, but a triumphant whoop.

"Thank you for letting me see your car," I said as she walked with me around to the front of the house."

"You're welcome. Maybe I'll see you at class again someday."

I nodded. "I'd like that."

Then, as if belated realizing she hadn't asked about any class members, she stopped and turned toward me. "How is everyone?"

"Mostly okay. Did you hear about Deb?"

"I haven't talked to anyone since the day we found Grace."

"Oh." I drew in a deep breath. "Well, Deb's gone, too."

The spark in her eyes went out. "Gone as in left the studio or gone as in . . . gone?"

"Gone."

"How?"

"Insulin overdose."

Nancy's mouth dropped open. "Like for your book?"

I gave a single nod of my head to indicate yes.

She turned her head at an angle and studied me. "Is that why you asked about my secrets? You think I had something to do with it?"

I wiped my brow with my forearm. "Not you. The cops think I did it, so I'm asking around in self-protection. But I have been worried about you. At the rate our class is disappearing, I feared you were a victim."

"Nope. I'm still here." She chuckled again, a pitter-patter that didn't sound very amused. "And here I'll stay until . . . you know."

"I don't blame you." I stepped forward to give her a hug, and this time, she allowed it.

She walked back to the house, saying over her shoulder, "Be careful!"

A strong gust of wind upended the blue recycle bin parked outside her gate. I pulled the thing erect, then gathered a handful of papers that swirled around my legs. As I stuffed them back in the bin, I caught the headline of the local newspaper dated two days previously, NO LEADS IN INSULIN TAMPERING CASE.

I turned to look for Nancy to ask why she'd prevaricated when I'd mentioned Deb, but I only saw a flicker at the front window, as if someone had peaked at me from behind a drape.

I dithered for a few seconds. Should I confront her? It's possible she had nothing to hide and simply refused to play the deadly book game. And even if she did have a secret, it couldn't have had anything to do with Deb's death. Nancy might have had means and even a motive, but since she hadn't been back to the studio in the past few weeks, she'd had no opportunity to switch the EpiPen in Deb's purse with the doctored pent.

Figuring I'd accomplished what I'd set out to do—check on Nancy's wellbeing—I turned and trudged back the way I came.

A mile from my dad's house, I faltered. Too much heat. Too much wind. Too little water. I saw a rare tree shaded curb, and I longed to sit and rest awhile, but I felt uncomfortable, as if people would think me a derelict. *Oh, the hell with that. They already think you a murderer.*

I lowered myself onto the curb and sat with legs stretched in front of me like a little girl who couldn't find her way home from school.

Although there wasn't much traffic, the fumes of the vehicles that did pass nauseated me. After about five minutes, I pushed myself upright, then staggered a few steps until the stiffness from sitting passed.

A vehicle pulled up next to me. A cop car. *Crap. Now what?*

A young cop got out and swaggered around the car toward me. I shook my head in disbelief. Officer Ungar, the writer. As if this day weren't bad enough.

"May I see your identification please?"

"Why? You know who I am."

He did a double take. "Oh, hi." Then in his formal voice, "May I see your identification, please?"

I patted my pockets. "I'm walking. I didn't bring my driver's license."

"You should always carry your identification with you, Ma'am."

I sighed. "So I'm a Ma'am? Great. Is that all you wanted? To see my identification?" I knew it wasn't smart to sass a cop, but I'd had enough. Enough heat. Enough wind. Enough lies. Enough death. Enough cops.

"We got a call about a drunk sitting on the curb. Have you been drinking, Ma'am?"

I pulled the empty water bottle out of my pocket. "The problem is I haven't had enough to drink." Seeing the narrowing of his eyes, I added quickly. "Water. I didn't bring an adequate amount of water."

"What are you doing here?"

"Resting. I walked five miles, and I still have a mile to go."

He hitched up his belt with all the cop paraphernalia on it, and looked at me in disbelief. "It's a hundred degrees out here!"

"So?"

"So I better drive you home."

I looked down the long winding street and back at the cop car. I absently uncapped the water bottle and took a sip of air, which only added to my dryness. As much as I feared getting in the police car, I feared even more being in the sun without water. Deciding that valor was the better part of discretion, I lurched the few steps to the squad car.

He scrutinized me as if trying to measure me for a jail cell, then opened the rear door and eased me into his vehicle. I don't know if he had the same car as the last time, but a few unfamiliar stains on the seat and on the floor made me think it a different vehicle.

But it still smelled of pine, vomit, and unwashed feet.

And the door handles still were missing.

Chapter 25

From grief I'd learned the dangers of being hungry, angry, lonely, and tired—they made it too easy to relapse into self-pity and depression—and I felt myself succumbing to all four of those conditions. I couldn't do anything about the soul hunger Jay's death had left me with, nor could I do anything about my cosmic anger at death, not just his but all deaths. Sleep eluded me, and loneliness had become a fact of my life.

The only thing left for me to do to break the cycle of self-pity was to satisfy my physical hunger. I checked all the cabinets and the pantry, but I'd done such a good job of clearing out that not even a single can of soup hid in the shadows. The refrigerator didn't offer much, either—a couple of eggs, half a carton of plain yogurt, a few bottles of water, and a can of Ensure left over from my father's stash. The freezer contained only one unappetizing frozen dinner.

After the police office had dropped me off at the house, I'd taken a long shower, and dressed in clean cotton slacks and shirt. The change revived me sufficiently that now a trip to the grocery store seemed like a wonderful adventure.

When had my life become so narrow that a simple errand thrilled me? Death, grief, and taking care of my father had helped catapult me into my current state. Lack of a place to go—and indecision— kept me in my constricted life. When you can go anywhere, where do you go? When you can do anything you can afford without having to check anyone's schedule, how do you choose?

Soon, though, will it or not, my life would change. The new owners would move in, and I would move on. But where would I go? What did I want to do?

After all these years of tending the sick and dying, I wanted an untroubled life so my mind would have freedom to roam and I wanted a carefree place to live so I would have time to write. But a desire for adventure and bold living warred with the glorious vision of a literary paradise.

Isn't murder adventure enough for you? whispered a voice deep inside, and I had to admit the truth of those words. For now, anyway.

My musings—and my vintage car—took me to the grocery store. I wandered the aisles, looking for things to treat my taste buds, and spoiled myself with an Italian theme. Pizza sauce. Italian sausage. Chicken. Grated parmesan cheese. My mouth watered as I envisioned some sort of pasta-less chicken parmesan with a salad. I grabbed a few fresh vegetables, along with a package of broccoli slaw, which looked like colorful spaghetti. I paid for my purchases and drove back to the house, feeling much more optimistic than when I had my encounter with Officer Ungar.

I spent a contented hour fixing my meal. I took an extra minute or so indulging myself with a pretty arrangement of the food instead of dumping it on the plate as I normally did. I perched on the stool and inhaled the delectable aroma.

This moment is my life. And it is very good.

I picked up a forkful of the bite-size chicken pieces and thinly sliced sausage in a zesty sauce over cooked broccoli slaw, and chewed slowly. Exactly what I'd hoped for. Something tasty and adventuresome and bold.

Then the doorbell chimed.

I could feel the woman's aura of power even before I opened the door.

"Yes?" I said by way of greeting.

I expected some sort of comment about my less than enthusiastic greeting, but Detective Arsalee Morales gave me a stern look I can only describe as an official stare. "I need to clarify a few points. May I come in?"

I opened the door wider and made a theatrical gesture to usher her inside. As she passed me, I heard the whisper of the lining of her business suit rubbing against the dark blue of her jacket, and I wondered how she handled the heat in that outfit. But maybe she spent all her time indoors, questioning recalcitrant witnesses.

She lifted her nose and sniffed, and the small quirk of her lips told me she liked the smell of my dinner. I thought of offering her some of my food since I had plenty, but decided it would be too awkward to eat companionably—or not so companionably—with someone who wished to put me away for murdering a human being. (I have murdered ants and maybe a spider or two, but that's as far as my homicidal tendencies go.)

But all sign of her pleasure died as she looked around the empty living room. She'd seen the place before and knew the house had been sold, so I don't know what she'd expected—that I'd done the reverse of steal the furnishings, and instead put them back, like a rewind?

I held out a hand to offer her the use of the stool, but she declined and positioned herself at the counter. I stood across from her, glad to have that three-foot slab of granite between us.

"Lucky me, two cops in one day," I said. "What's going on?"

"I hear you've been asking questions," she responded.

I smiled. "I hear *you've* been asking questions."

If her frown gave any indication of her mood, she didn't find my comment amusing.

"I cautioned you about investigating on your own."

"I didn't investigate." *Not at the beginning anyway,* I added silently to mitigate the lie. "People came to me." That, at least, had the benefit of fact.

"I heard you're investigating Grace's death."

I gaped at her. "No. That's . . . no."

She held my gaze with hers. "I suppose you think I'm one of those bumbling detectives you mystery writers are so fond of creating to make the actions of your amateur detective seem defensible."

Her accusation so shocked me, I blurted out the truth. "I don't think you're bumbling. I think you're terrifying."

She smiled, but not prettily. "You think I'm terrifying?"

"Cripes. Yes.

"And smart?"

"Ye-es."

"Then why the hell are you going behind my back and questioning people"

My heart pounded in response to the thunderous intensity of her question, but I managed to get my words out despite the adrenaline making my voice wobble.

"I have the right to talk to my friends."

"You have no right to impede an official investigation. You have no right to aid and abet a criminal. You have no right to withhold evidence."

A spell of dizziness hit me, and I leaned my belly against the counter to keep from falling. *This can't be happening.*

I said very slowly so there could be no misunderstanding. "I. Am. Not. Withholding. Evidence."

She hefted her briefcase onto the counter and snapped open the latches. I gasped, wondering if she were getting out a pair of handcuffs.

"Grace's death was ruled an accident," I said quickly. "You know that. When a case is closed, I have no obligation to tell you anything further about something that is not a crime. All I know is that a witness confirmed it was in fact an accident."

She took out a small recorder. "Do you mind if I record this interview?"

"Yes, I mind, but I give my permission." Yeah, I know. Stupid. But I wanted my truth on record. She scrutinized me as if she couldn't figure out if I were toying with her.

"What do you want?" I asked.

She spoke quietly, but I could hear the steel in her tone. "I want to know what you know."

"What I know? I don't know anything for certain."

"You know there was a witness. Who's the witness?"

"Deb. She admitted to being in the studio when Grace fell. She said she arranged the body to look like the photo I took for the book cover, then she went back outside and waited for everyone to get there. She said she planned to call an ambulance when we'd seen Grace lying there, but by the time Madame ZeeZee arrived, it was too late."

She did her Wonder Woman pose. "And you didn't think to tell me about Deb's confession?"

"Actually, I did think of contacting you, but what good would it have done? It wouldn't have changed anything except corroborate the official findings. Besides, there is no 'duty to rescue.' I consider what Deb did morally indefensible, but it's not illegal."

She smiled a "gotcha" sort of smile, as if I were a staked lamb and she a tiger. "You contacted an attorney?"

I giggled. I couldn't help it. "Yeah. An attorney named Google."

She rolled her eyes up to look at the ceiling and shook her head. "Google has a lot to answer for."

"If Deb had no legal duty to rescue Grace, then she didn't commit a crime, and I had no duty to report it."

"What else did you find out?"

"Gossip, mostly. Supposedly Deb killed her first husband and made it look like an accident, though I haven't had a chance to research it."

She managed to nod in such a way that I had no idea what she meant by the gesture. Encouraging me to continue with my response? Agreeing to my researching further? Acknowledging that Deb had killed her ex-husband?

"What else?" Detective Morales asked.

"Apparently, Deb blackmailed people, though again, that came to me by way of gossip. I don't know for sure what she did. Don't know for sure who she was except that she was the only true Janus-faced person I ever met. Her husband thinks she was the sweetest woman alive, which I'm sure she was—to him. I saw her as more of a lying narcissistic sociopath. But what's the truth? You'll have to figure that out if you want to find the person who killed her, because I don't have a clue."

"Who did she blackmail?"

"I don't know. Supposedly she forced a couple of the women at the studio to give her small gifts to keep their secrets, but I haven't confirmed it. I mean, I can't exactly stop in the middle of dance class and ask, 'Hey, everyone, what's your secret and what did you give Deb to protect it?'"

"Since you seem to rely on Google, I assume you researched the women at the studio. What did you find?"

"Saints. That's what I found. Two are extremely devout. One is a hero. One was a missionary. One is taking care of her husband who has Alzheimer's. The rest? I don't know, but there doesn't seem to be a murderer in the bunch."

She didn't ask the names of any of the women I had described, which made me think she was far ahead of me in the investigation. My spirits lightened, as if the dark specter of murder had been whisked aside. I had all of thirty seconds to savor the moment before Detective Arsalee Morales spoke and enshrouded me in fear again.

"So that leaves you," she said.

I could feel fear fencing with anger in the pit of my stomach. I did not have the social skills to keep those feelings from coloring my voice. "That is precisely why I've been asking questions. If you arrest me, I need something to bargain with. I don't know what you believe, but I know the truth. I had nothing to do with Grace's death, nothing to do with Deb's death. Any time you spend investigating me is time you are not spending on looking for the killer."

She clicked off the recorder. "Have you written any more of your book?"

"No. Why, do you want to be in it?"

She smiled, a small enigmatic curve that made me wonder about her secrets. "Only if I'm one of the saints."

I offered her my own version of a mysterious smile, but I doubted I pulled it off. "Depends on whether you arrest me for murder."

"Fair enough," she said.

"I do have a request, though. I love your name. It's different. And beautiful. Do you mind if I use it for a book? If you think it would be a conflict with your job, I could wait for a different story, maybe make you a bank officer or something like that."

"Either is fine. If you put me in your book as a detective, I'd like to see it before you publish."

"I can do that."

Then, as if to grab back whatever power she'd lost in that brief moment of bonding, she gave me a fierce look that deepened the lines between her brows, and she spoke harshly. "If you are telling the truth about having nothing to do with either deaths, then you better be damn careful. You might have found saints, but there is a murderer lurking beneath one of those haloes. In mysteries, when the amateur goes up against the villain, he or she almost always gets wounded. In real life, you'd get dead."

I shivered. "Then please, please find her. I'm having a hard time figuring out where to go when I have to leave this house, but neither prison nor death appeal to me."

"Thank you for your help." Detective Morales stowed the recorder in her briefcase, snapped the latches, and swung it off the counter. "I'll be in touch."

"Who told you I asked questions?"

"I don't know," she said in a fair imitation of my voice, and I realized she knew I'd fudged my responses. But had the lies I told to protect the innocent branded me as a murderer?

I walked the detective outside and waited until she drove away before stepping back inside and locking the door. I shoved my food in the refrigerator, and collapsed on the bed to take a nap, but I couldn't shut off my mind. Did the detective wish me ill, or could I simply be one of the numerous leads she had to follow.

In replaying the interview in my mind, I felt proud of not saying *you've got to believe me* when I proclaimed my innocence, especially since she didn't have to believe anything except the evidence.

But what evidence did she have? There couldn't be anything to implicate me since I hadn't done anything, but the question nagged until finally I dozed off.

I awoke wearier than before I fell asleep, and also hungrier.

I heated my abandoned meal in the microwave. The concoction still tasted delicious, but the Italian spices couldn't take away the bad taste in my mouth left over from the detective's visit.

Chapter 26

Monday afternoon found me outside the studio, waiting for class to begin. At two oh five, I wondered where everyone could be. At two ten, worry niggled at me. At two fifteen, I finally called Madame ZeeZee.

"Where are you?"

She laughed. "It's Labor Day. Did you forget?"

"Sheesh. Unbelievable. I guess I'll go back home."

Home. Wherever that was. Despite the accident of phrasing, my dad's empty house provided no home, but it did give me a place to stay. Would I ever find home again?

Refusing to indulge in such piteous thoughts, I headed back to the house. But not to my computer. On Saturday morning, I'd gone to my storage unit and rummaged for the box of books and pencil puzzles I'd kept, and had spent the weekend in bed, reading and doing Number Place puzzles. (Decades before Sudoku's re-introduction to the United States by way of Japan, I'd been solving the same puzzle under the name of Number Place. Not that the information has anything to do with my story, but this is the place in the story where an author normally throws in some exposition to give the reader a break from suspense.)

I heated the last of my broccoli slaw spaghetti, and retired to my room to continue pampering myself.

The phone woke me. (In case you're one of those folks who can tell a lot about a person by the ring they chose for their cell phone, I'll let you in on my secret—I picked the same ringing sound I'd grown up with.)

"Did I wake you?" the person at the other end asked.

"No," I said groggily.

"I got a message that you called?"

"Oh?" Then comprehension hit. "Margot! How are you?"

"Tired. We just got back from the beach."

"Then maybe this isn't a good time to talk?"

"No. It's fine."

And that's where the conversation stalled. The little speech I'd prepared when I'd originally called had disappeared from my head.

"Hello? Are you still there?" Margot asked.

"Yeah. I'm here. I have to ask you something, but I'm trying to figure out how to do it."

"It's that bad?"

"Maybe. I don't know. I was wondering if you could tell me about Margruta Jasikevičius." I'd checked with a video on Google to learn the correct pronunciation, so it wasn't my mangling the surname that kept her from responding right away.

"Where did you hear that name?"

"Remember Gerda who didn't want to dance with professionals? A friend of hers recognized you. Said you'd once been a Lithuanian ballerina."

"I'm not a ballerina anymore, Lithuanian or otherwise. But that's not what you want to talk about, is it?"

"Gerda said you murdered someone."

"And so you think I killed Deb? I never hurt anyone."

"I didn't think you did, but . . ."

"You had to ask."

I hung my head, though she couldn't see the shame on my face. "I'm sorry."

"It's odd. At the beginning, it was all I thought about, but now months go by without my ever remembering who I was."

"Like grief."

"Not *like* grief. It *was* grief. I lost my home, my passion, my job, my language, my place in the world."

"What happened?" My voice shook with the sympathetic tears her recital had stirred in me.

"I wasn't a great ballerina, but I was good. Good enough to be the understudy of the understudy of the prima ballerina."

I could hear the sadness underlying the pride in her voice, and the tears rolled down my cheeks unchecked.

"It was a total fluke. The prima ballerina never got sick, so when the understudy's father died, they let her go home for a couple of days. Then flu struck. The principals all got sick. So I played Don Quixote's Kitri to a packed audience. It was . . ." She paused, then continued in a barely audible voice. "It was magic."

She sniffed, and I thought she too had succumbed to tears. She drew in a ragged breath, and continued. "I didn't want the night to end, so I hung around after everyone left to savor my triumph a bit longer. I went out into the theater and sat in a mid row orchestra seat and tried to imagine how I'd looked on stage."

She paused again, and I took the moment to scrub away my tears and blow my nose.

"You always think," she said, "that major changes come gradually, like death from old age. But sometimes change comes so quickly, you're left wondering what happened. I'm still not sure exactly what took place. I heard a shot. The ballet master staggered onto the stage in front of the curtain. I got a brief glimpse of a second man in the shadows, but I couldn't tell what he looked like except that he was tall with big shoulders and had dark hair. I ducked in my seat. I don't know if he saw me, but I was afraid to leave in case he did. So I was still there when the Criminal Police came. They questioned me. I told them what I knew."

I pictured her, the pretty ballerina, still dressed in her costume, still feeling the dream, and then finding herself in a nightmare.

"It must have been terrifying," I said.

"It wasn't scary until I got death threats from some . . . I don't know. Gangsters, I guess. They didn't want me to testify. Apparently, the ballet master had stolen money from the ballet company, which had been funded by money launderers. There was no such thing as witness protection in Lithuania back then, so I protected myself. Came to Los Angeles to visit my aunt and uncle and stayed. Became a citizen."

"I'm sorry," I said for lack of anything more profound to say.

"Thank you. It was hard for a long time. I knew English, but I had an accent that made me stand out, so I took diction classes to learn to talk like everyone else in California. I took ballet classes and taught the babies at the studio. I worked for a while as an emergency medical technician. That's where I met my husband. He's a fireman. We have two boys. One's married with children, and the other is engaged. It's been a wonderful life. But . . ."

"I know," I said softly.

"It's hard to believe so much good came from so much bad."

"Are the problems at the studio bringing it all back to you?"

She laughed. "Not until you mentioned it. If anything, what's going on reminds me how blessed I've been."

"Us, too. I've always loved taking classes with you, though I must admit, I've also been intimidated at times. I mean, we're doing stretches on the floor, and you sit there with your legs spread out on either side of you in a straight line, and on your forearms on the floor as if it's the most comfortable position in the world. But now, I'll probably be too intimidated to even try."

"No you won't. You're doing so much better than when you started. You forget, you've only had a couple of ballet classes a week for two years. I had fifteen ballet classes a week for twenty years when I was young."

"So when I'm ninety-five, I can be as good as you?"

"Probably. I'll be eighty four then, and I have some health issues, so we could be on the same level. Madame ZeeZee will be a hundred and ten and still teaching."

We laughed at the image of us as aged ballerinas.

"You don't have to worry," I said. "I won't tell anyone about this conversation."

"It doesn't matter. Madame ZeeZee knows. And from what you told me, so do some of the others in class. I was afraid of those gangsters for many years, but I doubt they are still looking for me."

We said our good-byes, then before I disconnected the line, I yelled, "Wait. Are you still there?"

"Still here."

"Do you know anything about the ballerinas who disappeared?"

She let out a merry laugh. "You mean the ones the aliens stole?"

"Yeah, those," I said sheepishly.

"That blogger is a crackpot. Most of the dancers she claimed disappeared simply retired. A couple came here to the United States. A few died. One supposedly had some sort of UFO experience, but I'd met her, and she always had a bit of a fey quality. I think that's where the blogger got the idea about alien abduction."

"Rats." I said. "I hoped maybe aliens were implicated in Deb's death. I don't like the idea that one of us could have done it."

All humor fled from Margot's quiet voice. "Neither do I. Murder is a bad business."

Chapter 27

I lay back on the pillow, arms behind my head, and thought about Margot and me and how, through a convoluted series of events, we ended up in the same place.

Because every action impinges on every other action, even down to the most minute particle or wave, the confluence of our lives would have had to begin billions of years ago, when the universe burst into being. Through untold eons, the Everything developed increasingly complex life forms, and finally, it created a semblance of a human being. A million years later, our present species sprang forth, and many thousands of years after that, I was born in the United States of America. I—a bookish child with no talent or energy for physical activities— grew up, loved deeply, got married, became widowed, and traveled a thousand miles to Peach Valley to care for a dying old man.

One day, while waiting to meet a woman from my grief group for lunch, I noticed Madame ZeeZee's studio, took a chance, and went inside. I never had a list of things I wanted to do before I die (does anyone have a list of things they want to do *after* they die?) because I wanted the miraculous: a love I never knew. And that's what happened with dance.

Margot's individual journey started nine years after mine when she was born in Lithuania with a love of dance. Her life of physical and mental discipline ended in murder and a six thousand mile trip into the unknown. And somehow, those two cosmic journeys—that of the bookish child and the ballerina—intersected at Madame ZeeZee's studio.

Not a nightmare, but a marvel.

Could the lives of the murderer and her victim also have accidentally crossed years after the inciting event? Could the victim have done something recently to create the murderer? Or—I sat up at the thought—could the murderer have come to the studio for the sole purpose of meeting and then doing away with her enemy? Could the murderer have spent months, perhaps years, dancing with her foe before finally deciding to do away with her?

But what would have upset the status quo?

The book.

Always that damned book. Perhaps the manipulation of Grace's death proved to the murderer that Deb deserved to die after all. In addition, she had the perfect scapegoat—me.

If I had never found the studio, would life be the same? Or would the universe have taken a spin in a different direction?

I sighed. I might as well wonder how to drain the oceans or turn off the stars.

With a flash of insight, I understood why I'd become so addicted to solitaire after Jay's death. If the game didn't work out, I could roll fate back to the beginning, and try again, and again, and again, like an alchemist, searching for the secrets of the universe in repetition.

But I'm no alchemist. I haven't managed to transform myself into a higher form of life, haven't managed to turn atoms into energy.

Haven't managed to find one murderous old lady.

Something nagged at me, something I'd touched on in my reverie. And then it came to me. If Deb's treatment of the unconscious Grace made the murderer decide on the righteousness of her quest, how had she known about Deb moving the body? I hadn't told anyone until after Deb died.

But maybe the murderer had overheard Deb telling me what she had done. I pictured the scene, the two of us standing outside the studio, the heat of the morning, an open door. Why did I have an impression of an open door? Madame ZeeZee hadn't yet arrived, so the studio door remained shut. Oh, right—the door of the nail salon had been propped open. I vaguely remembered hearing voices drifting outside, and then silence.

Silence because they were listening. But who had listened? The dark and sinister owner, of course. The manicurist, perhaps.

And a customer.

I tried to remember the women I knew who had their nails done. Madame ZeeZee, but she used a different manicurist. Rhett and Michaela went to the salon next door. Who else?

Unable to dredge up any more images of wickedly long, professionally done fingernails, I called Madame ZeeZee. While the phone rang, I thought of how today's detecting—amateur detecting, that is—compared to the heyday of detective literature. With cell phones and computers, you never needed to leave the house. The world came to you.

"Hello? Hello? Is anyone there?"

I jerked myself to attention. "Hi, Madame ZeeZee. It's Pat. Do you know who has their nails done at the salon next to the studio? I know Rhett and Michaela do, but does anyone else?"

"I went once, but I got a toenail fungus from them, so I never when back. Allie had problems with them, too, but Deb and Nancy liked them. And Rose sometimes went there. Why? Do you think it's important?"

"It might be. Did you know about Deb's blackmail scheme?"

A long silence, then, "How did you find out about that?"

"Well, you did ask me to investigate."

A short laugh that sounded vastly different from her normal light-hearted giggle.

"Your investigation is not how I imagined it would be. I didn't know you'd find out all our secrets."

I could feel my brows pulling together. "What did you imagine? That I'd just sit down and write the murderer into being?"

"I guess I did."

"But who would you have chosen?"

"Someone I didn't know."

I blew out my cheeks. "Yeah, me too. But unfortunately, the murderer chose herself without any help from us."

"When I found out about Deb, I threatened to kick her out of class if she didn't stop. I wish I had kicked her out. Then she and Grace would still be alive. "

"Why did you let her stay?"

"She's always been a problem, but I felt sorry for her. She was so needy, so desperate for attention. Dance is like therapy. It brings people to life and life to people. I thought dancing would help Deb deal with her problems, or at least help her put them into perspective. When you come to class, you have to park your baggage at the door and let dance do its magic, but Deb always brought her problems and attitude into the studio."

"So dance as therapy is why so many women with horrendous backgrounds have found their way to your studio?"

"I believe God brought all of you girls here. You also have to remember, I have the only studio up here in the high desert that offers lessons in classic dances to seniors as well as children. The other studios only take kids."

"What do you know about Nancy? She seems an odd one to take classes. She doesn't act all that happy about dancing, but staying away doesn't make her happy, either."

"Nancy's problems have nothing to do with Deb, or I would have explained her situation to you."

"I'd eliminated Nancy because I figured she'd had no opportunity to place the doctored EpiPen in Deb's bag, but if she and Deb had been at the nail salon at the same time, she could have done it then."

"I hate telling you all the things people confided in me."

"Well, I hate hearing them. Would you rather I stopped asking questions?"

"No!" The single word exploded out of her with the force of truth. "I worked too hard to have my career end like this, and if there are any more deaths, it *will* be the end."

"Okay. Then let's get it done. Tell me about Nancy."

No response.

I waited.

Finally Madame ZeeZee said, "Nancy's daughter Beth took ballet from me for many years. Beth was very good. Got accepted to a ballet company in Canada. But it was hard, harder than she expected. She came from the desert, so she got sick a lot from the cold. The company didn't pay the dancers enough to live on, and Nancy couldn't afford to send her more than a small allowance. Beth had to sell her car. When that money was gone, she called Nancy and said she got a ride home with a friend. No one ever saw her again."

"What?" My heart pounded. "Is that true."

"Yes," Madame ZeeZee said so softly, I barely heard her.

"When did this happen?"

"Thirty years ago."

I felt like retching. "How does anyone live with the not knowing for that long?"

"Nancy pretends her daughter is still in Canada. That way she doesn't have to accept her death."

"But why come to class? Wouldn't she want to stay far away from you?"

I heard a small sound, as if Madame ZeeZee were sipping a drink or sobbing.

"She did stay away until a couple of years ago. It surprised me when she came and said she wanted to take dance classes. I think being at my studio comforted her. It's a link to her daughter."

"I can understand that." But did I? Could one ever understand the grief of another? Can anyone but the bereft herself see the Swiss-cheese holes loss had carved in her psyche?

Like Kim, Nancy seemed sane, serene. But did murderous impulses hide in the holes of her serenity?

"Is there any reason Nancy would have wanted Deb gone?"

"None that I can think of. Beth's disappearance happened a long time ago, and I doubt Deb knew about it."

"Deb had a way of finding out things, and she had no sensitivity. Could she have said something that hit Nancy wrong?"

"It's possible."

But would quiet Nancy with the pixyish twinkle in her eyes kill because of a slight, intended or not? It seemed too over the top. "I get the impression Nancy is as sick of death as I am. I don't see her killing anyone."

"I don't see any of you girls killing anyone. Dancers don't. We find the answers to pain in our passion for dance."

"I hate to ask, but in the interests of piecing together the truth, I should. What's your secret?"

Madame ZeeZee heaved a sigh that echoed through the ether. "My secret? Dance is my passion. I hate charging for lessons, but I wouldn't be able to keep my studio open if you girls didn't pay."

I smiled to myself. Leave it to Madame ZeeZee to have such a non-lethal secret, though in truth, it was no secret. She'd mentioned it to me before.

"What about Rose? I heard she had an online affair. Could she have killed Deb to keep her husband from finding out?"

"Her husband knew. He's the one who urged her to find a virtual lover. He wanted her to learn to talk dirty, but she couldn't do it."

"Oh, sheesh. Poor Rose. It's hard to believe that the people I dance with have such atrocious problems and sorrows."

"Why is it hard to believe? Aren't you the one who said we've lived a total of more than seven hundred years? There's a lot of living in that many centuries. No one lives to be our age without suffering."

"But there's so *much* pain!" I cried out.

"Well, you're looking for pain because pain is what kills. I'm sure if you looked for happiness among my dancers, you'd find much more joy than pain. Look at you, the difference between now and when you first showed up."

"I'll be glad when this is done. I hate wallowing in other people's angst. I have enough of my own"

"I know. But I'm relying on you to find the truth. Sorry, I have to hang up. Rico wants to watch a movie."

So we parted, she to her loving husband, me to my lonely quest.

Too depressed to do anything else, I lay down on my bed and shed a few tears of self-pity, though I knew in my heart things could have been so much worse.

Jay had disappeared out of my life, and though it had bothered me that I didn't know his whereabouts—at the beginning, I would wander the desert screaming, "Jay? Where are you? Can you hear me?"—I did know his earthly fate. He'd died of inoperable kidney cancer, with me by his side. I heard him take his last few ragged breaths. Watched his Adam's apple bob once, twice. And then that heartbreaking stillness.

But what if he had simply disappeared? Gone to the store, perhaps, and never come home? His death had been hard for me, so dreadfully hard. But not knowing what had happened to him would have killed me.

And yet Nancy had found the courage to live, to love again, to find joy.

I thought of the women I danced with, and how each of them faced grief the only way she knew how. Deb with desperate need. Nancy with denial. Rose with appeasement. Lena with dissociation. Rhett with relentless optimism. Margot with audacity. Kim with missionary zeal. Madame ZeeZee with dance.

Although I didn't know what sorrows Jackie, Buffy, and Michaela might have had to deal with, I knew them well enough to know their reactions. Jackie would accept her tribulations, publicly at least, with good-natured cheer. Buffy would face her problems with quiet style. And Michaela would find comfort in her religion.

Grace, I think, had found solace with her husband and her family and her seemingly charmed life.

But what about Allie? I only knew two things about her—she

had plastic surgery and she lied about her age. Is that how she dealt with adversity? With lies?

In thinking about the often silent woman, I realized I knew more about her than I expected. I knew her desperation for attention matched Deb's, but that Allie tried to hide her need, which in itself was sort of a lie. I knew that she'd once been a star on Broadway. And I knew she was happily married to a plastic surgeon. Or rather, an ex plastic surgeon. He must have retired a long time ago.

I jumped out of bed—well, no I didn't. I laboriously pushed myself upright and stood wavering a moment until I got my balance. Then I went to the computer, wide awake and eager to see what I could find out about Allie's husband.

I didn't know his first name and hadn't thought to ask Madame ZeeZee when I talked to her, so I Googled "Shaffer, plastic surgeon," and got a whole page of responses for Shafers, Shaeffers, and Shaefers, but only one Shaffer. Dr. Robert Shaffer in New York City.

Allie and New York seemed to go together. Hadn't Madame ZeeZee mentioned that Allie claimed to have seen her in New York?

I clicked on the link for Robert Shaffer and found myself at the website for The Shaffer Clinic. Though there were a dozen doctors listed, I didn't see a single Dr. Shaffer. I found the site menu and clicked on "about."

The Shaffer Clinic was founded in 1970 by Dr. Robert A. Shaffer, MD, to provide a high standard of excellence and to offer the most advanced procedures available in both craniofacial reconstructive surgery and cosmetic surgery.

After graduating from Johns Hopkins University, Dr. Shaffer completed a six-year integrated plastic surgery residency at The UCLA Division of Plastic & Reconstructive Surgery. He worked for ten years at Mount Sinai Hospital in New York before opening his own clinic.

There followed a long list of organizations to which the doctor and the clinic belonged, then, appended to the bottom, a brief note:

Despite the loss of Dr. Robert A Shaffer, who remained on the board after he retired from practice until his death, The Shaffer Clinic continues to operate at the highest standard of excellence.

Dr. Shaffer could not be Allie's husband, who was still very much alive. Or so Allie said. And I knew her for a liar.

Whoa.

Shocked by the direction of my thoughts, I searched for Dr. Robert A. Shaffer's obituary. According to the brief notice I found, the seventy-nine year old plastic surgeon had died three months previously. He was survived by his wife Alyssa Lynn Shaffer. Memorial donations were to be made in his name to The Shaffer Clinic.

Could Alice be Alyssa? I Googled "Alyssa Lynn Shaffer," but got no hits. I Googled "Alyssa Lynn on Broadway," and found a playbill featuring Alyssa Lynn in *Rum of the Mill* at the Theatre de Lys. The poster was up for auction at an exorbitant price. A note attached by the auctioneer said that all the original playbills had supposedly been destroyed when an accident at a preview prevented Alyssa Lynn from performing, but that a besotted stage hand had pocketed the playbill before it could be incinerated.

A search for information about *Rum of the Mill* told me the play was a delightful coming-of-age musical. I also learned that two of the female dancers in that production had gone on to fame, but I did not recognize either name. Could Alyssa Lynn have spent her life lamenting that she been not been one of those dancers?

The picture on the playbill was a drawing of a boy and a young woman. The woman, though beautiful, did not resemble the Allie I knew, but there'd been two major women's roles. The picture might have been the other woman.

When I could find no more traces of Alyssa Lynn online, I emailed Wanda. *Help! Can you find out anything about Alyssa Lynn who was married to Dr. Robert A Shaffer? I think this might be Alice Shaffer from dance class. I also found a reference to an actress Alyssa Lynn who had an accident in the early nineteen seventies that prevented her from performing in an off Broadway show called* Rum of the Mill *at the Theatre de Lys, but I can't find anything specific. Is this the same woman? Maybe your sources would have the information. Please? Thank you!*

Chapter 28

I did not know what to expect from dance class on Tuesday. Would the women hate me for prying into their lives? Would I hate them for their secrets?

Luckily, Jackie waited by the door of the studio when I arrived, and her cheery hello heartened me so that when Margot showed up, I was able to welcome her with a casual smile. I could detect no constraints in the smile she gave me in return, which made me relax even more.

I can do this.

Buffy arrived with her good humor intact, and her greeting seemed offhand enough that I knew she harbored no ill-feeling toward me for my revelation about her parentage. Rhett, strutting across the parking lot, looked as if she were back to her normal vibrancy with any anger she still felt for me well hidden. Allie, too, seemed her usual self, but instead of my seeing her as a reserved woman, I now sensed a person too stressed to speak. I wished I could comfort her, but I doubted she'd welcome either words or an embrace from me. Or from anyone.

When Lena arrived, she elicited surprised comments and compliments from all of us. She'd abandoned her wigs, and her own silver hair had been cut in a flattering style with bangs sweeping across her forehead. She looked younger, rested, at ease with life.

"Wow," Margot said. "Look at you."

Lena preened. "I finally did what the doctors suggested, and put my husband in an Alzheimer's care facility. He likes it. He doesn't always remember who he is anymore, but when he does, he's pleased to be there. He says he doesn't have to worry about me so much now." She laughed. "And there I was, worrying about him. I finally got caught up on my sleep."

"Hospice came to see my mother." Madame ZeeZee unlocked the door. "They said they could get my mother in a private home where she will have round the clock care, but she doesn't like the idea."

"We looked into a private home for my dad," Jackie said. "The place we saw smelled of rotting food and urine. There were three old men, and the only person there all the time to look after them was an elderly woman who should have been in assisted living herself. I'm glad we could keep my dad at home."

"I have a friend who wants to take care of the elderly in her home," Margot said. "She's a hospice nurse with all the connections. She's filled out the paper work but her house is not certified by the state yet. Do you want me to check with her?"

"My mom won't go." Madame ZeeZee stashed the keys in her purse. "She hates her apartment and complains that I moved her up here to the high desert against her will even though I had to—she suffered a stroke. But now she won't leave the place."

Jackie laughed. "These old folks. Can't do a thing with them."

Madame ZeeZee seemed to pose after turning on the lights, a lithe figure in her mauve tights and top. It looked to me as if she were making an effort to leave the troubles with her mother at the door. She padded as softly as a young girl across the wooden floor and parked her bag on a shelf in her office alcove. The rest of us found chairs in the small waiting area and slipped on our ballet shoes, talking and joking as if no shadow had ever dimmed our lives.

By the time Madame ZeeZee put on the music for our *grande reverence,* we were all waiting on the dance floor to begin.

To my surprise, instead of being intimidated by my knowledge of Margot's background, I felt no difference in my attitude toward her. Her experience as a ballerina had nothing to do with the pleasure I'd always found in taking classes with her, and I still felt that joy. She must have sensed there'd been no change in my feelings, because now and again she gave me an encouraging smile or word as was her custom. But mostly, we followed directions for the patterns Madame ZeeZee gave us and concentrated on getting the steps right.

Three-fourths of the way through the class, during a brief hiatus where Madame ZeeZee had disappeared into her alcove to change the music, Buffy said, "You're smiling."

"I am?" Realizing the truth, I repeated myself. "I am! We're dancing."

"Well, yeah." She laughed. "This is a dance class."

"I take it for granted now, but look at me . . . I'm dancing! Today it's more than that, though. The electricity is so strong."

She looked puzzled. "What electricity?"

"The energy that connects us. We're in sync today"

"I didn't notice any energy."

I tilted my head to study her. "You didn't?" I figured everyone felt what I did when we danced. I might not be as in tune with the music as Buffy was, might not always be able to pick out the right notes or the beat, but the group energy affected me. When everyone was doing something different, too fast, too slow, too overly dramatic, too forgetful, I felt as if I were slogging through mud. But days like today, when everything and everyone harmonized perfectly, I danced like a dream, the energy pulling me and everyone else in the same direction, all of us moving as one being.

It had been a long time since I felt that energy, that synchronization. Did it mean the group had healed itself, and we were in the forward place I had hoped for? Or was this merely a joyous interlude?

The music started again. I put aside my reflections to concentrate on the combinations Madame ZeeZee gave us. Between classes, though, when we went to the waiting area to don our belly dance skirts, I was able to resume my musings. It didn't seem possible, if one of the women in class were a murderer, that we could dance so blithely with no conflicts or negative energy affecting us.

Could I have taken a wrong turn in my deductions?

Or could it be that killing Deb had brought peace to the woman who had done the deed?

"So much for the smile."

"What?" I pivoted toward the sound of Buffy's voice. "Oh. I was thinking."

"Always a bad choice."

We laughed as we returned to the barre. We did warm-ups, which seemed ridiculous since I felt overheated from ballet class, but I knew such exercises also served to integrate our energies so that by the time we began to practice our dances, we were already in harmony with each other.

After Madame ZeeZee started the music for the first dance, she moved into line with us. No one in front. No one behind. All as one. I felt as if I were as light and free as the veil I danced with.

We performed perfectly.

"Good," Madame ZeeZee said when the music ended.

185

We wrapped our veils around us for the second dance, and the slow unveiling, when it came, felt sensuous and liberating, as if I were also shedding my worries. For the third dance, we again wrapped ourselves in our veils, and at the finale, when our veils fluttered to the floor in an undulating rainbow, the palpable energy held us rapt in a moment of silence.

As we put away our veils and cymbals and got out our *dandiya,* the sticks for our East Indian dance, I said to Buffy, "You really didn't feel that energy?"

"No. I felt we did well, though. Everyone was on the beat."

"Proof," I said, "that no one can ever truly take a step in another person's dance shoes."

"Who's dancing in another person's shoes?" Rose asked.

"Me." I laughed because in the two years of taking dance classes, I'd only bought one pair of shoes—my ballet slippers. The other shoes had been hand-me-downs from women who'd purchased them online and didn't want the hassle of returning the ill-fitting footwear.

We practiced "Dola Dola" a couple of times, then, to my regret, class came to an end. The other women took off their belly dance skirts, put on their street shoes, and left the studio. The energy drifting out the door with them. I waited until after Madame ZeeZee locked up, then I trudged back to the house, feeling heavier with every step.

By the time I secured myself inside the house, I'd reassumed the full burden of the dancers's deaths. The feeling that I might have taken a wrong step in my thoughts haunted me. Why hadn't it occurred to me that the women weren't the only ones who would have known of the EpiPen idea? The wives might have told their husbands.

Could Charlie have killed Deb in retaliation for Grace's death? But he could not have known about Deb's involvement. And anyway, the EpiPen seemed more of a woman's weapon.

Or a frail old man's.

Husbands were the usual suspects. Could Emmett have killed his wife? Maybe his talk of "Sweet Debbie" had been a smokescreen for my benefit. But he had seemed truly bereft. I'd sensed the energy of his grief, and such radiating pain could not be easily feigned.

No matter how many questions I posed, I didn't get any closer

186

to the answer I sought. I simply did not have enough facts to make sense of Deb's death.

Perhaps lack of facts, rather than an assumption of my guilt, kept Detective Arsalee Morales on my tail. Crime at a distance, such as the insulin-filled EpiPen, would garner little trace evidence. The killer never had to go inside Deb's house, and if the doer had seen even a single cop show or read a single crime novel, she'd have known enough to wipe her fingerprints from the device, maybe wrapping it in a facial tissue before depositing it in Deb's purse.

I didn't know anything about insulin or EpiPens, but if there were differences between prescriptions of insulin or if there were different kinds of pens, those would be traceable bits of evidence for the cops, but wouldn't help me at all.

I turned on my computer, expecting to spend a few mindless hours playing solitaire, but an email from Wanda waited for me. She hadn't found anything yet about the actress, but she attached a few photos from the New York Times society pages ranging from ten to twenty years ago, showing Dr. Robert A. Shaffer and his wife Alyssa Lynn at various functions, which confirmed my surmise that Alice Shaffer and Alyssa Lynn were the same woman. I felt excited at first, as if I'd solved my mystery, but then the truth dawned. Just because a person pretended to be younger than her years, pretended her beloved husband still lived, it didn't make her a murderer. It made her a sad old woman, one who couldn't face the truth of her aloneness.

I never pretended to anyone that Jay continued to live, but part of me believed he waited for me back home in Colorado, though in truth, that part diminished every day. I still kept his eyeglasses in case he needed them, and I'd donated his car to hospice, but I kept his extra set of keys, because how else would he get around?

Such is the quantum state of grief, where one's love is alive and not alive at the same time.

Did Allie find comfort in pretending to us and her Facebook friends that she still had a loving husband? I certainly was not one to look askance at how other people dealt with the unspeakable pain of loss. Although I'd never told anyone, at the beginning, I used to hug the box with Jay's ashes and pretend I was hugging him.

All the sad, lonely women . . .

Chapter 29

I woke to new resolves: no more drowning in other people's pain, and get on with the task of rebuilding my life.

An email from Wanda with photos of the three houses Alice Shaffer owned—a beach cottage on the outer banks of North Carolina, a cabin in the Adirondacks, and an estate in Connecticut—helped fuel my resolve. I knew rich people felt the same sorrows that we less financially fortunate folk did, but the rich had opportunities and possibilities that we lacked. Much of my extended grief hinged on the uncertainty of my future: how would I support myself in my old age? If I became infirm, where would I get the money to pay someone to look after me? What would happen if I couldn't afford a place to live? All problems Allie didn't have.

I got so caught up in my reasons for not being sympathetic to Allie, that it took me a while to ask the salient question: what the heck was she doing in Peach Valley? Maybe she, like Margot, had relatives in the high desert, and she'd come to visit them so as not to be alone.

Or maybe misery really did love company. Maybe only murder would help her pain. Apparently, it had worked for Deb—according to her husband, she'd wallowed in grief until the death of her ex-husband, a man she had allegedly killed.

Funny how after a tragedy, some people ran toward death, embracing it as a lover, and other people stayed as far away as possible. I didn't even want to consider where in that spectrum I fell.

I vaguely remembered hearing of a magazine for theater news. Billboard, maybe? I Googled "Billboard Magazine," and found a link for the archives.

I spent a pleasant hour in the past, reading about songs I'd never heard of like "Lucille has Messed up my Mind," "Blue Afternoon," and "Permanent Damage." I read about an opening of the store Tape Village in a Denver shopping center not far from where I grew up, and how they were going to emphasize eight-tracks. I read about The Johnny Cash show and the newcomers to the Nashville scene. And then it dawned on me, this was not a magazine for theater news.

So, back to Google. I eventually discovered the *Internet Theater Data Base*. I looked up *Rum of the Mill*, and found a list of the production staff, the cast, the type of show (musical), the number of performances (twenty plus thirteen previews).

At the bottom of the page was a place for user comments. Someone named Thtrlvr wrote: *I loved the preview of* Rum of the Mill *with Alyssa Lynn as the star. Fiona Parker, who took Alyssa Lynn's role after the accident, did resonate with me. Alyssa Lynn's makeup artist should have been thrown in jail, not just fired.*

Whoa. Makeup artist? Deb claimed to have been a makeup artist on Broadway, though I'd assumed she lied about that as she had about so many of her fabulous exploits. But could she have told the truth? What if she had been the makeup artist who had caused Alyssa Lynn's accident? If the mysterious accident had derailed the actress's career, that sure would be motive for murder. It had seemed to me the EpiPen as a long-shot murder weapon spoke of an old grudge, but why take action now after so many years had passed?

Of course. The death of Allie's husband. Had her grief derailed her sanity? Or did being alone remind her of what she could have been?

Although I searched the internet until I needed to get ready for class, I couldn't find out anything more. I emailed Wanda the link to the comment and added another plea for help.

When I reached the studio, I told myself that anything at this point was mere conjecture and to leave my thoughts of Allie as the murderer at the door. And, surprisingly, I did.

I already knew the Hawaiian dances Madame ZeeZee was teaching the beginners, so I concentrated on her hands, trying to make my gestures as smooth and sensuous as hers. I felt no electricity, but then, I never expected to. It would be months before muscle memory would take hold in the new dancers, enabling them to move smoothly and without thought.

The advanced class, however, did feel electric. We went effortlessly through our whole repertoire of dances. We even had time to change into sarongs and practice our Tahitian moves.

"You had some hip action going there," Rose said to me after class when we stripped off our sarongs. "I used to be able to move like that."

"I'm sorry," I said, but she brushed off my sympathy with a wave of her hand.

On the walk home, an odd thought struck me. Had Rose begun to lose all that weight when her husband demanded she learn to talk dirty to him?

It seemed to me the big mystery was not why one person murdered another, but how each of us found the strength—and joy—to make the most of our days.

Dance had become the answer for me at that stage in my grief journey, so even though I couldn't find it in me to care if it were Allie or a stranger who had killed Deb, I feared that if I didn't find out the truth, Madame ZeeZee's nightmare—losing her studio—would become mine.

Wanda's email brought disturbing news.

"I found a small article about Alyssa Lynn in a now defunct New York newspaper called On and Off Broadway. *It said only that Alyssa Lynn had been hospitalized when her makeup artist for* Rum of the Mill *used the wrong foundation on the actress's sensitive skin. The makeup artist swore she did not use the brand Alyssa Lynn was allergic to, but she was fired anyway. The woman's name is Doreen Prescott. I tracked her down. She lives in Omaha now. I even found her phone number.*

Despite my earlier thoughts about not caring who had killed Deb, I felt disappointed that my quest for the murderer had hit a dead end. Still, there was the mystery of Allie herself. Why so much pretense? Did her actress soul find the strength to make the most of her days through playing a role, if only for our benefit?

I called Doreen Prescott. A robotic male voice told me to leave a message.

I waited for the beep. "My name is Pat. I am a writer. I wondered if you would be willing to talk to me about the mishap with makeup that caused you to be fired from the show *Rum of the Mill*. If so, please call."

While I waited for her to return my call, I phoned Madame ZeeZee and caught her driving home from her children's ballet class.

"I have Allie's phone number," she said in response to my query, "but it's at the studio. If you can't wait until tomorrow to talk to her, I can tell you where she lives."

"That would be great. What's her address?"

"I don't have the exact address, but Deb told me she saw Allie going into the house three doors down from her. The one with the For Sale sign out in front. Does this have anything to do with Deb's passing?"

"Possibly. I don't know."

"Well, call me if you find out anything."

"Okay. Oops. Gotta go. I have a call coming in. Bye."

I disconnected from Madame ZeeZee and took the other call. "Yes?"

A hoarse voice said, "There was no mishap, you know. Someone fiddled with the foundation. They removed some of the allergy-free makeup from the jar and replaced it with the one Alyssa Lynn was allergic to. I used most of it when I applied it to Alyssa Lynn's face. Everyone thought I added a bit to the pot to cover up my mistake, but I didn't make a mistake. And Alyssa Lynn knew it. The stuff came from her own stash. She didn't trust anyone with her makeup. And she was right. Someone had it in for her, but it wasn't me." The bombardment of words stopped, and I could hear gulping as if she were drinking. When she spoke again, her voice sounded different. Softer. "I never found out who hated Alyssa Lynn so much."

"Maybe the person hated you, not her."

"I visited Alyssa Lynn in the hospital, and she said the same thing. Oh, man was she angry. Never seen anyone so angry. She wasn't a nice person. Played a few tricks of her own, you know. She said she could forgive someone if they had come after her, but she couldn't forgive anyone who turned her into collateral damage. That's what she called it. Collateral damage. And boy, was there damage. The pustules were so bad, there wasn't much of her own skin left. She had to have facial reconstruction surgery and skin grafts, though I think her plastic surgeon got carried away and did more than was necessary, you know, a Pygmalion sort of thing."

"Do you have any idea who switched the makeup?"

"No one hated me."

"What if it wasn't about hate? What if the result had been unintended?"

"It was intended. Someone purposely switched the makeup."

"I believe you. What I meant was, maybe someone didn't know

what the wrong foundation would do. Maybe she thought Alyssa Lynn would have a bit of reddening or a pimple. Maybe she just wanted to get you in trouble."

"Oh." A long silence. "Well, there was this one girl. She wanted to make a name for herself real bad. Wanted to be someone, you know? I didn't blame her. Isn't that what we all want? To be somebody? She was furious she had to do the makeup for the chorus. She didn't think it would advance her career, but that's how we all started. She didn't hate me. We were friends. Went to lunch, that sort of thing."

"Could she have pulled a prank?"

"A prank yes. But nothing worse. She just seemed needy, you know?"

"What's her name?"

"I don't remember. It was a long time ago. Donna or Debbie. Something that began with 'D' like my name. I do remember she lived in some desert town in California. She hated it so bad she said she'd do anything to stay in New York."

"Anything?" I asked softly.

Another long silence. "You think it was her?"

"Maybe."

"So, you're going to write this up for the newspaper, right? Clear my name?"

"I'm not a journalist. I'm a novelist."

A shriek. "What? You write fiction? Why am I telling you all this?" And then the slam of her phone receiver.

Deb. Alyssa Lynn. Doreen. Were all theater folk sociopaths at heart? It's a good thing, then, that I found dancing so late in life. It wouldn't have been much fun dealing with a whole world full of Debs.

Mindful of the impending culmination to my story, I took a shower and pulled on black pants and a clean black tee shirt, and accessorized the basic ensemble with an unbuttoned peach top and a black hat decorated with peach flowers. (Yes, panties and shoes and socks, too, but that should be understood.)

I drove to Verde Ranchero, entered the gated community behind an elderly man weaving all over the road, found my way to Deb's street, and spotted the For Sale sign a few houses down from hers.

Allie opened the door. She balanced on strappy silver heels, wearing a silky turquoise dress accessorized with what looked like vintage silver and turquoise jewelry. A faint smirk curved her lips without etching any lines on her face.

"May I come in?" I asked.

She walked into the interior of the house, leaving the door open, which I took as permission to enter.

The living room had the bare minimum of furniture, enough to give an idea of the room's size, but not enough to imprint on a shopper's mind. A coffee table squatted in the right angle formed by the beige couch and matching loveseat. A light fixture with fan blades shaped like leaves dangled from the center of the ceiling, and a large framed painting of a young woman hung on the wall opposite the couch, but nothing else relieved the sparseness of the room—no knickknacks, lamps, frilly pillows, or snapshots. I wondered if the starkness reflected Allie's taste, or if she'd rented the house as is. According to the real estate agent who sold my father's house, prospective buyers preferred to imagine their own possessions in the rooms rather than fixate on a stranger's décor.

Allie sat on the couch and waved me toward a loveseat. "It took you long enough."

I perched on the edge of the seat. "What took me long enough?"

"I thought you were supposed to be this hotshot detective. I expected you to figure things out days ago."

"I'm not a detective."

"Whatever."

I couldn't help wondering what role she was playing. Maybe *Clue* meets *Clueless*.

"I can't talk long." She lifted her arm, glanced at the broad silver bangle on her wrist, and widened her eyes. "Oh, my look at the time. My husband will be home soon to take me out to dinner."

I peered at the bangle, but didn't see a timepiece attached. I wondered if I should mention I knew her husband wouldn't be home any time soon, had, in fact, died three months previously, but I didn't know how deeply entrenched she'd become in her fantasy world. If she believed in her continuing role of dutiful wife, even halfway, she might slip completely out of reality and deny me a showdown, and I felt that only a satisfying conclusion to our confrontation would clear the murder out of my head. Besides, her husband, living or dead, seemed to have nothing to do with the issue at hand.

"Well?" she said, sounding impatient.

I smiled. Unwittingly, I'd fallen into Detective Arsalee Morales's method of letting silence do the speaking.

Allie played with her diamond wedding ring, twisting it around and around her finger. "Don't you want to know why I did it?"

"I'm listening."

"Isn't it obvious?"

All of a sudden, I didn't know what we were talking about. "Isn't what obvious?"

She spread her fingers, and held her hands close to her face. "Look at this!"

"I'm looking," I said, though I didn't know if she wanted me to notice her hands or her countenance.

She touched the tip of her fingers to her face. "This is what that bitch did to me."

"Did what?" I studied her features, the perfect nose, the lovely cheekbones, the delicate chin, the taut skin with not a single mole or blemish. "I don't see anything wrong. You're stunningly beautiful."

"You lie!" She jumped to her feet as if she really were as young as she pretended to be. She leaned toward me, her face a grotesque mask of hatred. "Everyone lies! Why do all of you act like you can't see how ugly I am?" She sank back onto the couch, and her face fell into its normal bland expression.

I held myself motionless, not wanting to give her any reason for another eruption.

She smiled tenderly, as if at a precious memory. "I used to be beautiful. Boys worshiped me. Men loved me. Women wanted to be me."

Fear unfurled in my belly. *What had I gotten myself into?* I remember once thinking she cultivated silence so as not to risk getting muddled over what era she'd lived in, but now I wondered if she'd stayed quiet to make herself seem sane. Furtively, I scanned the furniture and eyed her form-fitting dress, wondering if she'd hidden a weapon within reach.

Allie gazed at the painting of the insipidly pretty young woman. "See how beautiful?"

I studied the painting, and realized I'd seen the woman before—on the playbill for *Rum of the Mill*. I still saw no resemblance to Allie, but then, she'd had extensive surgery from a Pygmalion wannabe.

She shot me a tear-filled look that made her eyes seem huge and tragic. "What am I supposed to do now?"

"Take each day as it comes." I spoke softly as one does to a hurt child or to a wild animal that had crept too close.

"What do you know about anything? Fat, unattractive girls like you always pretend beauty doesn't matter but that's just sour grapes."

Unattractive? Ouch. I knew I weighed too much, but I looked pleasant enough, with bright eyes, a pretty smile, and a few laugh lines to add character. Did anyone need more than that?

She cocked her head as if waiting for a response. When I had no retort, she continued. "I'm too young to be a character actress, but with what that bitch did to my face, I'm too hideous to be an ingénue."

I wanted to clap at her performance, but kept my hands folded in my lap. Although I hadn't seen any sort of weapon, her long fingernails looked sharp enough to do damage if I riled her.

Fingernails. Nail salon. "You got your nails done next door, didn't you? I bet you told everyone you didn't go there so no one would guess you overheard what had happened to Grace."

"They fixed a broken nail, is all. I . . . I . . ." She looked down; her false lashes cast shadows on her cheeks. "I couldn't get up the courage to off the bitch, but after what she did to Grace, it was easy. I figured I was next, so I had to defend myself."

"Did she know who you were?"

Her eyes widened. "You don't think she did?"

"I don't know. You look so different."

Allie burst out laughing. "Oh, I like that! She died without ever knowing why." The gleeful laughter stopped abruptly as if the power had been shut off. "I thought it would make it easier if she were gone, but it doesn't make any difference."

"It still hurts, doesn't it?" I referred to her grief, but she missed the point.

"It always hurts being unattractive. But then, you'd know that."

Cripes. "What do you have against me?"

"Oh, let me think." She put her index finger to her temples in a parody of thinking. "Maybe because you're going to arrest me?"

I couldn't help emitting a short laugh. "I can't arrest you. I'm not a cop."

"Well, you called them, didn't you?"

"No."

Her brows drew together, but not a single line formed on her forehead. "What about the dramatic ending for your book? That's why you're here, isn't it?"

From where I sat, I could see both the woman and her portrait, and I had no answer for either one of them. No matter what happened now, that young woman would still be gone, altered forever by the fingers of time and her surgeon. And the old woman would still be mired in her losses, half-mad from grief.

"Why didn't you leave? Why did you wait around to get caught?" I paused for a response that didn't come. She might not know the truth and if she did, she probably wouldn't be able to admit that here, in this deadly little town, her husband lived both in her imagination and in the role she'd created for herself. If we, her audience, didn't know he'd died, then he lived, like an offstage character. If she went home, she would be confronted by the unpalatable truth of Robert's demise.

I wanted to hug her, to show compassion for the bereft woman hiding inside the carefully constructed carapace, but I feared getting too near her. I'd endured years of grief in my struggle to find a renewed interest in life, and I had no intention of wasting that effort by risking death.

Apparently, whatever had caused her chattiness had worn off, because she, too, seemed lost in thought.

I struggled to rise from the too-soft loveseat. "The real detective on this case is smart. She will find you. If you want my suggestion, contact your lawyers and see if he can arrange some sort of deal for you before she arrests you."

She flinched. "So you're going to let me go?"

"You don't want me to? Why not?" And then I knew. The excitement of a trial with her in the starring role would seem better than having to face an empty life. "I'm not planning on going to the cops. I don't want to be a bit player in your jailhouse drama. But if they come to talk to me, I'll tell them about you. Being an accessory to murder has no place in my future."

She lifted her head toward the picture, but I sensed her glancing at me out of the corner of her eyes.

"You don't have to get up," I said, though with the way her face had turned pale and her hands shook, I doubted she'd have been able to move.

I plodded to the door, and turned around. "Good luck." The words sounded inadequate, but I could think of nothing else to say. I opened the door to darkness.

The sun had set and I hadn't even noticed. I dug my keys out of my purse, and headed for my car. I stabbed at the lock a couple of times and finally managed to insert the key and open the door. I slid onto the seat, tried to put the key in the ignition, but I lost my grip and the keys fell from my lifeless hands.

I crossed my arms on the steering wheel, rested my head on my forearms, and wept.

After a few minutes, when my sobs died down, I heard the crunch of tires on the tarmac and the soft whirr of a well-tuned engine.

I peered over my arms.

A police car drove slowly past my bug, as if checking me out.

I fished for my keys. Trembling, I managed to insert the right key in the ignition and start the vehicle.

I drove slowly from the neighborhood with the cop keeping me company. I did not speed up when I lost sight of the car.

Chapter 30

I'd often thought a violent showdown at the end of a mystery a cliché, a scene that had been tacked on to show how hard-boiled the detective and how important the mission. And, of course, to prolong the suspense by giving the reader one last taste of gratuitous violence. But now I understood the necessity of a fight. It might be okay, as T.S. Eliot said, for the world to end not with a bang but a whimper, but a story needs a bang-up ending. The hero's adrenaline needs somewhere to go, and no self-respecting hero would be caught weeping to release tension.

But then, I'm no hero.

I stumbled from my car and into the house to use the bathroom, then dropped onto the mattress, too exhausted to do anything else.

The ringing of the phone roused me.

"Did I wake you?" Madame ZeeZee asked.

"No. I'm lying down is all." I always denied being awakened by the phone because I didn't want people to feel bad about calling me.

"How did it go with Allie?"

"Fine. How did it go with your mom?"

"She says she has her rights. She pays her rent and doesn't bother anyone, but hospice says she needs to be in a nursing home. I don't know what to do."

"It's a hard situation. You'll do what's right."

"With God's help," Madame ZeeZee said. "Did you find out who did it?"

My sleep muddled mind took a second to realize she'd changed the subject back to Allie. "Yeah. Karma. Chaos."

"Karma?"

"What goes around, comes around."

"I know what karma is." The unaccustomed asperity in her voice made me bristle, but I took a breath and forced myself to relax.

"The way I see it, Deb killed herself. She got too caught up in her own dramas and forgot that everything has repercussions. Chaos theory says that small actions can result in greater effects later on, and that's what happened to Deb. One of her little dramas built up into a great tragedy and it ended up killing her."

"I saw that movie. *The Butterfy Effect*."

"Yes. Like the movie. That's why Deb died. Allie never really admitted it, in fact, she seemed so out of it when I talked to her that I can't be sure what she actually meant half the time."

"Did you go to the cops?"

"No."

"You have to."

I don't have to do anything. "Don't worry. The cops saw me in front of her house. I'm sure someone will come to talk to me tomorrow. I think they've been keeping tabs on me."

"Why?"

"Who knows. Allie seemed to think I went to see her to find a finale for my book. Maybe the cops think the same thing. Or else I'm still a suspect." I yawned. "I better go. I'm really tired."

"Okay. Talk to you later."

I fell asleep immediately. Didn't brush my teeth. Didn't change out of my pants and tee shirt. I awoke to the sound of the doorbell.

I sat up groggily with no idea how long I'd slept, but the brightness of the room and the ghastly taste in my mouth told me I'd slumbered through the night.

Detective Arsalee Morales's impeccable dark blue suit and her clear brown eyes made me feel even worse than I'm sure I appeared.

"May I come in?"

"Can I stop you?" I stepped aside to let her in. "I'm sorry. I'm grumpy this morning."

"Bad night?"

"You could say that."

"I told you not to get involved."

"Yeah, well, a lot of people have told me a lot of things that I never heeded. My publisher calls me contrary."

She peered at me. "Do you need to make coffee or something?"

"I don't drink coffee."

She nodded as if I'd answered a different question, but I had no idea what that question might be. With any luck, she and her enigmatic ways would soon be out of my life, and I would no longer have to try to figure her out.

She walked across the empty floor and slung her briefcase onto the counter, giving me the strange sensation of déjà vu, but is it déjà vu when the action has in fact happened before?

"You do know I could have you arrested for obstruction of justice?"

I shrugged. Though the grogginess seemed to be wearing off, the lackadaisical attitude that had accompanied the blear remained. "I didn't obstruct justice. It seems to me as if justice arrived without any help from either of us."

She did her Wonder Woman thing, but the pose had lost its power to intimidate me.

I held out my palms as if in offering. "Poetic justice?"

"The law deals entirely in facts."

"Since when? The law is often about subverting facts and hiding the truth. Courts aren't about justice, they are about processing cases, and facts sometimes get in the way."

"Whether justice has been served, I still need to close this case. What happened last night?"

In my mind, I replayed the conversation with Allie, and I had to laugh. "She got me. Got me good. She never admitted anything. Never used Deb's name. Just danced around me as if I were a maypole."

"What specifically did she say?"

"Let's see. She talked about her husband coming home soon. Called me fat and unattractive. Screamed at me that I lied when I told her how beautiful she looked. Asked if I were going to arrest her for some unnamed crime. Accused me of wanting a finale for my book. I think that about covers it."

"And what did you say?"

"I told her you were smart and would discover the truth. Suggested she contact her lawyers and turn herself in. Said I'd talk to you when you came by because I had no intention of being arrested as an accessory." I giggled. "Accessory to her drama is all I'm guilty of."

No smile cracked the detective's stern visage.

The last giggle ended on a sob. "How do *you* deal with the pain of human frailty?"

"The job. Knowing I'm doing something important."

"I hope you can find enough evidence to make your case because what led me to Allie is circumstantial. A long ago accident with makeup. A husband who is or isn't dead. A woman derailed by grief. All that might be fine for a novel where a touch of ambiguity is acceptable, but it's not adequate for the law. She might confess, though. I think she will do anything not to have to deal with her husband's death."

"I can understand that." The detective spoke sadly, and for the first time, I got a sense of the woman beneath the professional exterior—a woman made hard by the world she lived in, a woman haunted, perhaps, by secrets of her own.

She claimed her briefcase, and marched toward the door. She stopped to let me open it for her. "Do me a favor. Don't write any more murder mysteries based here in Peach Valley."

I laughed. She didn't.

Chapter 31

I spent the weekend fighting sadness and searching for a place to live. Didn't succeed on either account. Sadness, a thing without wings, perched on my soul, and the potential abodes I visited gave me no hope of ever dislodging the pitiful interloper. The places I could afford were too small, too dark, too dirty, too depressing, and I knew I would shrivel if I lived in any of them. The nicer places, places I couldn't afford, seemed no more welcoming.

Was this to be my fate, stagnating alone in rooms too claustrophobic to let my spirit soar?

Maybe the people who bought my father's house wouldn't notice if I never moved out. But not even that facetious notion offered me a solution to my dilemma. His home hadn't been a happy place for me, and I would be glad to leave if I had somewhere to go.

Monday brought the first lightening of my mood. I had dance class, and I hoped dancing would give me a break from myself.

I arrived a few minutes late. Madame ZeeZee, Kim. Lena, Buffy, and Rose were huddled in waiting area, chattering with excitement. I stood silently by and listened to the commotion. Although Allie's arrest for Deb's murder had come as a surprise to them, what shocked everyone seemed to be Allie's pretense that her husband hadn't died.

After a minute or two, Rose noticed me. "How did you find out about Allie? Were you there when she got arrested?"

"I wasn't there," I said quietly. "I didn't know she'd been arrested. When did that happen?"

"It was on Facebook this morning," Lena said.

I shook my head at the way the social network had supplanted the media as a way of disseminating the news.

"It's true," Lena insisted.

"I believe you," I said.

"So the nightmare is over?" Madame ZeeZee asked me.

"Could be. I talked to the detective Friday morning, and they haven't contacted me since. I didn't really have much to offer, so I doubt I will be called as a witness if she goes to trial."

"I bet you're glad to have been part of the investigation," Rose said.

I smiled, a mere baring of my teeth, because I had no response for her. I had yet to figure out how I felt about the cascading misfortunes in which I'd become embroiled, but I doubt gladness played any part in my feelings.

"How could Pat be glad," Buffy said. "How can any of us?"

Kim nodded. In her purple turban, she looked mysterious, like a wise woman of a bygone era. "Poor Allie. Death turns your soul inside out, and you never know what you will find in that dark hiding place."

"I don't know how I will react when my mother passes," Madame ZeeZee said.

"You can't know," Kim said. "All you can do is try to enjoy your time with her, and if you can't enjoy it, then take comfort in knowing you're doing the best you can."

Madame ZeeZee nodded, then said, "Let's get started."

I hurriedly pulled on my jazz shoes and straggled out to the dance floor with the rest of the class.

"Where's Rhett?" asked Lena.

"She hasn't called," Madame ZeeZee said.

"I see her." Rose pointed to the parking lot where Rhett seemed to be gyrating to music we could not hear. "What's she doing?"

Rhett ran in, did a couple of quick chaine turns followed by a few kicks and hip wiggles. Laughing, she ran to me and threw her arms around me. "You did it! You did it!"

"Did what?" Madame ZeeZee asked.

"He's dead. Pat killed him. She promised she would and now he's gone."

The others turned to me, but I kept my focus on Rhett. "Who is gone?"

"My ex- husband. He cheated on that woman, and she killed him just as you said she would."

I stood as if in a vacuum, unable to breathe, unable to hear. It had been Rhett who proposed the scenario of her ex-husband's death, Grace and Deb who volunteered to be victims, Buffy who chose the murder weapon, and yet it had been my book we'd been discussing. Could I have the power to bring ideas to life?

I stumbled through the warm-ups and dances as best as I could with half my mind taken up with the confounding question. *Did I have the power to make thoughts come true?*

After class, I practically flew home, tossed my hat and purse on the counter, and opened the computer.

I sat with my fingers on the keyboard and thought about the life I would like to live. A new love? No, that I would leave to destiny, but the fates could use help in getting me the rest of what I needed. A writing life, of course, with enough income from my books to afford a soul-satisfying place to reside. A life of adventure and boldness, wisdom and joy. A life filled with . . . life.

While I waited for the future that would soon be mine, I would still have dance class, and this moment, and all the moments to come.

And oh, those moments will be good. So very good.

Acknowledgments

It might take a village to raise a child, but it takes the whole world to raise a book. My heartfelt thanks to the following people for helping me get the story right:

Kat Sheridan for a fabulous motive. Mary Strasser for help with dissociative personality disorder. Corkey Wohlers for a means of murder and a fun secret to uncover. Jan Blondet for volunteering to be the lovely victim and for being my covergirl. Dennise Manning for her enthusiastic support of the project and for a true story. Linda Miklos for the Lithuanian ballerina. My classmates for their forebearance. Wanda Hughes for letting me put her in the book. Arsalee Morales and Rami Ungar for their names. And most of all, Cecilia Rosado for her friendship, for teaching me to dance, and for all her wise counsel. Point your toes!

Other Titles available from Pat Bertram
and Indigo Sea Press.

A Spark of Heavenly Fire

In quarantined Colorado, where hundreds of thousands of people are dying from an unstoppable, bio-engineered disease, investigative reporter Greg Pullman risks everything to discover the truth: Who unleashed the deadly organism? And why?

More Deaths Than One

Bob Stark returns to Denver after 18 years in SE Asia to discover that the mother he buried before he left is dead again. At her new funeral, he sees himself. Is his other self a hoaxer? A doppelganger? Or is something more sinister going on?

Daughter Am I

A fortune in stolen gold.
A dying hit man just released from prison.
A young woman who will do anything to protect those she loves . . .

Light Bringer

Thirty-seven years after being abandoned on the doorstep of a remote cabin in Colorado, Becka Johnson returns to try to discover her identity, but she only finds more questions. Who has been looking for her all those years? And why?

Excerpt from Light Bringer

Tracks led to the house where a small gray creature huddled against the door.

She clapped her hands. "Shoo. Shoo."

The creature did not stir.

"Go on. Get," she shouted.

The creature still didn't move. Was it dead? This wouldn't be the first time a dying animal had been attracted to the warmth seeping from beneath the front door.

She approached gingerly, relaxing when she saw what appeared to be an old gray blanket that had somehow ended up on the stoop. She bent over to collect the wad of fabric, then straightened. Bad idea. Who knew what vermin had taken refuge in the folds.

Before she could figure out what to do, the blanket moved. She jumped back and stared at it. The blanket moved again, giving her a glimpse of a coppery curl.

She lifted the bundle, cradled it in her arms, and drew back the blanket. Two dark eyes, shining with intelligence, gazed at her.

She sucked in a breath. An infant, no more than nine months old.

As the infant continued to gaze at her, its eyes brightened to gleaming amber. Then it beamed at her—a welcoming smile, both joyous and knowing, as if it had recognized a dear friend.

Helen's face felt tight. "Who are you?"

The baby chortled in response.

"And who left you here?" She glanced at the tracks. They led in only one direction—toward the house.

Feeling dizzy, she crouched to examine the tracks more closely.

They were footprints. Tiny footprints in the snow.